Also by Vamba Sherif

Bound to Secrecy
The Black Napoleon
The Witness
The Kingdom of Sebah

Land of My

Land of My Fathers

VAMBA SHERIF

hope**road** : London

HopeRoad Publishing Ltd
P O Box 55544
Exhibition Road
SW7 2DB

www.hoperoadpublishing.com
First published in Great Britain by HopeRoad 2016

Original Dutch edition first published in 1999
Het land van de vaders by Vamba Sherif

Published by special arrangement with Uitgeverij De Geus in conjunction with
their duly appointed agent 2 Seas Literary Agency

Copyright © 1999 Vamba Sherif

ISBN 978-1-908446-49-7

eISBN 978-1-908446-54-1

Printed and bound by TJ International Ltd, Padstow, Cornwall, UK

To
The people of Liberia, the victims and the survivors
of the war. May we remember.

Book One

The Two Worlds

1

One morning, on a wet autumn day, I caught sight of the ship in the distance and hurried towards it. The salty sea air bore excited voices towards me, and it was not long before I became part of the bustle. Shouldering my luggage consisting of clothes, some valuable books and expedition materials, I climbed on board. The ship was crowded with men and women. There were no children. Among the passengers were carpenters, stonemasons, tailors, and a preacher. But the last was not the only one there who had embraced the word of the Lord. Seated or standing in groups, the men revelled in dreams of a better life in a republic with abundant land and the opportunity to establish a trade. Nowhere in the wide world was the freedom desired by black people of America fulfilled more than in the coastal republic of Liberia. As I edged my way to the berth that would be my abode for the coming weeks, I heard those dreams being exchanged with conviction and hope. Although I did participate in these conversations, my dreams differed from all the others. I cherished freedom and had longed for it all my life, but that was not why I was heading for Africa, for the land of my fathers. What made me trade America with all its promises for a distant shore was perhaps greater than freedom.

The ship set sail out of the crowded dock with the Atlantic winds guiding it. Well-wishers in their dozens waved from the pier, but I chose not to wave back. I was resolved to put America and everything about it behind me and to forge a new beginning for myself.

Yet, how could I escape from it all – the fields, the great house, Sarah, and the huge country where I had spent so much of my life.

2

I was born to a mother who raised many children who were not her own. One day, one of the children in her care fell into a well. I remember being with her when the incident occurred. We were drawing water when the child, a boy of six, tripped and fell head first down the well. Mother, who had sustained an injury to her legs that had resulted in a pronounced limp and who could not walk without a cane, used a ladder and climbed down the well to rescue the child. Such a woman was my mother.

One Christmas morning – I must have been eight or thereabouts and regarded my world with mother and stepfather as sufficient – a white man sauntered up to our cabin and shot me a look I had not seen in a face like his all my life. The man went on to ruffle my hair and called me by my full name. After sharing a few words with my mother, my actual father, our master, took leave of us to prepare for a sumptuous Christmas dinner at the great house with his daughters and in-laws.

We were all given a few days off from the fields and could visit relatives and friends at other plantations. We could attend to our little gardens, which produced things we could sell in the city; or we could come together to sing and narrate stories until dawn. And although we were not allowed to drink, we managed to forget the fields by doing chores that appealed to us.

The cooks and other domestics were busy at work preparing the best dishes of the year at the great house. Having no duties around the cabins, I walked over there, which I was allowed to do.

The house consisted of a small study, ten bedrooms, two of which were occupied by servants, drawing rooms, a lounge, a large kitchen, a pantry, and a verandah giving onto a beautiful garden bordered by cypress trees. As I approached it, I had the impression of entering a domain where everything, from the servants and others who occupied it, the rooms and gardens, contrasted in every way with our lives in the cabins. And of course this was true.

In the house, our master and one of his four daughters, Sarah, and some servants lived. Sarah was sitting on a bench on the verandah, reading aloud from the Bible, her whole attention riveted to the book. Standing not far away, I listened to her telling the story of Jesus. I found the story and the way she read it captivating, and whenever I paused to reflect on the moment I took to the Lord, I would always associate it with hearing Sarah's voice. She was reciting the story of Lazarus's death and the Lord proclaiming that Lazarus was but asleep and then waking him up to life. Despite my awareness of the danger associated with a person of my kind trying to acquire knowledge, which was thought to lead to recalcitrant thoughts and eventually to rebellion, I resolved to master those passages. I suppose, looking back on it all now, the Lord had held out his hand to me.

Sarah would now and then pause, perhaps to acknowledge my presence. At one point, she sat upright, closed the Bible

6

which rested on her lap, and gazed at me. There was mischief in her eyes. She was tall, lean, with bony hands, pale cheeks and long black hair. Both of us had piercing eyes, prominent foreheads and the irritable habit of toying with our fingers. Her three older sisters had married men who owned plantations. Their mother, a woman who had controlled the affairs of the plantation with an iron fist, had died a few years back, and Sarah was the only woman left in the great house.

She smiled now as I went on to the kitchen. We did not speak that day.

The kitchen was a beehive of activity. The head cook and domestic, Benjamin Johnson, called out to me when I entered. 'Come over here, Edward,' he said, and I approached him. The aroma of fried chicken and diverse sauces pervaded the air.

Benjamin Johnson was hashing onion, fresh tomatoes, cucumbers and boiled eggs to prepare salad. He was of amicable disposition, which he had cultivated and which, he told me later, was necessary for his survival on the plantation. Occasionally he visited our cabin, bringing some leftovers with him. Old now, but as healthy as a horse, he wore an expression that seemed to plead and deride at the same time. Benjamin smiled when least expected and during inappropriate times, throwing one into confusion as to how to respond to him. With seasoned hands, he now prepared the food, while at the same time issuing orders to other servants. He seemed at home in that world and yet, on more than one occasion, he had told my parents of his desire to escape. He was an important figure on the plantation and our master appeared to rely on his counsel regarding us. He would boast of his successes. Other servants consulted him on everything pertaining to culinary issues and to the house. Through the years, he had climbed the ladder of plantation life from a young man who tilled the fields to being head of the domestics and a cook bent on mastering an art form in which he took the greatest pride.

He offered me a drumstick.

'This will do you good, I know it, Edward,' he said, and I looked for an empty corner, eased myself down and bit into it. Benjamin Johnson was right. The food did indeed do me a lot of good.

Later, I left the kitchen. Sarah was no longer on the verandah. In those days I was wont not to head straight for the cabins but to stroll along paths that ran through the bushes, pausing to listen to nature, to the songs of birds or the cries of animals. During one of my wanderings I found a place in the bush, covered with dusty sand, a place so tranquil that it became my sanctuary, where I would retreat to take stock of my life as a child on the plantation, my head brimming with questions regarding my fate. I often wondered, in the light of the stories my mother told us about Africa, what had happened that resulted in us being cast away forever from our land. Why had we become the property of other human beings? Nothing I could think of could justify our circumstances and why they were being perpetuated for so long and by so many.

I avoided my sanctuary that day and took a different path, uncertain as to where it would lead. It was a sunny day, the sky the bluish colour of Sarah's eyes, and the air pregnant with the odour of the bushes. Now and then I would pause to gaze at the trees, as if they could communicate with me and answer the myriad questions that swirled in my head. Beyond a cluster of bushes I thought I heard hurried whispers, and on taking a closer look saw a gathering of men and women. I knew all of them. My stepfather was among them. What was unfolding intrigued me. My stepfather was teaching the slaves a language I had never heard before. It did not sound American, not even remotely. He seemed to have plucked it out of the void, and now, in a calm voice to which the men and women clung like children to a fairy tale, he recited a word or a sentence, which the group repeated. He brought such a solemnity to bear on the moment that I felt I was witnessing an ancient ritual brought over from the African world. But afraid of incurring his wrath, I stole away from the bush and headed for the cabin.

Mother was sprawled on a chair before the kitchen, a tiny wooden affair which stood beside the cabin, and was littered with sooty pots and pans. She was surrounded by a gaggle of her children, and at the hour of the day, in the fading light of the sun, some of the children were whining and demanding her attention as she prepared the last meal of the day. Her hair was braided in two rows, and she wore a long brown dress which seemed to merge with the color of her skin and which she wore for days on end. She was heavily built, perhaps once a beautiful woman, dark and tall like a tree, her strength depleting with the years. What remained of that strength she could harness in her eyes, which had the most effect on us, making us laugh or sob to the power of her stories.

I did not know how she and my stepfather met, for it seemed as if the two had been together all their lives. He could be a hard man, my stepfather, and that was why I had not interrupted him in the bush. He could not tolerate the rise of a voice in the cabin besides his own. His love for us, which he expressed in deeds only, was sometimes doled out as if it was a punishment, harsh and unforgiving. A bulky man, his height and build reminded me of what our ancestors might have looked like in those distant lands. He had a coarse voice that would disturb the atmosphere of the cabin on his return from the fields. And he was often hard on us, never forgiving an error. We feared him so much and held him in such esteem that we thought he was made of stone and never broke until my mother went down with a terrible fever one time and I saw him in tears and I knew then that he was just like us, a man susceptible to emotions. Nevertheless, on other days, he applied the rigid laws of the plantation on us. He never resigned to his fate but believed that slavery was doomed to fail, instilling in us the conviction that freedom was just around the corner and that one day we would all return to Africa, to our origins. He brought us news of activities of abolitionists, of acts and resolutions taken on our behalf, of every whisper connected to us.

One of the children in particular was demanding all her attention, a child of about three with a snotty nose, whose weeping voice rose above all the others. My mother's face had taken on that frowning aspect which indicated the depth of her exasperation. Any moment now, she would slap the child. 'Mother, let me,' I intervened, and she heaved a weary sigh. 'Edward, I can't concentrate on anything with this child around,' she said. I took the boy away and used the rags on him to wipe his nose and then helped calm him down. 'Now you all behave or you would go hungry to bed,' she said. The children lapsed in silence. Later, I sat outside with a group of them around a large bowl of beans, while my mother shared another bowl with the rest.

Later, my stepfather joined us. His mood was amicable. He sat in front of the cabin with a strange light shining in his eyes, as if his face showed that he was privy to a secret.

Soon, some men, women and children from other cabins came to a tree behind our cabin to listen to my mother's stories.

'In Africa where we came from,' she began, 'there lived a people who went a whole year without salt. Salt was as precious as gold, and they could not thrive without it. So they dispatched a group to the land of salt. It was a long and treacherous journey which few had undertaken before, for traders from the savannah always brought them salt which they exchanged for kola nuts and other precious goods. But that year, there were no traders. A year passed and those sent out to look for salt did not return. The people decided to dispatch another group in search of the first, but those never made it back either. The third and fourth batches were never heard of again. So it came about that whenever someone died children were told that the deceased had gone to buy salt, for those who went to buy salt never returned.' Mother stopped.

She seemed for a while like a great matriarch who had offered a modicum of her wisdom to her children and now paused to let it sink in. In the deep silence that fell on the gathering, her voice rose, solemn as a verdict, without a trace of emotion. 'You, you, and you,' she said, pointing at each one of us. 'My son, my husband and me, we are all of us descendants of the people who went to buy salt. We never returned.'

Of all the stories mother ever told us before and thereafter, none moved me like the one that night.

Later, after the story had taken deep root in us, we danced and sang, and I slept huddled in a corner on a plank with the story of the people who went to purchase salt on my mind and pervading my dreams.

Once Christmas was over, we returned to the fields. I went on running errands around the plantation or joining the men and women to till the fields. For a while, I forgot all about Sarah. But one day, I saw her elegantly dressed and with a parasol, strolling along a path close to the fields.

'Edward, come over here,' she called out to me.

My stepfather, seeing me about to respond to her, grunted his disapproval, but at her insistence I joined her.

We sat in the shade of a tree. For the first time I was introduced to the world of words. In a short time I managed to grasp the alphabet and was hungry for more. Sarah turned out to be a competent teacher.

The more I spent time with her, the more it upset my stepfather until one night he returned from the fields and took me in front of the cabin with a number of mother's children.

The man flogged me with a cruelty that shocked me, leaving welts on my back. It was the first time he had laid hands on me. Mother was stunned. In a burst of temper, he tried to explain his action.

'The key to our survival here is to know our place,' he said. 'The child does not know his place. He's putting all our plans in jeopardy.'

My mother was silent all night, which hurt him to the quick.

I could not sleep for the pain in my body. To escape the biting silence of the cabin, my stepfather headed for the fields at the crack of dawn, and he returned and sat beside me, trying to apologize but failing to do so, for the plantation was not a place for such sentiments.

One night he woke me up after everyone had retired to bed and the world was quiet. 'I will be the one to teach you,' he said.

My stepfather told me about a language he had learned from someone he had met at another plantation. 'There's a country called Liberia, where the people who were once slaves here in America live in freedom. Some of the natives of that country speak this language. It's called Vai. They say an Indian taught them to write their language down, but what we know for certain is that one of their people had a dream in which he was taught the language. It will be our language, Edward, the

12

one we will speak when we return to Africa. While teaching you the language, we will prepare for our escape. We need to keep our heads low. The closer you come to the likes of Sarah, the greater the risk of our plans being exposed. So avoid her as much as you can. Don't trust her.'

Though I was touched by his dreams and wanted to learn the Vai language as much as others who believed in him, I wondered how I would react were Sarah to offer to teach me again.

Our master, bent on making our plantation one of the best, drove us to work harder and longer that year. As he had no overseer – for ours was not a large plantation – he saw to everything himself. We left the cabin at the crack of dawn and returned late at night. Some of us would collapse in the heat of the scorching sun, but we were not given a moment's respite.

One day, while we were ploughing the fields, I saw my mother edging her way to our master, leaning on her cane, and with that burning look on her face that had on more than one occasion compelled me to confess my misdemeanours. She drew up to him, and said, 'The work is driving everyone to an early death. It's enough. Enough.'

Our end had surely come, I thought. My mother who had never defied the master was about to unleash a revolution. The silence that reigned lasted so long that I thought our master would end up slapping her. I had seen him flog people until they had passed out. There was a story of a woman who had succumbed to his whip. It was mother's turn, I was certain of this. But our master left the fields in silence.

The fieldworkers began to berate my mother. 'You should not have intervened, woman. Now he will return and make us all pay,' one of them said. 'You shouldn't have done this,' another said. My mother turned around and headed for the cabins, limping like an old woman.

For the first time in more than a quarter of a century on that plantation, our master caved in to the demand of a slave. We resumed work as of old. But that year was catastrophic. The crops failed.

Our master soon returned to his old ways, driving us like a herd of animals. When that failed to lessen his desolation, he took to locking himself in his study, refusing to see anyone, not even Sarah. Sometimes we would see him strolling along the border of the fields, head dropped and taking long draughts of a strong drink. My stepfather took over running things until our master returned to his old self. Sarah, ever the devoted daughter, attended to him. He delved into the Bible, praying and asking for repentance. When the new season dawned, he brought the Bible with him to the fields and made us pray before work.

Only Sarah remained unaffected by it all, which further strained her tenuous relationship with her father. She went on teaching me, now less often, but with the same zeal. I made sure that my stepfather was not around when I went to see her. Perhaps because I was an able and willing student, or she wanted to feel worthwhile around the plantation, while the number of suitors who once courted her waned, or perhaps to get back at a father who did not return her love, Sarah was resolved, in spite of his objections, to go on teaching me.

We often met behind the great house in her father's absence. Within a few years I had become familiar with some of the biblical stories, like that of Moses who fled with his people, just as my stepfather was planning to do with his people.

That Sarah, with her excessive love for her father, treated him as one incapable of caring for himself infuriated him. He regarded her constant fuss over him as an impediment to his ability to form a binding relationship with other women. Often, during his angry bouts, he would scream at her, saying: 'Why are you still single? Is it because of those bony hands and face? Who would want to have such a lean and sickly woman as wife?' For weeks he would not be on speaking terms with her, and he would lock himself up in his study where he had his dinner alone.

Tilling the fields or helping my mother with her children meant seeing Sarah less often than I wanted. Now a free woman, mother refused to move to the city and leave her husband and me.

Our lot changed when Benjamin Johnson, the head domestic died, and I was appointed head servant to the great house and could take better care of mother. More often than not I would be with Sarah who was now a woman long past her prime, and who treated me like a relation.

Life could have gone on uneventfully, I could have remained a servant till death or till I had acquired my freedom were it not for the fact that one morning we woke up to the news that my stepfather had escaped with eight others. They were quickly declared runaways. In his unyielding pursuit of freedom, my stepfather had succeeded in carrying out his plan. On a Christmas night when others were celebrating with drinks and our master and his daughters and their husbands were at the table exchanging reminiscences of youth and the old days, my stepfather and the others had taken flight under the cover of dark. His escape plan was so well executed that to succeed at it, he had not involved mother and me, perhaps because of my proximity to Sarah and our master.

Our master summoned us to the great house where we assembled before other planters, all armed to the teeth. Their dogs kept howling at us as if we were bait. We were questioned one by one. 'Tell us their whereabouts and we will grant you your freedom,' they promised.

The men hauled mother to the front and interrogated her. It was her husband who had escaped, wasn't it? Then she should tell them which route he and the others had taken. My mother did not flinch. One of the planters cracked a whip at her, hitting her across her face. She began to bleed. I broke away from the group to protect her, but when I reached her, her burning gaze stopped me. It seemed to convey that my outburst went against everything she had taught me regarding restraint. Mother bore the subsequent flogging without breaking, which emboldened me to do the same. The beatings now felt routine, our bodies beyond pain.

The planters went around laying out the strategy of curbing what they called the slaves' revolt and ridding us of any thought of future escapes. The first measure taken was to forbid us to gather in or around the cabins or to visit other plantations. Christmas would not be celebrated further and men were put on patrol to control our movements. Our master took to suddenly appearing in front of the cabins, counting the men, women and children, and looking sullen.

Not long after the escape, our master employed an overseer. 'No slave of mine will ever escape again, Edward,' he told me.

It was how Robert Curtis entered into our lives. Our master brought him one summer afternoon, both riding horses whose bodies glistened with sweat as a result of what must have been a long ride. Curtis was middle-aged, short and mean, and a tobacco addict to boot.

Our master literally flung him on Sarah. 'Because you are incapable of finding a husband and no one is willing to ask for your hand, I've brought you a husband,' he said. And Sarah was stupefied.

The new overseer seemed to make up for his deficiency in size by being cruel and spiteful. Within months of his arrival, he managed to turn our lives into a hell. His every word was followed by a cracked whip. He would work the men deep into the night and there were cases of some of them breaking down under the weight of work. He would force us to scrub the floors, to tend the garden, and to eat crusts instead of leftovers or a real meal. At midnight we would wake up to his footsteps and to his banging of doors, requesting all of us, the cabin dwellers and the servants alike, to present ourselves to him. We feared him so much that our behaviour became erratic. Curtis invented refined means of punishing us: he would flog a man and leave him to spend the night exposed to the elements. Not long after his arrival he did this to me.

One day I neglected to tell one of the servants to prepare his tea. As punishment, he stripped me naked and whipped me before the gaze of all the servants and field workers, and then he tied me like a bundle and left me out under the trees for the whole night. Whether our master was aware of our treatment, he feigned ignorance and paid little or no heed to our complaints. And the person who bore the brunt of this indifference besides us was Sarah, who took to confining herself to the house, hardly coming out of her room. Then, one day, Sarah vanished.

Her disappearance affected me deeply and I was resolved to never forgive that brute of an overseer. I decided to respond not passively as we were wont to do, bearing our burden and dreaming of a future when the chains around us would fall apart, but to carry on a silent rebellion. From the onset the other servants supported me; we decided to avoid taking the orders of a brutal and merciless master. We made up excuses so genuine that Curtis believed them. Seeing the success

17

of our strategy, the fieldworkers joined us, forgetting their grudge against me. As a result, the plantation fell into decline. That year's harvest was the worst ever. There were signs of dilapidation everywhere. Often, we would hear Curtis and our master arguing with each other.

I would sneak to my sanctuary to ponder on my relationship with Sarah. I missed her warm smile and gentle character and it pained me how much she had suffered the insults of her father and how she would sometimes burst into tears during our lesson.

Two years after her disappearance, while I was sitting on the steps of the verandah during a respite from Curtis's incessant orders, I saw a slatternly looking figure with long, tangled hair. It was Sarah. I darted towards her and was about to hug her when, horrified at what I saw, I checked myself. Her dress was stained, her face bruised, her hands dirty, and she brought the strong odour of the bushes and fields with her. She wore a haughty look that erased the smile of relief on my face. A fleeting look of recognition lit up her face when she saw me, but that was all, and then she climbed the steps to the verandah and sat on a bench, staring vacantly. I tried to strike up a meaningful conversation with her but to no avail.

That evening, her father returned from the city and went into the house without greeting her. A few days later, when all she did was sit outside and brood, Sarah began babbling to herself. She spoke in a language none of us could understand, because it was no language at all but a series of jabberings and howls that belonged to the animal kingdom that could be heard as far as the cabins. The whites of her eyes would be prominent then; she would roll them at invisible beings, her body shivering as though in the throes of a terrible fever or illness.

Her father realized that ignoring her was counterproductive and decided to plead with her to confide in him. Even Curtis was lenient towards us for a while, to please Sarah. I approached her one morning and held her hand, trying to get her to talk to me. She allowed me to hold her hand, which was as light as a feather, but she remained silent.

One day I went to the verandah only to see that her seat was vacant. There was no Sarah. I never saw her again.

Her disappearance awoke our master from his deep slumber of neglect. The first thing he did was dismiss Curtis. A few months later, he brought home a woman (accompanied by her son) with the severest expression I had ever seen on a face: a thin, hyperactive woman who communicated better with her look than with words. She was also a practising Christian. A year after her arrival, she built a chapel and told us that the plantation would be governed by the laws of the scriptures.

Her son, who listened to us, became the overseer. Now that he had a stepson as overseer, our master was often away and sometimes took me along with him. From then on, nothing that concerned our future escaped me. Not only did I note down conditions on other plantations and compared them with ours, but I became interested in the lives of freedmen elsewhere. I prided myself on the new opportunity offered me, for I was now in a better position to care for my mother. Every time I brought her news from other plantations, she would nod with satisfaction.

It was during one of the visits to a nearby plantation that I met a young woman who was waiting at a table. At one point we stood gazing at each other. She had a calm, almost languid expression on her face that compelled attention. I had the impression that she would break in my arms if I were to hold her. She was small, with delicate features, a smooth face, broad nose and raven-black hair that suggested an Indian and black ancestry. She had the habit of gazing at me as though she could read my thoughts. In the afternoon she displayed that gift. She revealed with accuracy my deepest fears and hopes, my fear of dying in slavery and my hope of leading a life with a house full of children.

Her name was Charlotte.

'If we had met a few years ago, we would have had a chance of a future together. Now it's not possible,' she said, in that matter-of-fact voice I would come to associate with her. Charlotte told me that she was to wed a freeman of some standing. 'So you see, you are too late, Edward.'

'I know a place you must see,' I said, undeterred by her words. No one had stirred me the way she did, not even Sarah. 'If you agree to see it, I will let you be.' I was convinced I wasn't asking much.

She was silent for so long that I thought she would burst into laughter, but I would learn later that she was someone who perceived life not through a hazy mist but through the clear light of day.

'I hope it's worth it or it will be our last meeting,' she said.

I returned to the plantation with the master almost in a daze. My head was filled with conflicting thoughts. How could I build a relationship that could eventually lead to marriage with someone who, like me, was not free? Was it possible to procure her freedom and mine? Where would we live? The future was strewn with uncertainties. I sought refuge in the Bible, in the words of the Lord when he implored us to knock at the door of salvation and we shall be received and to search and we shall find. I took consolation from these teachings as I retired to my bedroom.

'I've met someone,' I told my mother a few days later in her room in the great house, a small room that adjoined mine and which I could reach through a tiny door from my room.

Mother could hardly walk now. Her injuries which she had managed over the years had in old age resulted in swollen legs that limited her movements. I became her eyes around the plantation, the person through whom she saw and experienced the outside world. Sometimes, longing to see the children and when the urge to tell a story overwhelmed her, she would ask me to take her out to the cabins. She would lean on me, suppressing the pain, as I led her out of the house.

'Describe her to me,' she said.

In my mind's eye, I saw Charlotte, a fragile young woman whose appearance beleid her strength, but most importantly, she had laid bare my deepest fears and longings, a rare trait which had made me appreciate her and loved her more. And I conveyed this image to my mother, leaving out the fact that she was intended for someone else. Never could I imagine those brown eyes staring with affection at a face other than mine. I was certain that given time I could win her and together we could raise a family.

'May God make your union possible,' she prayed.

Not long after I took Charlotte to my sanctuary, which I had prepared a day before the meeting, clearing the sand of leaves and branches. Under one of the trees I concealed a jug of water and some provisions. Afterwards the product of my labours looked much like the interior of a well-swept cabin, a place to be at ease. Here was a piece of property that belonged to me in a world with which I was constantly at odds, and I wanted Charlotte to share that sense of belonging with me.

She appeared in a white dress, her hair tied into a knot under a hat that concealed parts of her face, and when I looked into that face I saw it lacked the playfulness of our first encounter. Something was amiss. She was all seriousness, as if we had come to conduct a transaction and not to discuss matters concerning the heart.

This explained my hesitation to hug her, for I had not been trained in how to behave with a young woman when it came to such issues as the one that faced me. But at the same time, she was there, at my sanctuary, in my world, which meant there was still hope.

'Edward, something has happened,' she said.

Charlotte informed me that her master, an abolitionist and an active member of the American Colonization Society, had given her and her family, consisting of a brother and three sisters, freedom with the sole condition that they went to settle in Liberia and nowhere else.

'I have no other choice but to migrate to Liberia,' she said.

For a while I was silent, and all of a sudden I had a moment of enlightenment. It seemed far-fetched but it was not impossible.

'What if I asked my master to grant me freedom, then we could leave for Liberia together,' I said.

For the first time, her expression changed. I told her about my stepfather and about the African language he had taught me. I realised then that I had not mastered it enough to be able to teach Charlotte. Had my stepfather succeeded in leaving for Liberia and settling there? Had he achieved his dream of turning Liberia into a republic with an African language as its lingua franca?

I had gathered from talks around dining tables at the great houses and from my stepfather before his escape, some information about Liberia, but not in detail. The country was founded in 1822 by a group of determined freed slaves, as a result of the injustice towards black people in America. Many were of the opinion that the freedom desired by the slaves could be realised not in America but in Africa. Some expressed their misgivings about the mixture of the two peoples. Some prominent black leaders opposed such an enterprise, arguing that the blacks belonged to America because they had built it and that resettling them elsewhere implied they had no place in American society. Despite this objection, a group of abolitionists and wealthy whites went on to establish the American Colonization Society. This society, later followed by others, was founded after a series of consultations with the government of the United States, which expressed its concerns regarding having a colony on another continent. The plan was to purchase a piece of land in Africa that would serve as a colony under the auspices of the Society and not the government. White agents were to accompany the freed slaves to Africa in search of a suitable place. The men were funded with enough means to purchase land for that purpose.

In April 1820, on a cold winter day, the ship *Elizabeth* set sail with more than eighty people on board heading for the African coast. That first journey, which was long and treacherous, ended in disaster when most of the men and women (including some white agents) succumbed to a mysterious fever. That incident delayed every attempt to settle there for a while.

But a few years later, I had been told, the first batch of freed men and women landed on the soil of what was to be called Providence Island. Life, as expected, was hard for the settlers, for they had many difficulties to contend with, especially the killer fever.

That was long before I was born, and Liberia was now a republic whose independence was declared in 1847. This was the country where Charlotte was to live. I was determined to join her.

'I will build you the biggest house in Liberia,' I said.

She drew closer to me.

'Tell me about the house,' she said.

'It will have a huge verandah where we would sit at the end of the day. It will have a number of rooms corresponding to the many people we will have around us: your family, my mother and our children. The house will overlook a river, it has to be a river, and we will speak African languages to our children. We will learn to appreciate the natives.'

'We will visit all the settlements, Edward, and forge a union between all the people. That will be our goal,' she said.

I nodded, gazing at her face, at her hair which she had loosened, and at her slender hands, and I longed to touch them.

Once again, when I took those hands in mine, I marvelled at the delicate bones and at her capacity to have such a profound effect on me. This wonderment, ever-present as I held her hands, heightened my longing for her. While the birds and insects sang within the trees and bushes that shrouded us, I guided Charlotte to the sandy ground.

There appeared on her face, in those half-closed eyes, a flame that swept over me, consuming me as I gazed into them. Her lips were smiling as they received mine and, as we joined together and became one, as I felt alive like never before, my body went into a sudden shudder, perhaps in awe of the moment. Charlotte's hands reached out to hold me. Her face, like mine, gradually relaxed in a dreamlike expression.

I met the master soon after that. From the onset, despite the blood we shared and my long service on the plantation, our interaction had been almost businesslike. My role had been carved out from childhood and there were legions of examples of what would happen to me if I were to give up my role, even briefly and for whatever reason. That I had promised Charlotte to accompany her to Liberia and be with her forever did not mean it was a settled deal. I was not blind to what my station was in life and to what I was hoping.

I had no hesitation when I entered the master's study and met him seated behind his table, attending to affairs of the plantation. He had aged. His hair and sideburns were all grey, and his hands were mottled, his speech deep, almost slurred. And he wore glasses. There was no trace on the wrinkled face, not even in the shape of the nose or lips to suggest we were ever related. What then had kept me chained to a person as frail and feeble as the one who sat before me? I realised it was not him that held me but the institution he represented. All around, his actions and those of his kind were condoned and perpetuated.

'Master, I come to you with a matter of grave concern,' I said.

He looked up from the papers.

'I came to discuss my freedom.'

He looked at me over his glasses for a long while, and then he took them off and brought his hands to rest together on the table.

'Your freedom?' he said.

I knew then that it would be difficult.

'You gave my mother her freedom, and I thought if we discussed mine we could come to an agreement.'

'But I need you here, Edward. I've allowed you to be closer to me, I discuss all matters of the plantation with you, isn't that so?'

I agreed it was so.

'Your mother needs you here.'

It was futile to continue the discussion.

'I've met someone. She's leaving for Liberia, and I want to join her. You've heard about Liberia, I suppose,' I said.

'I don't believe Liberia will work. Your place is here.'

With that he put on his glasses and turned his attention to the papers. I left the study and went to see my mother.

'Don't lose hope, son,' she said. 'You will reunite with Charlotte, if not in this world then in the next. You will be with her.'

Despite this setback, Charlotte and I often met prior to her departure for Liberia. With her, during that brief period, my world was filled with joy. At the plantation, I found my tasks easier with her on my mind. Often, after meeting her, I was left with an insatiable hunger heightened by the knowledge that we would meet soon.

Months later, at my sanctuary, Charlotte bade me farewell without shedding a tear, for she was convinced that we would meet again.

'I will wait for you, no matter how long it takes,' she said, and those were her last words to me. The way she uttered them, her matter-of-fact tone, dispelled my fears and armed me with the singular purpose of one day reuniting with her.

For more than fifteen years, I waited every year and month, every day and night, to unite with Charlotte. At first we exchanged correspondence through our master in which she told me about conditions in the settlements in Liberia. But because of the distance and the difficulty of sending and receiving letters, the correspondence dried up. Hoping that providence might guide my letters to her, I continued to write, but received no answer. This burdened my heart with worry.

Mother died a few years after Charlotte's departure for Liberia. On her deathbed, she told me she was meeting the ancestors without fear, for she was leaving her greatest pride behind her. 'You are my pride and joy, Edward. Follow your heart wherever it leads you,' she said.

The freedom I longed for all my life came only after the death of our master. His wife, who followed a few years later, granted us our freedom shortly before her death. Now that I was free, I was struck with panic. Everything seemed suddenly strange to me and even my thoughts were clumsy. I found that I was unable to cope with the world outside the plantation. I could not meet Charlotte in such a state, for I would not make a good partner. I had to prepare myself for that eventful day.

Distance from my beloved hardened me. I was like someone detached from the reality of his longing, dissecting it like a surgeon, playing out the various versions of the moment I would reunite with Charlotte. My thoughts would drift towards the woman with feeble steps, and I could not sleep for thinking of her. Why couldn't I forget her and choose another woman here in America? Why had distance failed to smother my longing? Why had time not succeeded in severing our ties?

I moved north with the purpose of studying theology. It was a whole new experience. I met freemen who had skills of their own and were prosperous in their own trades. There were also learned men who were pioneers of our cause. I made acquaintance with people I would later sail with to Liberia. On completing my studies, I felt more than ever that I was ready to meet Charlotte and to embrace my destiny.

3

The duration of the passage and the perils associated with it had prepared us for the worst, but the first few days of azure skies and blazing sun dispelled our fears. We sat on deck at sunset to while away the time, hardly ever sleeping for our excitement, and sometimes we sang and talked of life on the plantations until dawn. I would lean against the rail to relish the pleasant sea breeze and to gaze at the gleaming waters stretching endlessly around us. Occasionally, the sound of the waves lashing against the ship would reach me like a song from far across the ocean, soothing my nerves, and dispelling my fears of the unknown. Meanwhile the ship edged on, pushing through the churning waters, moving further away from America and heading steadily towards our destination.

There were days when I would choose to keep myself to myself, refusing to join others for prayer. Prayers were led by Reverend Robert Barclay, a remarkable man. He was born a freeman and had acquired a sound education and was now on his way to Liberia to set up and lead his own church, 'to convert the natives,' he told me. His brother was a prosperous trader in Liberia, exchanging goods with European merchants and importing scarce commodities from America. Reverend Barclay would come on deck and share his experiences and those of his father with me. He told me that his father had bought his freedom before the age of thirty-five and had married a freewoman. The reverend was a gifted orator. He was endowed with a booming voice and the ability to hold a person with his portentous and sometimes frightening sermons on things to come.

By now I had acquainted myself with all the passengers on the ship, most of whom were surprised that I was a reverend myself. We exchanged personal histories that were often very much alike, varying only in the length of time spent on the plantations and our struggles for freedom. Some of the passengers had relatives in Liberia, a few were returning after a brief sojourn in America, but the bulk had not been to the country. There was an entrepreneur who was now transferring his thriving business to Liberia. The women were reuniting with their husbands and relatives.

We were on friendly terms with Captain Rupert West and his crewmen. The captain was my age, forty, or thereabouts, a squat fellow, with a bushy beard and fat, seafaring hands. His father, a former planter who owned one of the biggest plantations in the south had set all his slaves free and sent them in this ship captained by his son. Captain West had been to Liberia several times, transporting people and goods between the two shores, and he knew its short history like its inhabitants.

One quiet afternoon, while on deck, I asked Captain West to tell me about Liberia, but he turned to me and said:

'Wait until you see it for yourself.'

The first days were uneventful, but one morning we awoke to a violent storm. The ship lurched sideways, rocking back and forth, an experience I found frightening, for I had come to set much store by this life as a freeman. Our captain went on giving forlorn orders to his men, as all of them struggled to keep the ship on course. We kept below, gathered together, praying fervently to the Lord to make true his words that he would deliver his people to the Promised Land. The storm raged on for a whole night and day.

On the morning of the next day, five of the passengers, two men and three women, became seasick and before dusk their condition had deteriorated. While the skies still cracked asunder, Reverend Barclay and I kept vigil beside them, praying constantly for their recovery.

Our prayers, however, failed to save two of the five sick people, who were women. They expired on the morning of the third day.

The ship mourned them. Some of the passengers, distressed by their loss, rushed out onto the deck to vent their rage at the elements. They screamed and called it names. The prospect of a better future in Liberia became a remote one. Some even contemplated returning to America on their arrival in Liberia. That side of the black republic about which I knew little was then revealed to me: Liberia, I was told, was a land founded on uncertainties and with a haphazard economy. Settlers roamed the streets of its capital without a skill, and the few with skills could hardly find work. The whole attempt to set up a colony on a disease-infested continent had been a failure, an unrealistic dream.

But after some feverish sermons by the ever-energetic Reverend Barclay and me, the bedraggled and disheartened passengers kept faith. Reverend Barclay and I said some prayers, and then performed a sea burial. Crowding around the bodies, we wrapped them in sheets of white cloth and added some heavy objects for weight. One of us offered a Bible which was divided into two and wrapped with them. The winds blew hard, whining like lost souls. Then, bearing the bodies to the windward side of the ship, we committed them to the sea. We watched the bodies being teased by the ravenous waves, nibbling at them once, twice, and then sweeping them away in a single violent lurch.

We stared in contemptuous silence at the ocean. As if we had quenched its hunger with that ceremony, the ocean soon calmed and a bright sunshine broke upon us. Life returned again to the ship. Some of us could now dare to smile and laugh. Our confidence was fully restored and we could sing hymns of praise to the Lord. Even the captain and his men joined in the festivities. As the men sang, my mind went to my beloved Charlotte in Liberia. I remembered our meetings at the sandy spot. The memories of those moments together I had nurtured even during those periods when every hope of ever seeing her had waned. I was also anxious to meet the natives who featured in my mother's stories, especially the Vais. Perhaps I would meet my stepfather, if he was still alive. Not only was my mission to reunite with Charlotte and to propagate the words of God to the natives, but to observe their customs, to learn their ways and their stories.

After three weeks of seeing nothing but the endless expanse that was the ocean, the men gave up their songs and nightly revels. We now gazed at the ocean with accusing eyes, anxious to be delivered from the grip of its vastness. Sometimes Reverend Barclay and I would stare ahead of us in silence for a long while, and then we would retire to our sleeping corners. Sometimes, from being pure and clean, the air would change to a pungent smell that assaulted our noses, causing breathing difficulties. As a result, I became seasick for two days, but fortunately to the relief of everyone on board recovered. Now in our fourth week, the excitement of approaching our destination was evident on our faces. We talked about Liberia as though we had already landed on its soil. One afternoon, after more than forty days at sea, we caught sight of the shores of Liberia.

There was Monrovia, the capital, named after James Monroe, the fifth president of the United States, stretching out into the sea like a peninsula. The city was surrounded by an opulence of verdant, exotic bush. Palm fronds edging its shores danced to the winds, and birds circled the skies, perched on the fronds and then took off into flight.

Then and there, I knelt before the Lord to express my profound gratitude for leading me safely to these shores, to Charlotte.

We disembarked. Because of the bustle of activity and the confusion around the ship, I did not have time to bid farewell to Reverend Barclay and the captain properly, both of whom had been of tremendous help to me during the passage. On setting foot on the shore, Reverend Barclay was swept up in the throng of people who had come to receive him. Shouts of recognition rose every time a passenger saw a relative among the crowd.

Besides our ship there were other vessels docked at the port, probably English or French. The two great powers, Captain West had told me, traded in this part of the country and ruled over lands, north, east and west of Liberia, causing much insecurity to the existence of the tiny country. A large chunk of land which Liberia had hoped to include within its sphere of influence one day had already been taken by the French and British. There was a constant dispute between them and the Liberian government regarding trading posts and the payment of customs duties when traders called at a port on the Liberian coast.

I searched around desperately, trying to figure out a way through the crowd, and my eyes fell upon a young man with a haughty look. He was dressed in a long frock coat and a black topper. I drew up to him and asked him about a woman named Charlotte, adding some information about her. On hearing Charlotte's name, the young man's face clouded with irritation, and he turned away from me and sucked his teeth. His indifference and strange behaviour angered me, and I was about to deliver him a slap but restrained myself. There was something about him that suggested his anger might be a shield of sorts to protect his own vulnerability, so I went up to an old man to enquire from him.

The old man, a tall and big black man, who reminded me of my stepfather on the plantation, was dressed in the manner of the young man, differing only in the colour of the frock coat, which was grey. His searching eyes seemed to drink in the sight of every passenger. At the mention of Charlotte's name, hesitation passed over his face and he turned to the young man who was still staring at me, as if I were a source of fascination. He was silent for so long that he began to get on my nerves.

'Please speak to me,' I entreated him, now fearing for the worst. Charlotte must have passed on, I thought, but to my relief the man nodded and said that he would lead me to her. I threw my scarce luggage across my shoulders and followed him.

Monrovia surprised me. As we hurried along its dusty streets, I saw houses built of wood, spacious and grandiose and with front gardens, much like those in America. Here and there were stores trading goods imported from America, alongside African merchandise like camwood, ivory and palm oil which were sold to European traders. The churches were gracefully built as if the country was founded on a stone-hard faith. The people of Monrovia were keen on appearance. Women walked the streets in dresses that were in fashion in America, and as if to compete with them in elegance, the men wore black silk toppers.

We saw the home of the president, one of the most beautiful houses in the city. This was the heart of Liberia, the dream of the freedmen. I was certain now, long before reaching my final destination, that I could make this land my home, this America in this paradise of trees. I could thrive in peace here and practise the word of the Lord according to my ability. Here I could preach with the zeal and passion that I felt must accompany such an endeavour.

The sun, fierce and hard, beat down on us and the air was unusually sultry, peppered with the fiery and oppressive odours. Drenched in sweat, I followed the guide, hardly keeping pace with him. Perhaps once upon a time in America he had been a hard overseer, a relentless and feared slave trader, or a skilled plantation worker favoured by his master. Now he walked in huge, determined strides that suggested a man of strong will who condoned no foolishness. Out of courtesy or the fear of being rebuked, I refrained from asking him questions.

We had now traversed the main centre of Monrovia and were heading for the outskirts. The grandeur of the houses diminished to be replaced by mud-walled thatched huts. Some of the huts were huge and could house ten or more people, but most were small and dingy. Children in rags and in the poorest of condition played outside.

My guide stopped at one of the huts, the worst in that area, its door falling apart, its thatched roof riddled with holes. Hordes of flies buzzed about an uncovered bowl of food, and a stench rose up that compelled me to pinch my nose. Was this Charlotte's home?

My heart skipped a beat when he exchanged a greeting with someone inside. The occupant's language sounded like English but was slightly different to the ear.

Giant trees with hollows at the roots as huge as caves towered over the earth, and on both sides of the path there were impenetrable thickets of vegetation. I had the unusual feeling that we were being followed, but whenever I turned around I saw no one. Strange birdsongs rent the air, and I heard the barking of a dog somewhere close by. The fear that my guide was some madman leading me into grave danger now took hold of me, but in the middle of the forest he led me to a solitary house with a garden. It was newly built but of mud. Thinking that this was my beloved's home, I stopped. But the old man moved on. I could bear it no longer and called out to him. He turned to me with a hard gaze intended to put an end to what he perceived as my childish behaviour.

The path we now walked was a narrow strip with intertwining bushes on both sides, which at times hindered our progress. A snake slithered from one side of the path to the other. I trembled with fear. There was no sign of a house. Emerging from the thickets, we entered a sugar-cane plantation twice the size of the fields of our plantations in America. Voices echoed from it, tired and worn out, fading into the depth of the lush greenness. We saw men harvesting sugar cane, which the women bundled and carried to the mill. The old man exchanged greetings with them and moved on. At a certain point, my mute guide took up a song I had not heard in years. It was a plantation song.

I thought of America with a heavy heart.

We took another path. A profound and almost palpable peace reigned over that place. The path led to a wooden house, unlike the houses in the centre of Monrovia, but equally elegant.

The old man pointed at the house. I thanked him and tried to hand him a coin, but he sucked his teeth as if I had insulted him by offering the coin. Then he turned to head back to Monrovia.

I took a step towards the house, towards Charlotte.

4

It was as if my heart was about to wrench itself from my body. With every step I tried to persuade myself that I was exaggerating the importance of the moment and that I should move in steps befitting a man of my age and experience. But my heart reproached me. It brought to bear my nights of solitude and the years of tilling arid soil and picking cotton, and of seeing Charlotte's face in my mind's eye, taunting me about my failure to remember her features, the shape of her nose and lips, her eyes, her touch, and her arms. And of how that first time at the sanctuary had felt as I held her in my arms and guided her to the sandy ground.

On approaching the house, I encountered nothing but silence. The aroma of delicious cooking wafted about. The house was a one-storey building with a verandah whose pillars were decorated with vases of plants and flowers. A simply carved wooden crucifix with the agonised face of the Lord guarded the door. Chairs made of reeds, probably the work of the locals, stood here and there on the verandah. Hanging between two trees in front of the house was a hammock. Somewhere around the house, perhaps at the back, a faint, almost ethereal voice rose with a song.

I went up the front steps and paused before the door and called out, but received no answer. I gazed into the face of the Lord as if to ask permission. Pushing the door open, I went the length of the passage and stopped at the opened back door to listen for a presence in the house. Except for the sound of the song somewhere, it was silent.

After going down some steps, I looked around but saw no one except a garden of eggplants and collard greens on one side of the house, and a coop with a hen and its chicks. I walked on until I encountered the form of a woman bowed over a scrubbing-board, washing clothes in a bucket of water. She was humming and singing a song softly.

I paused to drink in the whole sight: the ochre earth which she stood on, bearing secrets that were thousands of years old; her hands wringing out the clothes with great deftness, and her song that was once composed in a different tongue in the heart of this continent and then borne by strong and careful people across the Atlantic and brought back centuries later to its root, unchanged, undistorted by time.

The wind sighed through the trees, wafting the pleasant smell of the cooking to me. Somewhere, a bird chirped a single note.

I drew myself up to my fullest height.

'Charlotte,' I called.

She went on washing and singing. She had not heard me.

'Charlotte,' I called again.

It was as if the world had ceased to move. Charlotte stopped, bowed, fixed in her posture, but her hands were trembling.

'Edward!' she said without turning to me.

It was a call tinged with sorrow and surprise, relief and hope. Slowly, she straightened herself up.

'Edward!'

She called me now in the tone of one who had expected this moment all along but was now not sure it was happening.

'Edward Richards!'

She turned to me, her hands wet with soapsuds, her mouth agape in surprise and wonder. A long silence ensued as we faced each other. Her once frail, slender body was now plump and shrouded in a simple blouse, her face beaten, her breasts sagged. There was a faint presence of grey in her hair. From the way her feet stood firmly on the ground, they had become much stronger now, the delicacy gone. She was shrouded in the mysteries of this land, in the grip of its terrifying beauty and she seemed edgy and on her guard.

But she remained the same Charlotte. Her eyes had not changed. They were accusing in their steadiness, yet forgiving, berating yet soothing, telling me of the longing that had pinched her face, and that had sucked every warmth and joy out of it and had hardened it to deal with the harshness of living in a place filled with mysteries, questions and riddles.

I moved towards her and flung my arms clumsily about her, sniffing the warmth of her body and relishing the kisses with which she covered me. We stood entangled in each other without words, each understanding what the other had gone through, and why I had to forgive her for the silence, and she me for times endured without me.

We could have remained like that, perhaps forever, were it not for a voice, terrible in tone, which called out her name.

'Charlotte, what is this?'

It was a man's voice. We disengaged with some difficulty.

A man wearing a permanent frown on his face and dressed in working clothes emerged from the house; he came down the steps with his eyes looking me over as though sizing me up.

The hen had left its coop, followed by its fluttering chicks as they pecked the ground for crumbs. The leaves rustled to the rise of the wind. The sun blazed as after a brief rainfall.

'I told you about Edward many years ago,' Charlotte said.

Her voice sounded strangely calm.

The man sucked his teeth, his gaze fixed on me.

'What is he doing here?' he asked.

I wanted to speak, but Charlotte said: 'He left America to come to me.'

'He should not be here.'

I stood there aware of the power of time to crumble and build, to bring together and divide. Charlotte moved towards me, but stopped short of touching me. Her eyes wet with tears, she pleaded to me to understand.

But how could I understand this life?

It was with a sense of dismay that I left the house with Charlotte calling after me. My heart raced with thoughts, but it pained me to think. I thought of returning to face Charlotte and hear, in her own words, what she felt about me, but brushed it off. It was obvious that she had shunned me with her accusing eyes, sent me off with her silence.

Now I began to doubt the eternity of love, and of its power to survive all odds. Yet, there was that suffering face of the Lord on the cross along the road, staring intently at me. How could love not be eternal? How could it not survive time that was merely the dawning of days and the fall of nights?

5

A miasma of foul air lingered over Monrovia. It was humid and the pricking sweat stung my eyes. Smoke rose from homes, and the wind bore the smell of the sea and the marshlands. With its sparse population, its provincial air, the city seemed like an abandoned settlement, a sluggish and isolated plantation which, after years of boisterous activity, was now left to the mercy of insects. Needing solace and some form of consolation, I sought refuge at Reverend Robert Barclay's home. My church in America had given me an address here in Monrovia, but with the sudden turn in events, I did not want to be confronted with the tiresome ceremonies that went with meeting new people.

The reverend's home was not hard to locate. It was situated in the town centre, a two-storey house with all the grandeur of a successful trader that his brother had become. On seeing me soaked in sweat, troubled, Reverend Barclay chose not to question me and immediately showed me to the guest room upstairs. His brother, John, the owner of the house, was at his store negotiating the sale of leather and palm oil to Europeans, and his brother's wife was visiting a relative at one of the settlements.

I slumped in the bed. Even though the window was ajar and I had got out of my shirt and shoes, I still sweated. An army of mosquitoes disturbed me. I was thirsty but had no desire to call for water or for anything else. I wanted rest. There was a leather-bound Bible lying on the table by me. A map on the wall indicated various settlements that constituted Liberia. The king-size bed had not been used for a while, I thought. But I did not mind.

Later, a young woman with tribal lines etched on both cheeks knocked at my door and informed me that my bath was ready. I queried her about the marks on her cheeks and she informed me, in simple language, that they were sacrificial marks and were etched on faces at birth or during special ceremonies to celebrate adulthood.

The young woman belonged to the Vai people, whose language my stepfather had once taught me. Her mother was of the Gbandis and hailed from the north, and her father, born in Bopolu whose king Sao Boso Kamara had played a major role in the founding of Liberia, had brought her to Monrovia to be an apprentice to the Barclays. This was a common practice during those days. In exchange for her services as a housemaid, the Barclays helped with her education. Her name was Tenneh.

I spoke a few words of Vai, which had suddenly come to me, and Tenneh's eyes lit up. She could not believe I had arrived that day and could already speak her language. I told her my story, and she nodded. She spoke to me in her language, but I could not follow her.

'You will learn,' she said and left.

I headed for the bathroom, a small four-walled mud cubicle erected outside the house. The bath was refreshing. I relished the cold trickle of water on my back and the slight rise of the wind.

By the time I had finished, dinner was served. Robert and his brother John were already at the table. Robust-looking, with amusing eyes, John, who smacked his lips when he talked, was a jovial type and wasted no time in proving it. On seeing me, he began to poke fun about life on the plantation, about the hard work, the overseers, the treacherous means employed by fieldworkers, drivers and servants alike to gain favours, and about the betrayals and hopes.

'Tell me, Reverend Richards, how did you survive it all to become what you are today, a preacher like my brother?' he asked.

I tried to laugh off his question, for my stomach growled with hunger. The table was decked out with a panoply of foods, some of which were new to me. Different dishes like collard greens and gravy, spicy, native beans cooked with palm oil and meat, and bowls of rice. There were fruits like pawpaw, avocado, bananas and slices of pineapple and oranges, evidence of the sumptuous lifestyle of the prosperous of Monrovia.

In a far corner of the room, a large and well-made cupboard stood. Next to a cross on the wall was a framed seal of Liberia with the barrow, the shovel, the shore, the ship, the palm tree, the dove and with the legend *The Love of Liberty Brought Us Here* inscribed upon it.

As guest I was asked to bless the food. We dined first on deer meat which, according to Robert, was caught by the natives who were great hunters. The sauce was palm butter. We discussed the passage and the difficulties we had encountered. John asked all the questions, his voice crashing like waves across the silence in the house, laughing at matters that Robert and I thought were serious.

At length, the subject of the natives came up.

'The militia is going to launch a punitive campaign against a village in reprisal for killing two Liberian traders.'

'The militia?' I asked.

'The militia protects the security of the country by arresting those hostile to it. And there are many who are hostile to us here.'

'Are the natives hostile to the settlements?' I asked.

'Not all of them,' Robert said.

'But we are the same people,' I said. 'We are here to bring them new ideas. We owe them the sharing of our knowledge.'

Silence descended on the table, the cause of which I could not fathom. Had I made a wrong remark? Tenneh entered with a bowl of cassava, which went so well with the pepper sauce that all I could do was nod my appreciation to her. Tenneh spoke her language to me, and I attempted to answer her, which further deepened the silence.

To change the subject, I said, 'Today, I heard a man speak with an accent that sounded like ours, but not quite.'

'He's one of the Congos,' John said.

I threw him a questioning look.

Robert said, 'They are Africans who, after the abolition of slavery, were recaptured from the ships of obstinate slavers. Because they didn't know their origin in Africa, they were brought to Liberia in their hundreds. They want very much to be like us.'

'How is that?' I asked.

'They go to church like we do and pride themselves on being Liberians,' the reverend said, scooping a spoonful of rice. Then he added, 'In that respect, the Congos are unlike the natives.'

This was followed by a long silence.

'What's your mission here, Reverend Richards?' John asked.

'I am here to convert the natives to the Lord.'

John let out a peal of laughter that rocked his body and the table, almost tipping over the bowls and plates. Tears dripped down from his eyes. Robert stared at his brother, annoyed. John wiped his eyes with the backs of his hands and said: 'I told my brother this before and will tell you now, Reverend Richards, you are in for a difficult mission.'

He expected an objection on my part, but I remained silent.

'Since the founding of Liberia, we've had but a handful of converts,' he said. 'The people are very stubborn.'

This surely can't be true, I thought to myself.

As though he was trying to refute his brother's claims, Robert said, 'Some of the natives like the Vais and the Mandingos are Muslims, and I think we could be partners in building Liberia because, unlike other tribes, they read and write and know Jesus.'

'They know Jesus?' I asked.

'He's one of their revered prophets,' Robert said.

'Why don't we start with them then?'

The table was silent again. I began to worry that my remarks ended up hitting the wrong nerve every time. I had to be careful.

We heard a woman calling Tenneh, announcing her presence. John's wife had returned. She came into the dining room, and Robert hastened to introduce us. She was a woman with intelligent eyes and a calm disposition. It was obvious that she had great influence over her husband, for his jovial mood changed the moment he saw her.

When the wife retired to her room, we went out and sat in front of the house, below the verandah, relishing the setting sun and fighting the mosquitoes. The two brothers sparked up a conversation on politics.

John dreamed of becoming a senator. 'To be a senator in this country, you must belong to the elites,' he said.

44

'Who are the elites?' I asked.

'Traders like me, preachers like my brother and politicians like our president. Liberia was built on the muscles, sweat, and intellect of those men and women. That's why we survived when the whole world thought we would fail,' he said.

Tired and dazed by the stinging heat, I kept largely out of the conversation and soon found myself nodding off to sleep. I excused myself and retired to bed. Despite the worries of the heart, the unbearable heat and the whining mosquitoes, I slept soundly that night.

6

Reverend Barclay and his brother were not in the house when I woke up the next morning. The reverend had gone to church and John to see the militia off into the interior. Mrs Barclay and I had breakfast together. We sat on the verandah, sipping tea and enjoying the sunrise over Monrovia. Tenneh served us cornbread with butter, and thereafter she took a seat in a corner, participating in our conversation with nods and smiles.

Mrs Barclay queried me about my mission to Liberia, which I expounded on in great detail, expressing my wish to see the natives as soon as possible. Later she went on to tell me her life story and that of her husband. She was a freewoman of colour. Her father, who was white, had loved her mother and bragged about his English ancestor who he claimed was of noble descent. He had died leaving one third of his inheritance, a considerable sum of money, to her. She was not old enough to inherit it and her mother was not comfortable with material things.

She had met John, a freeman with a rudimentary grasp of reading and writing, but with a dream of becoming one of the wealthiest black men in America. Mrs Barclay was taken by the fire in John's eyes whenever he talked about his dreams. She had educated him, and he in turn had taught her to confront her fear of the world. To every problem it seemed John had an appropriate solution. When she told him about the inheritance, he thought about it for days, including the possibility of opening up a huge store in America, but he realized he needed double that amount to be able to pull off such an enterprise.

The idea of migrating to Liberia came to him when her mother refused to consent to their marriage. The couple arrived in Liberia only to discover that after the expense of building a home they were left with little or nothing. John joined the militia and quickly rose in its ranks. He was admired and adored by his mates, so much so that the president of Liberia, who had followed his heroic deeds, brought him into his circle of friends. John was now ready to realize what he had wanted all along, a business of his own. And it had thrived. In the span of a few years, he succeeded in building a reputation as a man with the ability to introduce scarce goods to the country. His store was one of the biggest in all the settlements. The European traders found it profitable to trade with him. At one time, the president suggested that John become an ambassador to a European country, but he declined, claiming that his country needed him on the ground. The truth was he did not want to abandon his business, which was not only lucrative but also the greatest source of satisfaction for him.

He had a command of many native languages, but was at odds with their ways. He was not without his own reasons. According to him, the natives had failed to appreciate the goods the settlers had brought to them: Christianity, civilization and the sincere will to help them abandon their heathen ways. He traded with them, exchanging palm oil and camwood with guns and spirits, and he knew how their kings were chosen, their wars fought, their disputes resolved. He had discovered

– he was one of the few to do so – that all the natives traced their origins to outside of that part of the world. Stories were common among them of movements of such and such people at such and such periods.

John argued that the natives were ignorant of the fact that the people they had sold into slavery centuries ago had now returned to lay claim to a meagre portion of what was once theirs. John could not understand why the land had to be bought by the settlers in the first place. Why didn't the settlers randomly choose a place in Africa, anywhere in Africa, to stay and make it their home? Why purchase a piece of land? Why should the settlers bother with such an issue if this was once their home, the land of their fathers and mothers? These were the questions John pondered when he led the militia against the tribesmen.

He abhorred their trading in slaves, and he could not imagine being connected to people who perpetuated such a business. So when he fought the natives, it was not only to strengthen the foundation of the republic but to put a halt to that fiendish trade. And he fought bravely and with passion. He joined the British and American vessels patrolling the Atlantic in search of slave traders. It was how his fame grew and how he was admired by the settlers and feared by the natives.

'My husband is a hero,' Mrs Barclay said. Then added after a while, 'But sometimes he can be a simpleton, an idler.'

She went on to cite an example of John wanting to run for a senatorial position. Though he had launched a series of successful attacks on the natives and had led a famous assault on a group who had nearly succeeded in defeating the settlers, thereby preventing them from ruining years of work, John had chosen not to campaign but to wait until the last day before the elections. He got up early that morning, telling her that he had had a dream he was a senator.

Here Mrs Barclay stopped and glanced at me. 'Do you see now how a man could easily lead himself to ruins?' she asked. Were it not for her, she told me, John would be a destitute, bowing and scraping to the elite of the country. Here Mrs Barclay digressed from her story.

'Are you married, Reverend Richards?'

'I am not,' I answered.

'Sad for a man of your looks and knowledge,' she said.

I didn't know what to say. Tenneh threw me sideway glances, suppressing her laughter. I toyed nervously with my fingers.

'Are you in love with someone, Reverend?'

Mrs Barclay's gaze was fixed intently on mine.

'I am, Mrs Barclay,' I said.

'That is better, much better. Don't you think?'

'You are right, Mrs Barclay.'

I listened to her, relishing the quiet tone of her voice as she lauded herself for the successes of her husband.

Tenneh interrupted us, asking if we wanted more of her cornbread. The two of us nodded. Tenneh left for the kitchen. We sat for a while, waiting for the delicious cornbread. Soon Tenneh came back with slices of cornbread on a tray.

We ate slowly. I enquired from Mrs Barclay about my stepfather, mentioning his name and his passion for the Vai language. She had not heard of him, she told me. Perhaps he did not cross the ocean. Or if he did, he might have settled somewhere along the coast.

'Where can I meet some of the natives,' I asked her.

After some hesitation, Mrs Barclay told me where to find them.

'They are to be found in villages around Monrovia,' she said.

Not long after, having thanked her again and nodded to Tenneh, I found myself on the dusty roads of Monrovia, following the directions Mrs Barclay had given me.

7

The natives lived in villages surrounded by walls several feet high. In these villages, behind the huts were little vegetable gardens often tended by women and children. I saw a man tapping palm wine, a popular beverage I would learn later. I gathered that the natives were steeped in the worship of carved wooden images, and I was amazed to see a man offering food to an image. I almost shouted at him. But something about his dedication to it, his well-practised ritual, fascinated me. He sat before it, chanting and offering crumbs of food to it, rubbing it with his hand, pleading to it.

A celebration of sorts was going on in the village. Young girls dressed in raffia skirts and with their bodies painted with kaolin and coal danced to the beat of a drummer. A procession of men and women surrounded them. Shouts of joy rose from everywhere.

I asked one of the participants what was happening, and I was told that the girls were coming of age and the whole village was celebrating the event.

I found that the villagers spoke various languages and that the languages were similar to each other. This suggested that perhaps they had a common ancestry. There were tribes from all over the interior thriving here. Some could speak English. In the midst of the huts, I saw a few homes built in the style of those in Monrovia. A young woman with a good command of English told me that her grandfather had married someone from the house of one of Liberia's ministers.

Doors were open to welcome me and I was invited to share in the meals. Although I had been warned of the danger to my health if I yielded to such lavish hospitality, I did not hesitate to accept and relish the food. My conclusion was that the natives were fascinated with the new ways but had their qualms. They feared that with the coming of the settlers they would lose their way of life. The villages were already a hodgepodge of American-Liberian and native cultures thriving together. I saw a man with an American topper and baggy trousers proudly sauntering around. Some spoke English mixed with their mother tongues. These were encouraging signs. John's assumption that converting the natives was impossible seemed fallacious to me. The evidence to the contrary was to be found here.

On my way home that day, I was light-hearted, sure that with love and patience, the two greatest virtues of the Lord, I would lead some of the natives through the gate to the Kingdom of God. Or I would show them at least that we meant them no harm, not in the least.

Not long after I had got home and Mrs Barclay and I were sat outside, John returned. He told us that the villagers, one of whom had killed the two Liberian traders, had handed over the perpetrator without even being asked. The villagers had then proclaimed their allegiance to the government of Liberia anew and forever. To prove their commitment, they had given the militia rice, smoked meat, leather, calabashes of palm oil and many other things. John broke into laughter. 'That's the way to treat them,' he said. 'With force and without mercy.' And his wife sucked her teeth.

John, a member of one of the oldest associations, the Freemasons, could not stay for dinner, for he was to attend one of their meetings. But I knew he was escaping the wrath of his wife. He went to the bedroom and emerged dressed in a black suit, a top hat and tailcoat and left while his wife rolled her eyes at him.

'What did you see today, reverend?' she asked.

I recounted my experience, beginning with the festivities that went on in the village, and I told her of my general impression of the natives and the fact that my mission could certainly be accomplished now that I had met with some of them. Although she was delighted that I felt that way, Mrs Barclay warned me not to be over-optimistic.

'Many before you have tried and failed,' she said.

Reverend Barclay returned. He asked me when I was going to call on my church to see how I would go about doing my work. I needed some time, I answered. He said that he was leaving soon for the settlement of Harper, Maryland. We conversed for a long time that evening, and I thought that the Liberians were now different in many ways from their brethren in America.

I frequented the native villages around Monrovia, seeing the whole venture as a kind of orientation for my missionary work. Tenneh, ever-resourceful, was of tremendous help to me. She confirmed what I had thought, that her Vai language was similar to other native languages, and that names and counting had similar words, with one group counting to *tan*, which was ten, and another to *pu*, which also meant ten.

For two months after my arrival and the incident with Charlotte, I made no attempt to see her. My work helped to take my mind off her. Whatever illusion I might have entertained about our relationship was shattered with that singular experience at her home. It would be better if I put her and our past behind me, like I had done with other aspects of my life, and to dedicate my life fully to the service of the Lord.

Despite being in this coastal town for a while, the oppressive climate wore me down and I could not sleep from the assault of mosquitoes. Bumps and abscesses, evidence of their bites, were strewn all over my hands and face. My body itched so much that often I had the maddening urge to scrape off the itching spots. Besides fighting the parasitical insects, my nights were spent worrying about my mission and the natives. All these factors led to what transpired.

On my way from one of the villages, having completed my day's work, I was taken by a sudden headache. My head throbbed with such pain that I struggled to keep myself from falling. By the time I reached home, my body was shivering with a fever that had once threatened to wipe out the entire population of Monrovia. I went immediately to bed.

Having suffered from loose bowels the whole night, I was as frail as a feather the next morning. Unbearable pain surged up my joints and I was often in violent convulsions. One minute I was comfortable and the next I was throwing up. My spit tasted sour and the water I drank tasted like a bitter drink. Food was unpalatable. I could not sleep, could not lie still. I floated in between life and death.

Tenneh and Mrs Barclay attended to me. Days passed but with no great improvement in my health. My end, it seemed, had come.

One afternoon, a week into my illness, when I was in one of my deliriums, Tenneh came in to announce that a woman named Charlotte wanted to see me. 'Don't let her in,' I managed to convey to Tenneh, gesturing widly. 'Tell her she's not welcome. I don't want to see her.'

She left and returned saying: 'But she insists on seeing you, Reverend.' I rolled my eyes at Tenneh.

'Tell her to go away.'

But I heard Charlotte's footsteps.

She came in the room dressed as if she was heading to church. She felt my forehead and caressed my body. She was silent. A strange smile coalesced around her lips. What she then did astounded me: she undressed, and I saw her like I had not seen her for a long time. She lay beside me, her body's warmth sending a shiver through me. We were together again, in one bed, in a strange house and country. As I was too frail to hold her, Charlotte held me, whispering soothing words. While she snuggled close to me, I suddenly realised I could never betray the longing of my heart and that I needed her. There she was, soothing my trembling body, sharing in its feverish warmth and taking in the nauseous stench of my breath. We were one again.

Charlotte told me of her early days in Liberia. In the beginning she had to cope with intimidating men who chided her for opting to wait for a man who had not survived the cruelty of plantation life. She waited for years. Her days were unbearable without me. She wrote several letters but received no reply. Waiting had broken her heart, tortured her and worn her down. It was not out of love that she chose her husband, but out of fear that the Monrovian Society might shun her for refusing her fiancé, who had loved her enough to build her a house that was the envy of many, and a farm that yielded valuable crops. Even during her marriage, she hoped that one day we would meet again.

Her voice was serene and soft, easing my heart and steadying my breath. She stayed the night with me. When I referred to her husband and how he would react if he knew she was with me, Charlotte said: 'He knew all those years that my heart was elsewhere. I didn't conceal my feelings regarding you. I told him today that I was going to see you. He has to learn to live with that. You are here now, Edward.'

With Charlotte beside me, I forgot my illness. I forgot everything. She was ever-present and ever-caring the next day and during the weeks that followed. She did not leave to attend to her husband and we never discussed him. In the morning, she bathed me, prepared soup and fed me. Urging me on to eat and gently chiding me, she made sure that I drank all the soup. I managed a laugh and could not remember laughing so heartily for a very long time. When I fell asleep, Charlotte nestled close to me. I felt some kind of elation while in the grip of the illness that I had never felt before, and I knew then that I would not succumb to it. I would survive it to be able to love her.

No one objected to Charlotte's presence in the house. Indeed, it was welcomed. It seemed that the household had now worked out my reason for being in Liberia. I was a preacher who had taken the mighty words of the Lord as his guide but who had chosen to follow the longing of his heart as far as this shore. Instead of shunning me, the house honoured me. Although the two of us deferred on issues concerning the natives, John would visit me every evening, cracking jokes to make me laugh. He would be joined by Mrs Barclay and Tenneh.

Reverend Barclay wrote from Harper saying that the Lord would not forsake his servants and I should, therefore, not lose faith.

Within two weeks, I was on my feet again. In six months, the most precious of my life, I saw Charlotte almost every day. She would leave her home in the morning before sunrise and was at the house before I had awoken. Together we saw the natives and together we preached and prayed. Charlotte was versed in the scriptures and preached so convincingly to the natives, whose language she could speak, that we boasted a few converts in less than a month. I was able to understand her during that period and to understand myself and our relationship.

It was Charlotte and no one else who encouraged me to answer to the incessant call of the Lord to carry on my missionary work. She would love me forever though we were not destined to be husband and wife.

I couldn't ask for more. But I was to get more.

8

As part of my preparation for the journey to the interior, I hired the services of two young Congo men as guides and to help with my luggage. One named Patrick had been to the interior several times, while Matthew had a relation among the natives. They were glad to be my guides, and assured me of the safety of the interior. Nevertheless, because of rumours of bandits who often attacked travellers and difficult rulers who impeded further penetration into the interior because of their own trade interests, in slaves and otherwise, and because of fear of the unknown, I was compelled to have several guns in my luggage. I also took medicines, presents of clothes, perfume, knives and spirits I had bought from John's store. A traveller to the interior could not do without a sextant, a thermometer and sheets of paper and notebooks to jot down observations.

I chose not to confine myself to the surroundings of Monrovia, but to head deeper into the forest, to Tenneh's mother's birthplace. She told me that her mother's people lived in a place so remote that they had not heard a single word of the Gospel in a thousand years.

I was not blind to the difficulties and did not underestimate them. But instead of flinching away from them, I wanted to confront them head-on. Armed with the teachings that true faith could move mountains and allow one to walk on water, I prepared for the journey.

Mrs Barclay tried to talk me out of it. It was a perilous adventure, she said, a reckless attempt on my part which, she was sure, I would not survive. John could not conceal his obvious worry. He knew the interior. It could make or break one, he told me; it was like a mystery that could choose to reveal itself to a traveller at once or wait years to show its true face. It could punish an intruder on the spot or choose to forgive. To survive it, you had to withstand its biting claws until such a time that it chose to ignore you.

Pleased that I was carrying the Gospel to her people, Tenneh however warned me that they might not comprehend it, or that I might not cope with life there. 'I am going in peace, Tenneh,' I told her. 'I am going to tell them that we are brothers and sisters. Those of us from America have returned home.'

Reverend Barclay wrote to me, advising me not to venture deeper into the forest but to confine my work to villages around Monrovia. A work of God was a work of God, he wrote, and it was unnecessary to expose myself to dangers such as the interior.

Only Charlotte stood firmly behind me. Nothing, she said, could harm one who had chosen the Lord as his shepherd.

On the day of my departure, the young man I had encountered months ago behaving foolishly at the port paid a call on me. He had come with a message that his mother wanted to see me.

'Who is your mother?' I asked.

'You will know if you follow me,' he said.

He was remarkably docile that day. I brought up the subject of our encounter and berated him for his lack of manners. His silence emboldened me to go on reprimanding him, and it led me to thinking that perhaps he was not a spoiled young man after all. I tried to inveigle him into parting with information regarding his mother, but he would not respond. He led me out of Monrovia, following the same path that the old man had taken nearly a year ago, the path to Charlotte's home.

We met Charlotte seated in one of the chairs outside the house. There was a strange calmness about her that hinted that things did not augur well for me, but in her eyes there was a burning light that contrasted with her calmness. It was a quiet morning, the sun mild and the wind pleasant. The air was fresh with the scent of the bush. The young man stood a distance away from us, toying with his fingers.

'I sent for you, Edward,' Charlotte said.

'He refused to tell me,' I said.

'He's angry,' Charlotte said, looking at the two of us.

'What on earth for?' I asked.

'Because he'd not known his father all his life.'

'His father?'

Charlotte dropped her gaze.

'Who is his father, Charlotte?' I asked.

She looked at me square in the face and said, 'You are his father, Edward.'

I couldn't speak. Words failed me. Then I turned to the young man. Here, in front of me, with the height and resemblance to me, with the angry eyes and the habit of toying with his fingers; here in every way the spitting image of me, was my son. Why didn't I see it before?

'Charlotte!'

'I kept my end of the bargain, Edward.'

'But you never told me!' I said.

'I named him after you.'

I was silent.

'Try to love each other,' she said.

I moved towards young Edward to hug him, but he would not allow me. Anticipating such a reaction from a son whose existence I had until that very moment not even known of, I held out my hand to him. He took it. I knew then that it would take a miracle to bridge the gap between us. At that moment, I cancelled my trip to the interior with the purpose of winning my son's approval. As expected, it proved a formidable task. He was a different person, hardened by longing and forlorn hopes.

Though he was frequently in my company, he refused to open up to me. He accompanied me to the villages and listened when I preached to the natives. Sometimes he would withdraw into himself, his mind preoccupied and it would pain me to see him so sad. I reached out to Charlotte.

'I don't know what to do to make our son regard me as his father,' I told her on one occasion, and she gazed at me for a long while.

'He's never had a father for so long. Give him more time,' she said, and promised to talk to him. But even after her intervention, that time and many other times, Edward Jr remained passive.

Whatever it was that he harboured towards me, anger or perhaps rage, it seemed to consume both of us every time we were together. He would not confide in me, nor relax in my presence, and I could only conclude that perhaps the image of the father he had held on to did not correspond with the reality. Perhaps my presence pained him.

'You are my son, and I am here now,' I told him one day as we headed to one of the villages to talk to the natives.

'But for how long?'

'What do you mean?' I asked.

'You will leave soon.'

'I will never leave you.'

'We will see.'

With that he once again left me in the cold. He refused to debate the subject further.

A year went by like a fleeting wind, and I had not succeeded in igniting in my son the love I felt for him.

Charlotte told me, 'Edward, I've talked to our son and failed. But don't give up on him now. It's possible he's testing you.'

'But I don't seem to succeed with him.'

'You will succeed, Edward.'

'I feel I am alone in this, Charlotte.'

She shook her head.

'You are not alone, but I can't force him to love you.'

Yet the Lord, in his capacity as the Most High, the omnipotent and omniscient, came to my aid and answered my prayers in an unexpected way. The words of the Lord had touched young Edward. With that miracle, that sudden transformation, love came pouring into his heart towards me. I had sowed love with my love of the Lord, and now I was reaping it. When I informed her of the changes in Edward, Charlotte shrugged her shoulders.

'It was meant to be,' she said.

At fifteen, Edward had left school when he was told that he had a father who was probably alive in America. He chose to linger around the port whenever the ships docked and wait for that father. When he finally saw him, his anger at his father's absence had consumed him.

My son went back to school and I stayed a year more in Monrovia to instruct him in his studies. Sure now that he was on the right path and I had made my peace with him, I decided to carry out my other task in this world.

It was time to leave for the interior.

9

This time, along with Patrick and Matthew, a young man named Joseph was to make the journey. Joseph was not a Congo but a product of the union between a settler and a native woman. His mother's village lay on the way to Tenneh's mother's village. Over the years, the attitudes of many settlers had evolved from hardly condoning marital relationships with the natives to accepting it. Of the three accompanying me, Joseph was the boldest. He mocked the other two over their lack of knowledge about the interior. His boisterous spirit, his enthusiasm, were enough to assure me of a safe and energetic trip.

Things were different regarding my son. Having got used to calling me father, to addressing me with a slight tremor in his voice, perhaps afraid of losing me, my son found it hard to accept that I would leave him. Only after long conversations with him did he agree to let me go. Even so, when he saw me off he was bereft.

Charlotte had been calm when introducing Edward Junior, and appeared so again when bidding me farewell. Her turbulent emotions could only be detected from the throbbing of her heart while she hugged me. She wore a resigned look, which in hindsight conveyed the inner peace of a woman who had learned to accept life as it was, not as it should be. In the nearly two years of our relationship in this coastal town, she had taught me, among other things, that it was better to express love in silence.

We would sit in the shade of a tree for hours, recalling the moments spent in the embrace of my sanctuary in America. We would linger in that past and then return to the present, to the two of us seated under the tree, holding each other, holding on to each other. We talked about Edward and how we would raise him, talked about food, the meat or fish, the sauce she would prepare for us. We talked about life.

When not with Charlotte, I would sometimes dream about her walking towards me hand in hand with our son. I could not stop being amazed at how she had adapted to this climate and to this setting. She was one of the few settlers who spoke some native languages. Indeed, she had gone as far as dressing like them, wearing a tunic and wrapping about her long pieces of cloth. Only occasionally was there a hint that she had once crossed the ocean and was one of the settlers. When the men and women of Monrovia dressed in full regalia to celebrate Independence Day, my Charlotte was not with them but somewhere with the natives.

Once when we were together, somewhere on the outskirts of Monrovia, seated in the shade of a tree, our silence disturbed only by the sound of insects and the songs of birds, she told me she was so taken by the beauty of the coast that she had gone on a mission to persuade people to work together with the settlers, just as I planned to do. Well aware that she was bound to encounter difficulties on both sides, she had nevertheless carried on. It was her idea, not her husband's, to move outside Monrovia to be closer to the natives and learn their ways.

That morning, with utter composure, Charlotte bade me farewell. She joined my son, the Barclay family, including Tenneh and Reverend Barclay, who had briefly returned to Monrovia, in the dining room, and we prayed for a safe journey. We hugged, and I left the house to join my three companions who waited outside, their impatience obvious.

Just when I was about to join them, Charlotte's voice rent the air with my name. There was panic in the call. She came rushing forward and flung her arms around me. Her body shook in my arms and her tears wet my chest. Confused, overwhelmed, I held on to her. Her silence, our silence regarding our hearts' song was broken. I learned then that silence was not enough, that sometimes we needed words to formulate our thoughts and feelings. And Charlotte decided to voice her feelings.

I led her to the verandah. Charlotte told me that she was the favourite of her father whose mother was an Indian. During her childhood she would dream of joining her grandmother's people. Many a time, an old man would appear in her dreams, and he would hold out his hand to her. It was her ancestor, an Indian leader of his people, calling her to join them. As she approached adulthood, the old man disappeared from her dream. No matter how hard she tried, he failed to appear again.

She had survived slavery by hoping for the return of her ancestor. After years of waiting, he appeared to her. He conveyed his displeasure at her condition, a slave in the homes of others with the remote chance of ever joining her people. Then he disappeared again. She did not see him again until the day she stepped on the coast of this continent. The old man wore a smile that lacked warmth.

She knew something was amiss. Years drifted by without any sign of him. And she had learned to forget him. On the day I returned, she told me, the old man had appeared to her and talked to her. Her people had forgiven her for abandoning them, he had said, and that she should pursue freedom whenever and wherever in the world. A happiness the like of which she had never experienced before had filled her. Afraid that by telling me the dream she might lose the full significance of the feeling, that it might wear off or lose its magic, she had kept silent.

'I wanted to tell you this story before you left, Edward,' she said. 'You brought back my ancestor. Thank you.'

Charlotte stood up and let go of me, wresting herself from my hold. I managed to walk away from her. She waved me on.

10

My companions and I headed northwards as bright tropical sunlight bathed Monrovia, blowing life into the luscious green of its vegetation. With all the uncertainties accompanying this enterprise, I was not sure I would ever see the town again. So I turned to gaze at it. Monrovia was proof of man's inherent right to freedom, of his irrefutable desire to make his own way in life. It was the answer to the dreams of freedmen, but at the root of its founding lay questions whose answers were as important as the freedom it now gave. How could Monrovia forge a way forward without fully addressing the question of its indigenous people? How could it marry its Christian values with those of a large population whose way of life contrasted and in some ways opposed those values?

I raised my hand to wave at Monrovia. Perhaps the gesture was meant for the bluish sky, for the verdant forest stretching out to the horizon, and for the town rising from sleep to get ready for another day's challenges. Or maybe it was for Charlotte, who'd had the strength to survive without me, or for my son Edward who had waited for me to cross the sea. It might have been for them all that I waved.

My companions looked on in silence. We headed on. It was not long before we were confronted with the grandeur of the interior. Trees gazed at us in eternal repose and plants brushed against us and clung to our clothes. We journeyed for miles without seeing a single soul. On the crest of a mountain strewn with low brush, we paused to drink in the view of the forest spreading out like a closely knitted canopy of a density such as I had never seen before, not even in dreams. 'The forest could be a friend or a terrible foe,' Joseph said, and I believed him.

We descended the mountain. Now and then we would hear voices coming to us from places Joseph told me were villages. Just before dusk, we arrived at such a place. The mud huts were dark grey, and it was quiet at that hour of the day, the only noise the sound of pestles hitting mortars as women cleaned rice. On our way to meet the chief, we saw a very old man lying in a hammock, swinging it slowly, his eyes closed.

We met the chief dining in front of his house surrounded by a group of elders. He made us wait until he had finished eating before granting us an audience.

'Chief, we are in need of a place to pass the night,' I said, and Joseph interpreted for me.

The chief replied in a stammering voice and with wild gestures that we were not welcome in his village. Then he had some of his men move towards us to chase us out of the village.

'Men with your attire are harbingers of war,' he said.

I protested: 'We came to persuade you to work together with us, to build peace between us.'

What did he mean by men of our attire? Did he mean the Liberians on the coast or the white men? Harbingers of war? What kind of war? I found his behaviour unacceptable. I had not come to fight but to share what I had learned with the people of the interior and to learn from them.

We made our way out of the village escorted by his men. Joseph told me that past experience had made some rulers apprehensive of settlers.

'That chief was once a notorious slave trader,' Joseph added.

I couldn't believe my ears. I had heard of such people before, but I never thought that I would come into contact with them. I was trembling with anger.

'You say that man traded in slaves?' I said.

'Yes, and he was not the only one,' Joseph said.

I pushed past the men who were leading us out of the village and went to confront the chief, my rage boiling over. So it was true, I thought, so there were men who sold their own kin. I had moved so quickly that I was sitting on the mat facing the chief before his men could stop me.

Not a muscle in his face twitched.

'Tell me, did you trade in human beings?'

I had thrown all caution to the wind and realized I was addressing him in English. I turned to Joseph, who was now yelling at me to leave.

'You don't know these people,' he said. 'They can be dangerous. Mr Richards, please, let's leave. We are not safe here.'

I did not budge. I was ready to get into a fight with the chief, and I was amazed at my own courage, my anger egging me on.

'Tell him exactly what I said.'

'What are you saying?' the chief asked after Joseph had delivered my words to him. He stood up, his face furrowed with anger, and I jumped to my feet too, prepared to face him head on, to throw myself at him if need be.

'Did you sell your people?' I asked.

'My people?'

'Yes, your people.'

'They were my enemies. And I was being merciful to them.'

'Merciful? You call selling people merciful?'

'I did not kill them, for that's what we do with enemies, stranger, kill them. Be careful now or you will become my enemy.'

A hoarse laugh escaped me. 'So you are not denying that you sold people to be slaves?'

'What is wrong with this stranger? Has he lost his mind? Tell him we are not afraid of his kind, however armed they may be.'

His armed men, who numbered in the dozens, surrounded me.

'Let's see now, stranger, whether you have a tongue to speak.'

He was so close to me that I could smell his breath, which was harsh and pungent, but I did not budge. By now, my three travelling companions were begging me, pleading to me to back down.

'They could kill us here, Mr Richards,' Joseph said.

I ignored him.

'Do you know what happened to those you sold into slavery? Have you ever wondered,' I said, and when Joseph translated the chief laughed.

'Get them out of my sight,' he said, and gestured to his men to lead us away out of his village.

'You are lucky I slept well last night, stranger,' he said.

'Mr Richards, if you go on like this, we will not survive the interior,' Patrick said when the village was far behind us.

But I was so upset that I did not respond. If such men had not collaborated with slavers, I thought, we could not have been uprooted from our homes, our lands and continent. I loathed his sort with all my heart.

Meanwhile night had fallen, and we were yet to find a place to sleep. The night was alive. All kinds of beasts seemed to have awoken and were intent on gobbling us up. Their calls resounded through the darkness. The young men told me of frequent cases of leopard and lion attacks in the forest. We held on to each other, moving one pace at a time, stopping when we bumped into trees or tree trunks that lay across the path. The wind would howl, carrying the cry of a tortured animal. We waded through streams and negotiated bridges that were in fact ropes tied from a tree on one riverbank across to another on the other side.

We arrived at the second village just before dawn and met its chief preparing to receive horsemen from the savannah. The chief was a bulky man who struggled to breathe, and was drenched in sweat on that cold morning. He listened to our story.

'You are most welcome,' he said, and referring to our encounter with the old chief who traded in slaves, he said: 'Some rulers survived and still go on selling human beings. I don't tolerate it, and there are many like me.'

I caught myself beaming at the chief.

He shifted on the mat and sat upright.

'Your bath will be ready soon,' he said, and asked his wives to prepare one for us. As we waited, he told us about the horsemen.

'They are emissaries of the emperor Samori Touré. Samori's built the largest empire in this part of the world, and his men are on their way to Monrovia to meet the Liberian government to discuss the possibilities of supplying Samori with arms in his fight against the encroaching French and English,' he said.

Samori Touré must be one of those African heroes who populated my mother's stories, I thought, the ones who spoke

71

in voices of thunder, and I couldn't wait to know more about him. But by then one of the chief's wives announced that our bath was ready. Later, after a refreshing soak, we joined the chief, who was sitting in the shade of a tree with the Samorian emissaries.

'Tell me about Samori,' I asked the men.

One of the emissaries spoke: 'His capital is Bissandougou, a journey two or three weeks away from here. It's a walled city, the most fortified in all the lands of the black-skinned people. Besides Sundiata Keita and Mansa Musa, Samori is the greatest ruler the world has ever known.'

The men went on to tell me about his birth and ascendancy to power.

Their detailed description of their leader intrigued me. It was evident that Samori was an extraordinary man. I promised to keep my eyes open regarding the man and his ambitions. When the emissaries left, I presented the chief with a bottle of perfume, some drinks, and a knife.

'Thank you for these gifts,' he said. 'You are one with whom we can trade. You are one to be trusted.'

'I am a trader in the word of God, chief,' I said. 'I purchase the consent of men with the promise of the Kingdom of God.'

The chief listened without interrupting me until I had finished.

'You sound like Muslims, some of whom have married my daughters. I understand what you say, but I've chosen to remain worshipping the gods of my ancestors,' he said.

Since my encounter with the slave-trading chief, I had learned to be careful and patient with the people of the interior. I did not want to anger the chief by attacking his idols. Perhaps one day he would see the light.

'You've been kind to us,' I said.

He nodded, and said, 'Your lodging is ready.'

During the night, we stayed indoors and were surprised by the songs of children accompanied by clapping hands. On enquiring, I was told that it was the moonlight dance. Boys and girls would gather to tell stories and to sing and dance, just like we had done on the plantation.

Early the next morning, we bade the chief farewell, thanking him for his generosity, whereupon he said that he would like us to visit again.

We headed toward Bopolu. Along the way, we came to the village where Joseph's mother was born, and the old chief welcomed us like relatives. We stayed on for a few weeks, a period that gave me the opportunity to observe the customs of the people.

The men rose before cockcrow and headed for their farms, returning before dusk. Most often, the women accompanied them or stayed at home to prepare a meal and then took it to them. The elderly stayed at home, cared for by their working children. Often, they played a part in rearing their grandchildren and proffered advice on matters relating to the village. Although the bulk of them were farmers, the villagers nevertheless went once a month to the market of Bopolu to sell their crops, consisting of palm oil, palm kernel oil, rice and vegetables. The people traded in iron money, a tiny iron bar an inch long. Those who could not afford the currency swapped their goods.

The village practised polygamy, with the men dividing the night equally between their spouses. All the women adorned their waists with beautiful tattoo patterns and the most privileged wore huge gold earrings. Beauty was celebrated here as I suppose it is in all the villages of the interior. The most beautiful of the women or girls were greatly admired, and their beauty drew men from all over the interior and down to the coast.

After a fruitful stay, we pressed on with our journey. At one village, we heard the peculiar story of a man who could camouflage himself as a forest creature, throwing the hunted animal into confusion. We met the men returning with a kill. It was a leopard. As customary, pregnant women were not to see it for fear that their offspring might bear the countenance of a leopard. To protect those women, the leopard's face was covered with a piece of cloth. Horns were blown to welcome the great hunters. But on the outskirts of the village, people could not agree whether to bring the kill into the village or not. Some were against it, while others were for it. At last, as it was bound to be, those who favoured the bringing of the leopard to the centre gained the upper hand. And the kill was brought in with cheers and uproar.

The chief served us palm wine. Later we headed on. Joseph warned me of the next village, which teemed with sorcerers, a place where a cooking pot was nowhere to be found, for the witches used invisible pots. We passed through there without seeing a single soul.

That same day, we reached Bopolu. It was a large town, perhaps bigger than Monrovia. It was market day. Dozens of people roamed about, selling and bartering goods: kola nuts, vegetables, gold, silver, guns, knives, perfumes, clothes and a host of other things.

My companions led me to the king's palace. It was huge and plastered with cow dung. He was a giant of a man with a calm disposition and a soft voice. Among his retinue was a praise-singer. The chief received us as though we were not strangers. Indeed, he told us later, he had met some government officials from Monrovia before and had worked hand in hand with the government.

74

He told me the history of the town. The famous king Sao Boso, his grandfather, was a friend of the settlers and had helped them to acquire much needed land. But the settlers had not responded to the needs of the natives when they had asked for help. He mentioned Samori, who had asked the Liberian government for help several times but to no avail. I told him that I had met Samori's emissaries. The king expressed his hope that the government would accept Samori and his gesture of friendship.

The praise-singer now began to tell me about Bopolu's past. Most of what he said was interpreted and I gathered from his gestures what he was trying to convey. Flipping his hands about him, playing his musical instrument accompanied by songs, he lamented the past, which was greater than the present. Suddenly he stopped and took a bite of a kola nut. He was sweating from the effort. Bopolu, he said, was the link between the forest and the savannah, along a trade route that went as far as Timbuktu and beyond. It occurred to me to bring up the subject of the salt people in my mother's stories. While my words were being interpreted to him, the praise-singer was nodding.

He knew the story of the salt people. 'In our society', he said, 'children are not told the stark truth regarding death. They are told instead that the dead have gone to buy salt. That is because a people who had once travelled to buy salt never returned. The salt people were the people of the borderlands and the Arabs themselves. Traders brought us salt. But at one time, the supplies ran out. Some of our people went in search of salt to a kingdom once ruled by Sundiata Keita but they never returned, and those who followed met the same end. Rumours then spread that they had been snatched by people who had come in boats from across the sea.'

The puzzle fitted. My mother, without us realizing it, had been telling a story that was still alive here. While the people of this land did not know the lot of those who had gone to buy salt, we knew, we who were on the other side of the sea. I thanked the praise-singer.

Later on in the day, we saw the king again. When the conversation came round to the subject of Muslims, he mentioned that he was one himself but was not as educated as the imam of the mosque. I asked to have an audience with the imam. The king answered that it could be arranged. Someone was on hand to take me to him. The imam, dressed in a tunic, was austere-looking and surrounded by his students who were reciting words written on wooden tablets. He received me kindly. I asked him if he had anything in his religion about Jesus. To my amazement, he told me about Mary and the miraculous conception of the Lord. When he was finished, I said that I had brought him the word and told him about the kingdom of God about which, surprisingly, he knew a great deal. He accepted my teachings. And I thought that we needed such people to build a unified Liberia, for that was the future, for us and for them.

During my stay at Bopolu, I learned more about its people. It was a heterogeneous society with many of the tribes of the interior dwelling within its walls. I also began to learn some words of the language to prepare me for my final destination.

Every day I asked and was granted the king's audience. He would tell me about the customs of the land and ask me questions about America. On my second visit to the imam, I learned how his religion was introduced into the interior. Traders and clerics like him took the religion to many parts of the forest; some of them settled and intermarried. Most had risked their lives, like I was doing, to propagate the teachings of God.

Months after our stay in Bopolu, my three young travelling companions decided to return to Monrovia, their task of guiding me completed. Joseph had been the most helpful. Not only could he speak his mother's tongue but also three languages spoken in Bopolu, including Gbandi, the language of Tenneh's mother's people.

Joseph, Patrick and Matthew taught me all they knew about the ways of the natives. The three found it sad to part from me, for they were given the same respect as I was. Each was allotted a home and young women sang their names at night. One day, Joseph told me that he had fallen in love with one of the young women and was planning to stay in Bopolu. Although I did not see the young woman, he never ceased talking about her. Patrick and Matthew went with some men every day to tap palm wine, as if they had lived there all their lives. But when the time came to return to Monrovia, the three were ready. I took them to the king who expressed his disappointment at their departure. I thanked them for their help and escorted them to the outskirts of the town.

With my companions gone, I found it increasingly difficult to extend my stay in Bopolu.

A few days later, I decided to leave. My ever-generous host, the king, appointed four ably built men, one of whom could speak some English, to carry my luggage.

My departure from Bopolu was celebrated. The elders, including the chief, came to see me off. Young women, led by the praise-singer, sang my name. I went to see the imam. The cleric held my hand and prayed for me; the serious and seraphic tone of his chanting affected me so much that I broke into a prayer. The king declared that I was one of the few who had come to his town with a sincere heart, and he reiterated his joy at receiving me and promised that as long as he lived

I was welcome there. That moment, I had an almost sacred sense of belonging to these people and of being part of their world.

We journeyed through many villages and for many days before reaching a town in the Loma country where we were confronted, for the first time, with the masked being. On hearing the cry of one of his retinue, a cry that announced its presence, my travelling companions rushed to the bush for cover. I stood there flabbergasted. One of the men, trembling with fear, took me by the arm and led me away, berating me for my foolishness. That was the unseen masked being, the dreaded masked being, he told me. Ensconced in the cover of the bush, I did not see the masked being or its retinue.

Later, when we were sure it had gone, the men told me that the ritual of initiation into adulthood and the cult of the masked beings were pervasive in most tribes of the interior. Seeing one without being an initiate could result in certain death. People's lives revolved around the initiation ritual. Children were told about the masked beings from early on and prepared for the time when they would be initiated. No one, not even the Muslims who did not adhere to the cult, could mock them, for they did not distinguish a believer from a non-believer. They were all powerful and fearsome beings that sang like birds or shouted like thunder. They could read thoughts, tell the future of a whole people. Their source of power was the might of the ancestral spirits. Though they had little in common with the Muslims, they wore their protective amulets, thereby possessing the most powerful weapon of Muslims and Christians alike: the words of God.

So touched was I by these stories that I chose not to stay a moment longer in the village despite many pleas from its good-hearted chief.

We travelled the whole day and arrived at another place where I wrote down a journal of my observations. Relative peace reigned in the land. Except for few instances, the people were generous. Curious to know us, they asked many questions, sometimes verging on naivety. They wanted to know about America, about Liberia, about how we conducted our relationships, about our food, our women, our climate, and our means of transport and our homes. Whenever I answered a question, one of them ended up asking me the same question again.

The land was fertile. One had but to throw a seed anywhere, even on a hard-worn path, for it to grow. The future of Liberia lay in working together with these natives and in the yields of this soil. The climate, at first hostile to a newcomer, could be very favourable with time.

We were now far to the north of Monrovia, according to my sextant, in a fortified village that had just survived an attack from its bloodthirsty neighbours. A day's rest saw us on our way to our final destination.

It was a beautiful day and the sun was bright. My companions were in a merry mood. More than ever since the beginning of this journey, I thought of Charlotte and my son Edward, but was content with the choice I had made. I had had the opportunity to love them.

We arrived at our final destination at noon.

On the outskirts of the town, I encountered a man tilling his land. Handsome and with penetrating gaze, his eyes affected all who looked at him, including me. He welcomed me and held out his hand, then asked me in passable English the reason for my visit. Using my rudimentary grasp of his language, I answered that I had come to settle down in his town, Leopard Town, and to bring peace to the people. This pleased him so much that he held my hand and would not let go.

The village, nestling under a chain of mountains, looked mysterious, plucked out of a bygone era. I saw a few people coming out of their homes in ones and twos, walking with nervous steps and casting curious glances at me as though they had been confined to their homes for some reason and were coming out now it was safer. Did it have to do with the masked beings or with fear of war? I wondered.

My host led me to his compound and introduced me to his wife, Miatta, and his son, Salia. I had reached my destination.

The man's name was Halay.

Book Two

Dance of the Masked Beings

1

I've decided to tell you my story in order to explain the choice I am about to make, one which will affect the course of our friendship forever. I see no other way. There are no other ways. That you happened to be among us here in the forest, far away from America where you were born and bred, is perhaps as remarkable as the circumstances that led to the man I've become and to the decision I must make. So bear with me.

I was born in this town, a momentous event for my parents, perhaps for the land, because the months preceding my birth were characterized by frequent incidents of many parts of the forest bursting into flames. Our ancestors had left no traces in their songs and stories of such events ever occurring. Rice fields and vegetable gardens, ripe with the promise of good harvest, would catch fire and burn to the last seed. Every once in a while, as the day edged on towards dusk, a storm of dust would sweep across our towns and villages as though it was at war with the people. There were so many presentiments of a terrible misfortune about to befall that my people slaughtered animals in elaborate sacrificial rituals meant to soothe the earth and appease the gods, and they poured libations and consulted the oracle, over and over again, all to no avail. Something had gone terribly wrong. The earth was about to erupt into violence of a kind never witnessed before.

My mother was on her way from the farm and was resting on a rock on the summit of a mountain, below which the land spread out like a river, when the first pangs hit her. She had decided to pause and make up her mind regarding her condition. But the pangs, having taken firm root in her, compelled her to hurry down the mountain, and as she did so she felt as if the tall trees along the path would collapse on her and the road would roll up and bury her. In front of her, to the left of the path, there was a colossal tree whose branches she thought might offer her sanctuary, but she realized on approaching it that she did not have the courage or the knowhow to deliver me alone. As the shadows lapped up the sunlight and the trees blended with the shadows, heralding the night, my mother panicked. The road suddenly seemed longer, the hills and mountains yet to climb innumerable, but the fear of losing me compelled her to move on.

After what seemed like forever, my mother arrived late at night in our town which, nestled under a mountain and with light burning from hearths, seemed innocuous, detached from her reality.

'On reaching home, Halay,' she would tell me years later, 'the strength that had held me together abandoned me, and I fell on my knees in the dust.'

The women of the compound led her into a hut. One of them left to fetch the midwife. The old woman, whose age was unknown even to the oldest in the land, tiny and spry, the skin of her forehead as tight as a drum, entered the compound with a knife and an amulet wrapped up in a sheet of white cotton cloth. The knife was meant to sever me from my mother and the amulet to protect me against malevolent spirits.

84

The old woman was believed to have been born to a mother from the land beyond the great river and to a father who disappeared before she could begin to remember him, leaving behind a strange, musky scent she would come to associate with traders from the savannah who purchased kola nuts from our forests in exchange for salt and other goods.

She met my mother spread out on a mat, deep in the throes of labour. 'The dust,' my mother was saying. 'The dust is strangling me.'

The dry season had by then reached its zenith, and at that hour peppery dust poured into homes, swept up by the ever-present winds, which brought mysterious death, choking breath and unleashing havoc among my people, carrying dozens away in the process.

My mother began to shiver, caught in a paroxysm of fear. 'Don't panic. Take hold of yourself,' the midwife said, and she went to work, her face set in a frown, now and then encouraging my mother but without sentiment in her voice, for a woman in labour required strength not unnecessary compassion. From somewhere deep within her, at a moment when everyone, including the midwife, had given up on her, my mother found the strength to guide me into the world.

Four days later, as custom prescribed, my mother presented me to my father. 'I met your father standing at the edge of the valley, facing the huge mountain before him, his patience at breaking point. "Here's your son, Kollie," I said, as though I was done with you, Halay.'

My father was slight of build, broad-shouldered, and in the habit of crushing palm kernels with his teeth. He was known to cover long distances on foot, carrying heavy sacks of rice or kola nuts on his head or shoulders. On encountering him for the first time one would conclude, as so many did to their detriment, that a man of his build could not be endowed with extraordinary strength. But this was a man who, in a war that would define him and seal his fate and that of the land forever, had captured the ruler of the people across the river and had married his daughter, my mother, to facilitate peace between the two peoples.

My father wrapped me in his arms and whispered his dreams in my ears, like his father had done before him – a tradition that could be traced back to a group of people who, determined to forge a new beginning for themselves, had crossed crocodile-infested rivers and had fought strange beings and lost companions in the process and, exhausted and unable to press on any longer, had decided to settle in the embrace of these forests. 'You will take after me, my son,' he said. 'You will do whatever it takes to protect this land.'

Soon after my birth, my mother would tell me, a cold wind swept across the land followed by a downpour that lasted days. Homes quivered under the weight of the deluge, the land gasped for breath, frogs littered the roads, and the clutch of death released its hold on the people.

One day, I must have been seven, my father met me dawdling over my meal of shrimps prepared in a sauce of mushrooms and served with rice. He presented me with a bird he had cut down with a single catapult shot. 'Just for you, now eat, namesake of my father.' But I refused.

My mother sat me on her lap and narrated one of the stories of the ever-cunning spider. 'Some villagers were about to punish Spider for a crime he had committed,' she said. 'Spider claimed he could not swim and preferred being burnt alive. The townspeople decided to go against his wishes by throwing him in the river. Spider quickly swam to the other side and turned to the villagers, saying, "Stupid people, didn't you know that I was a born swimmer."'

Then my mother set me down and urged me to eat. 'Just wait until you have a brother or a sister, then you will stop this foolishness,' she would say. But seven years had passed without a brother or a sister. I had ceased to believe her. I had become adept at holding her attention, at making her world revolve around me, so much so that when I refused to eat, my stubbornness would drive her to tears.

'What is it, namesake of my father?' my father asked. 'Are we not hungry today? Then let's drop by your friend, Koilor.'

My eyes lit up with anticipation, for I was about to see the man I admired most beside my father, the blacksmith.

My father and I went through the town, which was surrounded by a chain of mountains, mysterious and fecund with ancient lore. One story was that our founder, a woman whose story had become a legend, stood on the peak of one of the mountains, beckoned to the sky and it descended and touched her fingertips. 'Her footprints are found somewhere on one of the mountains. She guards over our town, Halay,' my father said. Hard-worn paths divided the town, which consisted of several quarters, each bearing the name of a family or a place. Where I lived with my parents went by the name New Town. 'The new town came about because the children of our founder, who were twins, went to war over the right to rule Old Town,' my father said. 'As a result the young brother left and set up his town across the stream.'

The town was quiet except for the sporadic sound of the smith hammering away at a piece of metal and the chanting of the Muslim scholar and his students. Someone would throw a greeting across the road, and it would be answered with a voice in the deep thrall of midday lassitude, and then the chanting and the sound of the smith's hammer would take over again. Seated on my father's shoulders, in the embrace of his

87

strong arms, I felt secure, invincible, loved, which allowed me to break into laughter for no reason at all. Perhaps it was because I was the son of a man who bore the burden of his people with such pride.

Smoke rose from the smith's workshop perched on the slope of a hill in the distance. Some of my friends came running towards me.

'We want to play with Halay,' they said.

'Can I join them, Father?'

'What do you want to do, play or see Koilor?'

'I want to see Koilor first,' I said.

Just then, I saw my father's rival approaching, the man who craved his position and made no secret of it. His name was Mambu.

'So where are you off to today, Halay? Isn't it about time that you let this child be a man, Kollie? In a few years, he will be initiated into the Poro Secret Society. You have to prepare him. What would happen if the child were to come face to face with the masked beings?'

'What I do with my child is none of your business.'

'Your father is insulting your uncle, Halay.'

My father ignored him and climbed the hill toward the smith's workshop. On turning around, I saw Mambu winking at me, smiling.

'What are masked beings, Father?'

I had heard of the masked beings but every time one of them appeared in the town we children were told to stay indoors.

'When the time comes you will know.'

The smith was cross-eyed. Every time his gaze alighted on me, he would nod or blink, though the look was meant for my father. Sometimes he would go into a fit of coughing or sneezes, sending his hammer or anything within reach flying to the other end of the shack.

'You've brought my friend with you,' he said.

Koilor shoved his work, the cutlasses and hoes, into a corner with his bare feet, creating space for me and my father.

'Look at these rifles, Halay,' he said. 'I've repaired more than two dozen of them. In a few months we will be ready.'

And he handed a rifle over to me.

'Don't touch it, Halay,' my father said, snatching the rifle from me. 'We won our last battle with such a rifle. The enemy was crushed before the battle was even joined. Once upon a time courage was measured by the ability to face the enemy and defeat him. Now all you need is the skill to hit him with a single rifle shot. Times have changed.'

'I've heard there are better ones on the coast,' the smith said. 'The Liberians on the coast and the English on the other side of the river trade in better rifles. All I can do is to repair them.'

'These will do, Koilor,' my father said.

'After this battle, you will have no choice but to expand your family to include more wives, which means more children, Kollie.'

'Let's not discuss war before the child. He's here for your stories.'

The smith smiled. 'Did I ever tell you that I defeated every wrestler in the land, Halay? I was hired by towns and villages to fight for them at wrestling matches. After defeating my opponents, women would line the road to welcome me and sing my praises,' he said.

The smith began hammering with strokes that seemed aimless at first but meticulous as the metal took shape. And he recalled a time he admitted he would never relive again. 'Those were the days, Halay,' he said.

'But there was a man you failed to defeat in your many encounters with him, Koilor,' my father said. 'Do you remember?'

'You will make the child stop respecting me,' the smith said.

'Tell him the truth.'

'He doesn't have to know.'

'What is it, Father?'

'Your father was the man I failed to defeat. He might be small in stature, but he's the strongest in the land.' The smith paused. 'But if we were to fight today, I would defeat him very easily. He's losing his edge.'

'Let me know whenever you are ready,' my father said.

'I don't want to shame you before the child.'

The smith moved the iron from the furnace to the anvil and back to the furnace again. Gradually I began to see the metal take shape, from a crude form into a smooth pot, which he would later adorn with beautiful images of animals or shapes. I turned to my father with a pleading look.

'I want to be a smith, Father.'

The smith nodded as if he understood me, and I went on to name things I wanted to fashion from metal – trees, animals and people. 'I want to make the biggest pot in the world, Father.'

'Not a bad idea, Halay,' he said. 'But you must know that smiths are makers of utensils, cutlasses and weapons, not the world around them. Moreover, I hope you will succeed me one day.'

Later, after we had left and were on our way to the town hall, where my father held court and settled disputes, he suggested that we see his friend the blind man, Tellewoyan, who had become ill.

Tellewoyan looked handsome, his shaved head and smooth face belying the fact that he was blind and older than my father.

'Come here, Halay,' he said. He was sitting outside his hut, in the shade of a tree. 'Who told you I was sick? My enemies begrudge me my success with women. Tellewoyan, sick, never! Come closer.'

Addressing my father he said, 'Let the child come to see me every day. Did I ever tell you about those mountains whose peaks were clouded with whiteness, Halay? Yes, as white as clouds.' The blind man told me of huge canoes that transported people to distant lands. 'A white man on the coast in Freetown told me about those lands. The man also taught me to read and write before a cobra spat in my face. If not for the incident, I would have gone to England. I want to share what I know with you, Halay.'

'We will see,' my father said.

'Times are changing. The child needs education.'

Tellewoyan insisted I shared a breakfast of boiled plantain with him. 'The child will not leave my home without eating some of my food,' he said, and I ended up consuming all the food.

'And you say he refuses to eat,' the blind man said. 'Bring him to me next time and he will eat, Kollie.'

We got to the town hall, which was a round structure with a thatched roof; it was an open space large enough to hold more than fifty people. Despite my age and protests from some who brought cases to my father to be settled, he insisted that I attend the sessions. 'It would help him avoid making mistakes in the future,' he said. I watched him at work, settling marital squabbles and disputes over farm borders or misunderstandings over the wrong use of words.

It occurred to me then how people, even those who are close, were often at odds, some even hurting or murdering the other. I could not imagine leading such a life. I would not allow it.

On returning home, we met my mother preparing the evening meal. Though our compound was full of family members, including uncles, all of them were related to my father, none to my mother.

'What did you do all day?' she asked.

I told her about the smith and the blind man.

'Why do you let the child listen to stories of war and fighting? I don't want anyone talking about war in this house, Kollie.'

'War brought us together.'

'Yes, but war resulted in the death of my mother and in losing my language. No one speaks my language here.'

'The war is over, Siah.'

'Yet you are preparing for another war. If this goes on, I will have no other choice but to return home with my son.'

'There are enemies out there threatening our very existence. I cannot bear the thought of losing you to an enemy.'

My mother spoke our language as though she were a newcomer, which often amused me. One day I laughed at her attempt to articulate a particular expression, but the laughter froze when I felt her hand sweep across my face with a force that sent me crashing in the dust.

During the meal, which I ate seated across from her in front of the hut that I shared with her, my mother went into one of those occasional relapses which resulted in her staring vacantly for a long while. But unlike other occasions, she began to mutter quietly to herself, as though she were conversing with invisible beings. It fascinated and terrified me at the same time, and I was about to rush to my father when she turned to me with a panicky face and then a smile. She reached out and cuddled me, as if she needed some assurance.

I decided not to think about it, but it kept bothering me. There were rumours she was haunted by an evil spirit who had fallen in love with her and wanted her for himself. I retired to bed that night with her face – the sudden panic and then the smile – in my mind,.

The hut had few ornaments – a few pots, calabashes, clothes – for my mother set no store by material things. Once a week, she would change into a different tunic and wrappers, which covered her lanky frame, and around her neck hung a simple necklace, but her face, the most remarkable aspect of her – for it seemed permanently youthful – was often furrowed into a weary aspect. She seemed to pass through life as though it were a path to a better destination, bearing her past with her and refusing to share it with anyone, including me. Her constant worry about my well-being sometimes frightened me. I wallowed in her attention but would shy away from it whenever it threatened to suffocate me.

But that night, after what I had witnessed, I had the urge to be close to my mother. I refrained from playing with my friends in the moonlight to be with her, to listen to her voice, which was often soothing.

'Don't let your father involve you in his talk of war,' she said, while lying on a mat in a corner of the hut. 'Never, Halay. There are other ways to live than waging war. Remember that.'

'Mother, I want to be like the smith Koilor,' I said.

Outside, the voices of my friends rose with a song accompanied by clapping hands. 'That smith is as hungry for war as your father. I will ask the blind man to teach you to read and write,' she said.

What did reading and writing mean? I wondered, and how would Tellewoyan, a blind man, teach me? I couldn't wait to find out.

2

That night I had a dream, and in the dream I saw the masked beings. There were four of them, two with the carved wooden faces of women but terrifying in their beauty. One had no pronounced features but a smooth slab of wood flanked with long tresses of yellowish ropes. Another had the muzzle of a crocodile with huge plumes of feathers as hair on its head. These masked beings were all floating in the stifling void around me, beings that belonged to the Poro Secret Society, a society of adult men, the counterpart to the women's Sande Society, to which a child had no access. Every time they dived towards me, about to sweep me off the mat, I felt an oppressive weight that denied me speech. At one point I could see the thatched roof and the pouches my mother had placed around the hut to deter malevolent spirits, which meant I was awake and not in a dream. Not only were the masked beings dancing about me, but gradually I felt them becoming part of me, as though I were a fish net through which they were gliding like water. The fear I would become part of those beings, whose presence was as unbearable as a burning fire, compelled me to scream so hard that my mother awoke and the compound with her. She did not enquire as to the nature of my dream, as if she was privy to it, as if she had expected it, or had passed on her afflictions or whatever made her so out of this world to me. All she did was cuddle me in her embrace and stay with me for the rest of the night. The next morning, she prepared my bath, which I had standing at the back of the compound, facing the valley, the soothing movement of her hands across my back as she soaped me, reviving me.

I would have consigned this experience to oblivion were it not for the reaction of others in the compound. Most kept their distance or were quiet, including my father who wore a solemn, almost funereal expression on his face. 'It was a bad dream, Halay,' he said when I attempted to share the dream with him. 'It's over now.'

Seated on a mat across from him, before a bowl of rice porridge, I could feel eyes boring holes in my back, and I wished my old father would return and my mother would stop worrying her head about me.

'I will take you to the blind man,' my father said.

Tellewoyan did not touch on the issue of the masked beings although my father or someone else must have told him. Instead, he sat with me under a tree, while the morning sun burned our backs.

'You are going to learn how to speak first,' he said. 'That means I will say the alphabet and you repeat it after me.'

The blind man had kept some books from his days in Freetown. 'I got these from the white man who taught me,' he said. 'One day you will learn how to read all of this.'

Weeks drifted by punctuated with luminous lessons from the blind man, whose patience made me acutely aware of his handicap, so much so that occasionally I would stare at his dead eyes for a long while, and in the silence, perhaps sensing what

I was doing, he would break into laughter, his face sweaty from embarrassment.

'Return to your lesson, Halay,' he would say.

I often wondered who prepared his meals, especially when I saw him one morning boiling cassava in a clay pot. 'There are enough women willing to prepare a meal for this blind man, child,' he said.

Leaving him, I would join my father in the town hall or head for one of the two rivers that flanked the town.

One day, after a bout of swimming, I had gone in search of firewood in the forest near the river. I was on my way home with a bundle of wood on my head, when I saw a figure standing with its back to me, erect like a carved god. The ominous figure was attired in long raffia, its hard breath distinct within the silence that had descended on the forest, as if every creature was aware of its presence.

Then it turned. The figure was the masked being from my dreams, the one with the features of a crocodile. It not only followed me home but it also sneaked its way into my dream. It came to me in the form of a storm, chasing me while I tried to escape it. On opening my eyes, I noticed that my sleeping mat was wet with rainfall. There was no sign of my mother. I crawled out of my corner and when I stood up, a fit of sneezing caught me, and the world around me changed into a haze of crimson shades, which took a while to recede. I anticipated another sneeze, which did not materialize. What came was another wave of the masked being's presence, and this time it lashed me against the wall of the hut. The being approached me in terrifying silence and then opened its marbled eyes. There was fire in them. I tried to shut my eyes, to force the image out of my mind but couldn't. Employing the scarce strength left in me, I attempted to move, but the masked being went on prancing about. My chest was numbed, my feet frozen as it gnawed away at my being. It was at this point that I saw its drooling beak and teeth, and then it bore me out of the hut and flung me right before my mother.

For a while she did not budge, and then she broke into a scream and made hysterical gestures, followed by a sudden loss of consciousness. For the first time, I began to take the whispers that accompanied my mother everywhere seriously, whispers that she was haunted by malevolent spirits, which made her not of this world or the other, and that perhaps those spirits had set their gaze on me in the form of the masked beings. I began to be apprehensive of my mother.

Meanwhile my father went about the compound picking fights, saying, 'Who is out to harm my son?' On seeing his friend the smith, he pounced on him. 'Koilor, tell me that my son will be all right. Tell me.' But the smith sucked his teeth and shoved him aside, approaching me.

The sun had broken on the world, and the smith was sweating as he knelt beside me, his gaze intent. 'The child needs some water,' he said, and someone went to draw water from the pot before our hut.

By now I was sitting up on the dusty ground, with the smith holding me in his embrace. 'Tell me what you saw, Halay.'

'I saw a masked being with the face of a crocodile.'

'Describe him fully to me.'

The smith listened as I delved into my dream.

'What did he tell you?'

'He told me nothing. He talked in signs.'

'What signs?'

'I saw fire in his eyes, I saw images. Stories were told in those eyes.'

'What stories?'

'I saw a man. He was standing on a hill. I saw seven long white forms pointed at him. The forms looked like spears.'

'Spears? White forms?'

'The forms shone and dripped dark blood.'

'Dark blood?'

'I think they were tears, Uncle Koilor.'

The smith shook his head. My father broke into a litany of curses directed at enemies he believed had cast an evil eye on his son. He hit everything within reach – the walls, the ground, and the roofs – with his bare hands until they bled. His voice turned into a wail. 'Yes, they are out to get me. I know that for a fact now. They are out to hurt my son.'

The smith sucked his teeth, saying, 'Enough, Kollie.' The smith mashed some herbs he had brought with him in a tiny mortar until they turned pulpy. 'Get better soon, Halay, and I will teach you smithery.'

'Can I make the things that I see?'

'Yes. Get better first.'

The smith took a handful of the mashed herbs. 'Open your mouth, Halay,' he said, and squeezed the concoction into my mouth.

The liquid plunged me into a fit of dizziness. My father's rival, Mambu, entered the compound and rushed up to me.

'Tie the child up to prevent him from hurting himself.'

The man approached me, his gaze tinged with mockery. The compound was quiet. My father had by then regained his composure. The smith, on the other hand, stupefied at my reaction to herbs intended to cure me, looked on helpless as Mambu touched my forehead and rubbed my shoulders and legs. 'Tie him up, I say. Bring me a rope.'

Mambu's words were directed at no one in particular.

'You are meddling in our affairs, Mambu,' my father said.

'We are relatives,' he said.

'You are not related to us.'

'The child is mine, too. I am his uncle.'

'You are corrupting our past. We are not the same people.'

'Our stories have been told by the wise elders from time immemorial. You cannot shun a relative.'

Mambu's words were meant to tease my father, to work him up into anger, and it worked. My father now bundled up all his grief and pain into a fistful of rage directed at his rival.

'Leave my house now, Mambu,' he said.

He was about to hit him, but Koilor intervened.

'If ever I see you in this house again, the land will know once and for all who its ruler really is. I will kill you, Mambu.'

But Mambu ignored my father and went to my mother, who seemed to have come out of her stupor.

'Your husband, my brother, is angry with me. If you need me, let me know,' he said.

My mother nodded, her strength depleted. She would have stood up to Mambu and defended her husband in the past, but now she accepted the rival's mockery as though it was normal. My old life seemed like a shelter being scorched by the fire of the day's event.

The old midwife entered the compound. Since my birth, she had ceased to interfere in our lives, but everyone in the town listened to her. 'Why don't you take the child to the great herbalist across the river, Kollie? He will know what to do,' she said.

'Which herbalist?' my father asked.

'The one who cures the sick without touching them.'

'I will take my son to see him.'

'No, you must stay,' the old lady said.

'I want to be with my son.'

99

'You will be leaving for an uncertain length of time. Never underestimate an enemy such as Mambu. Because his father was once our ruler, he thinks he has the right to be king.'

'I must see to it that my son is better.'

My father told her that he would leave the affairs of the land to his best friend, Koilor. But the old lady said, 'He is incapable of ruling, Kollie. You must stay.'

But my father would not listen to her. She left, shaking her head. 'You will regret this, Kollie,' she said, 'but by then it will be too late.'

That night, we prepared for the journey. My mother packed a sack of dried meat and rice, a tin of oil and some vegetables in one bundle, and in the other she deftly laid out our clothes, then she bundled up the two into one. No relative was accompanying us. 'This has to be done by the two of us, Siah,' my father said, and my mother agreed.

3

The townspeople came to bid us farewell, a large crowd which spread across the road like ants. It was a solemn affair. The wind whistled a mournful tone as though it were sweeping across a deserted place. Turning to look at the town, I wondered whether I would ever see its mountains and its many paths again, its trees under which elders rested at midday. At the main junction where the road forked into four paths that formed the main thoroughfares, I saw the blind Tellewoyan being led by a relative. Behind him walked the smith, avoiding me perhaps because he thought he had failed me. 'Halay, don't forget your lessons,' the blind man said. 'Return good and well and we will resume.' Some of the boys with whom I had played in the moonlight or had swum in the rivers were also present. So were the Muslim cleric and his students. Moving past the courtyard, the smith's workshop, on our way towards the river, we came to Mambu's large compound, with its many huts and granaries. Mambu was standing in front of his home, wearing a white tunic and exuding an air of importance.

He waved to me and I waved back. My father refrained from berating me and simply ignored his rival.

We parted from the crowd at the great river. We exchanged hugs and muttered wishes in quavering voices. On stepping into the river, which was flanked by trees that threw a large canopy of shadow over it, the mild water climbed to my chest, but I waded through it with little effort. Would anyone, including my parents, understand that all that troubled me was the presence of the masked beings? I wondered. Or was this perceived as illness? Would the herbalist exorcise their presence and relegate them to a realm where they would never haunt me again?

The crowd vanished around the bend, and all I could see was a vast stretch of forest, with trees overlapping one another, here and there blocking out the sunlight. My father seemed lost in thought, and when I held his sweaty hand, he clasped his tight around mine. Under a huge bundle of our belongings, my mother looked as lean as a cane, her gaze fixed before her, her lips moving as though she were conversing with the masked beings who tormented me.

At a shack along the road, we encountered a group of men dressed in what I would later learn was khaki clothing. Their leader, a tall black man with a pipe in his hand and wearing spectacles, stretched out his hand to greet my father. Through an interpreter, the leader said that he had been dispatched by the newly founded republic of Liberia on a journey far into the interior to look at the possibility of including more people in the new black republic. It was an ambitious project. I noticed my father's unease, as if the message did not go down well with him, and I was too young to understand then, but I know now that he was keen on protecting his land from anyone bent on usurping it. The language the leader spoke was the same one that Tellewoyan had been teaching me. My curiosity as to what kind of people the Liberians were was aroused.

We continued our journey. The heady fragrance of the forest sometimes threw me into a fit of sneezing. Every so often a bird would chirp a note, and whenever we thought it had abandoned us, it would make its presence known with a flurry in a nearby bush. Then, suddenly, the bird was gone and we were confronted with the silence of the forest, with its shadows, which at times felt like large cloaks covering us, intent on stifling the life out of us.

The first village came into view, hewn out of the forest as if by accident, or as if it were a mark left by romping elephants. There was no sign of people. At a place marked with a line of white clay, my parents removed their sandals and beckoned to me to do the same, and we followed a tiny path that led through the village. We stopped to rest beside a spring and to shower in its cold water. My father assembled a bed of leaves as a sleeping mat for mother and me, and he erected a temporary shelter, which we rested under and waited for night. 'Don't be afraid of what you encounter in your dreams, Halay,' he said. I had a bite of the dried meat my mother carried in the bundle, and I lay awake, listening to the forest and awaiting the return of the masked beings. My mother sang me to sleep. I awoke at dawn to find myself bouncing off my father's back as he hurried to reach our destination. He carried me all day long.

We arrived four days later. The journey was marred with difficulties. It had lasted four days. Whether it had to do with my dreams or not I couldn't tell but I kept coughing and sneezing. My mother, whose every action came across as solemn, as one about to quake under an unbearable burden, with her face covered in a fine layer of dust, looked like an initiate into the women's Sande Society. She went on cursing a place that had no river close by where one could wash and put on decent clothes. We met a quiet village, the houses shut.

My father pulled me tight to his back and my mother covered her face. We waited at the centre of the village, bewildered by the silence. Suddenly, a string of roars sliced through the air and then ebbed away. My father's grip slackened, and I could not believe that a man I had associated with great strength could quake under any pressure. But that was not all. He broke into a run, with me on his back, and my mother followed suit. We had hardly covered a few metres when another sound crashed around us.

An enchanting song swelled, dissipating our fears. The song was about a boy, the song was about me. I could not see the singer until he was close to us. It turned out to belong to one of the masked beings from my dreams. My mother fell to her knees and buried her face in the dust. The masked being moved on stilts and was so tall that it gazed down on rooftops. There was another with a woman's face a beautiful woman, whose ringed neck lengthened until it reached the height of the masked beings on stilts. A third was the most fascinating of all: it had multiple faces, each as ancient as the other, and I could not tell whether the faces were staring at us or not. All the masked beings were adorned around the waist with long threshes of raffia. But a particular masked being with the crocodile face, the one from my dreams, had amulets and tablets inscribed with ancient scripts, which I would later learn were Arabic, dangling from his shoulders. Stitched to his raffia dress, from head to foot, were little mirrors, which reflected the afternoon sunlight. This masked being glided towards us and spoke in riddles. His retainer, a man who deciphered his riddles and interpreted his hodgepodge of languages, held a bell whose tone evoked fear. He had a bulging face, a terrible scar on his right jaw, and when he approached us and circled us, glaring at us, while ringing his bell, he bared a yellowish set of teeth, about to pounce on us. Meanwhile, behind him, the masked beings had squatted in the dust.

A tense silence settled on us. The masked being on stilts, now reclining over a rooftop and swinging his staff, jabbered a sharp, bird-like tone. The long-necked masked being with the feminine countenance spoke in a language I had never heard before. In a strident voice, it announced through its retainer that we had broken the law of the land. 'The child has seen beings forbidden for his eyes. Open your doors, good people of this place. The masked beings are about to depart.'

We were summoned to a gathering of elders. Before ageing men whose speeches were interrupted with coughs, my father was asked to explain himself. Hardly did he begin when a handsome man, the youngest in the gathering, sucked his teeth, saying, 'You are a clever one indeed.'

'He disrespects the law of the land and tries to come up with an explanation. This is new to us,' another elder said.

My eyes swept across the crowd and alighted on a man with the broad forehead and height of my father, and like my father he bit his lips when angry. 'I will take care of this,' the man said.

'It's none of your business, Tamba,' the handsome man said. And Tamba bit his lips. 'He comes here and says he is equal to us, doesn't he?' The gathering nodded. 'Then let him explain himself.'

'Leave this to me, Chief Kiazulu,' Tamba said.

'You heard him,' Chief Kiazulu said. 'Let him explain himself.'

Resolved on playing a part in deciding the fate of the strangers, Tamba said, 'I am of this place. I need to have a say in this.'

'I am telling you for the last time, Tamba,' the chief said. 'You shut up or you will be thrown out of this place.'

The town elders turned to us, bent on punishing us.

'Well, we are waiting,' the chief said.

My father did not speak. Chief Kiazulu shook his head and said, 'There are families among us whose histories have been corrupted over the ages. They are related to us in many ways. Our daughters are wedded to their sons, our sons to their daughters. Our farms border theirs, and our languages and ways of life have fused. I see a member of one of those families seated before me whose looks tell us more about him than he knows about himself. They tell us that he's an outsider.'

Chief Kiazulu turned to us as if what he was about to say only concerned us. 'Your relative sits before you, strangers. But, alas, he will be of little help to you today. Our law has been broken ...'

I heard my father say, his voice quavering with supressed defiance, 'My son has not reached the initiation age, and he's unwell. That's why we are here. We came to meet the great herbalist.'

The possibility of me being initiated, which meant coming face to face with those masked beings for months on end – beings who had harangued me in and out of my dreams – troubled me so much that I began to tremble and gasp for air. A child's fear comes in many layers, and it often takes on exaggerated proportions. I was sweating now, and my eyes were clouded with tears and terror. I gazed at the handsome chief, hoping his verdict would be lenient, but he remained adamant.

'Halay has to be initiated,' he said.

An anxiety seizure attacked me.

4

'The child is too young to be initiated into the Poro Secret Society,' Tamba told my father, as he led us to his home. 'He's not yet even ten, is he?' he asked, and my father shook his head.

Tamba's home consisted of a cluster of huts surrounded by a wall, and the place crackled with buoyant voices, as women and children went about their chores.

'By my ancestors, I will not let it happen,' my father said. He held my face in his hands. 'Halay, I will never allow anyone to force you into initiation. No one will take you away from us. Once you are better, we will leave.' He turned to my mother, who seemed to waste away with every passing moment. She had become so feeble, so withdrawn, that I thought an illness of any sort would be enough to sweep her away. My father looked into her eyes. 'Siah, believe me, our son will live. If I have to fight the whole town, so be it.'

The hut that was allocated to us was a simple affair without ornament, but my mother turned to our host and said, 'You make us feel as if we didn't leave home,' and Tamba looked away in embarrassment.

Our host spoke a variation on our language, which we understood and which my father would later tell me had to do with the same people settling in different places and their language altering over the ages.

'We are leaving to meet the elders again. The herbalist will come to see you later on today,' my father told us, and he left with Tamba.

The herbalist came strolling in with effortless strides, a huge man with beads dangling from his neck. Cowries were pinned to his short tunic, which had been dyed the colour of munched kola nut. On his forehead was a dark mark, and he had applied a thin layer of pounded herbs to a dent on his bald head. I could not take my eyes off the dent. The herbalist noticed my stare and glared at me. Seated with crossed legs, facing him, I could not bear his smell, which was pungent, but when I moved my head sideways, he forced me to gaze straight in front of me.

He filled my ears with a litany of incantations, he spat into my face three times, and then he staggered up, stumbled backwards, and darted towards a bush at the rear of the compound. A crowd had already gathered around us, and after a while the herbalist returned with bunches of herbs and leaves, and he asked my mother to fetch a pestle and mortar.

He spread himself out on the hard ground on his back and rested the mortar on his stomach. 'Pound the herbs,' he told my mother.

But she hesitated.

'I say pound the herbs, woman. It won't hurt me.'

'But I could end up killing you.'

'You are questioning the powers of the ancestors. A bad thing for a woman who wants her child healed.'

His words won her over.

'Pound as though you are pounding rice from your husband's farm. Go on, pound the herbs.'

My mother drove the pestle hard into the mortar. As the pestle rose and fell, the herbalist hummed a song. Later he fed me the concoction, but instead of making me better, it transformed the world around into different colours: my mother's eyes were red, and the crowd's yellow. Then the colours merged into blue. The voices subsided, and a strange calmness settled on me. I was certain now that I had defeated the masked beings. I felt no pain, not in my head or in my body, and I had the sensation of swimming in a stream of lightness. I must have fallen asleep, for on opening my eyes I found myself alone in the hut with an urge to drink. I crawled to the container and filled a calabash with water. But as I drank, I choked. Something thorny seemed to have lodged in my throat, and when I found my voice, I screamed. My mother came rushing in. 'What is wrong, Halay?' she asked, but I couldn't answer her – all I could do was point at my throat.

She left and returned with my father, who knelt before me, caressed my throat, shook his head and sent for the herbalist.

The man came, gazed into my eyes, felt my throat with a puzzled look on his face, and then said, 'Your son is a bearer of misfortune.'

'You shouldn't say that,' my father said.

'It is true. The likes of him are rare.'

'But this is temporary.'

'It lies in your deeds. Search your past and you will find that you've wronged someone who's returned to visit this evil upon you.'

'We've always been good,' my mother said. 'Kollie, tell him how good we've been to others. This cannot be true.'

'I cannot treat him,' the herbalist said.

My parents, including our hosts, decided to treat me themselves. Every day, the three came up with crude prescriptions, snatching them from their own experiences and from quack herbalists.

'We will not return home until he's well, Siah,' my father said. 'When he is, I will fight the elders to keep him from being initiated.'

The next day news reached us that some khaki-uniformed strangers, armed to the teeth, had replaced my father with his rival Mambu.

'I will not leave you and your mother, Halay. Don't you worry, when we return I will set things right,' he said.

Meanwhile, the herbalist had become a permanent presence. One day, I heard him telling my father, 'Last night, I cast the cowries. I am afraid to tell you what they revealed.'

'Please, tell us,' my mother said.

'They told me the child came to wreak havoc upon you.'

'But how?' my father said.

'I will answer your question with another. When did you last have peace of mind since he came to the world? Let the child go.'

'But he is our only child.'

'You will have another.'

'He will be cured,' my father said.

'I've warned you. He will strip you of your powers.'

'We will keep him,' my mother said.

My parents spent the night conversing in low voices that rose into shouts as the night crawled on towards dawn. The two were fighting.

The silence that lingered in the hut as the two attended to me was as sharp as a hunter's knife. At one point, when my father knelt in front of me, his eyes blood red, perhaps from lack of sleep or perhaps steaming with rage at what I had become, I thought he would slap me. I closed my eyes, waited for the inevitable, but the slap did not land.

My mother fed me the leftovers of rice we had had the other night, and then while holding me in her arms she became hysterical.

She shoved me away from her.

'Where is my child?' she said.

She turned to me with a strange look on her face.

'You are not my child.'

She scooped up dust outside the hut and began to consume it. Loosening her plaited hair, she sprinkled it with dust, and let out a scream that attracted a crowd to the house.

My father came running, grabbed her, cuddled her in his arms, and whispered soothing words to her.

'Leave,' my father growled at the crowd. 'He will be cured, Siah. I swear it. Halay will be as well as before.'

'Father,' I said, and when the two turned, I snapped my fingers three times, vowing to combat whatever was wrong with me.

I fought the masked beings by blocking their presence from my existence, and I fought the weakness in my legs and denied the jagged feeling in my throat. Soon I could afford to sleep with the presence of the masked beings confined to the far margins of my consciousness. My progress was like that of a child in the process of moving beyond the crawling stage to walking and running. A few weeks later I was running around the compound. My mother would take me with her to the outskirts of town and we would pick fruits and she would tell me about her people, about her life as the eldest daughter of her father, a king, and about the war my father had fought and how it had affected her.

'Never fight in a war, no matter what happens, Halay,' she said. 'War changes everything. It makes orphans of people.'

My father now worried about the next challenge before us: my initiation. But Chief Kiazulu would not budge.

'We will pick him up soon,' he told my father, who returned with his mind made up.

'We leave tonight, Siah,' he told my mother.

We escaped that night with Tamba as our guide. He took a less-known path, which he thought was safe. 'If the elders were to discover you were gone, they will send people after you,' he said.

'What will happen to you?' my father said.

'Don't worry about me,' he said.

And he was gone.

5

Back in our land, in our town, we found my father embarked on the precarious task of recovering his power. The task proved formidable from the outset. In our absence, when his attention had been focused solely on me, some of his people had sided with his rival Mambu and were determined to make him ruler. Mambu claimed he had the support of the English in distant Sierra Leone and of the Liberians who hoped to hold sway over our part of the world one day. On our arrival, my father summoned a gathering in his compound. I remember that it was a dry seasonal day, the heat demanding complete surrender to it, but the town seethed with defiance. Thousands of people from surrounding villages and hamlets had poured in, thousands from places as far as the borders.

My father suggested employing peaceful means to end the dispute.

'Despite our differences, we are the same people,' he said.

His words were thrown back in his face.

'Restoring you to power is not up to you alone,' the smith Koilor said. 'No, it's not about you alone. It never has been.'

I had always thought that the smith was timid and that he fabricated stories of valour for my own pleasure as much as his own. But at the gathering, arrayed in leopard skin, he whirled his rifle around as though he was the one most wronged.

'We made you what you are, Kollie,' the smith said. 'Power does not belong to you alone. It's ours too.'

One of the elders in the gathering said, 'Don't forget that we witnessed your mother's birth and watched her grow up into a beautiful young woman. We attended her initiation ceremony. Some of us held you in our arms when you were a child. We made you.'

'You owe us, Kollie,' a third remarked. 'Having power gives us the assurance that we matter and will continue to do so.'

'We've all been challenged, and a true man must never waver before a challenge,' another said.

The smith fired his rifle in the air and burst into a war cry, '*Seyenga yor yor*,' and the gathering responded, '*Yor*,' and repeated this until the clamour rose as though war was imminent.

The old midwife who had presided over my birth entered the compound, and the gathering lapsed into silence. Her cheeks were sunken, her chest flat, and her legs as slender as poles, but her eyes were clear and full of wisdom. She told the gathering in a feeble but steady voice about the men and women who, fleeing war and drought, crossed difficult lands in search of home. The children of our founder, the twins, she told us, had ended up fighting each other. 'It was because both hungered for power and wanted to be ruler. But there can be only one ruler.'

The gathering was silent.

'I can tell you with certainty who first peopled our land.'

'Tell us, guidance of our heritage.'

'Here is one of them, our chief.'

She pointed at my father. The crowd broke into war cries, tapping the ground with their feet until dust rose and covered the compound.

'Mambu's story is based on a lie. His people came here not a hundred moons ago. They are strangers here. They do not belong.'

The crowd got to its feet, and a wave of people burst out of our compound and poured onto the road, intent on confronting Mambu's people. Never had war been as imminent as at that moment.

I sneaked out and went to see Mambu in Old Town, choosing a route along the outskirts to avoid confrontation. I found him in his compound surrounded by men armed to the teeth with rifles, cutlasses, spears, daggers, hooks and hoes.

'What are you doing here, child?' he asked when he saw me; the crowd around him parted and I went up to him.

One of his daughters was with him, a strikingly beautiful girl about my age who was gazing intently at me. I could not bear her gaze.

'You are well now, I see,' he said. 'I should have come to visit you when you returned. How's your mother?'

I told him she was well, and he reached out to pat me on the shoulders, smiling. 'She's a wonderful woman, isn't she? I am the only one who seems to see that she should not be what she is – a prisoner.'

'My mother is not a prisoner,' I said.

'Then why doesn't your father let her visit her people?'

I had not anticipated the question. Mambu laughed.

'My daughter Miatta takes to you,' he said, and the girl gazed down, and I began to sweat, trying to take hold of myself.

'Uncle Mambu, the people chose my father as ruler.'

'Not all of them, child. These people you see here and thousands of others believe I am the rightful ruler of the land. Look around you.'

'Your father usurped power,' one of them said.

'He's a crook.'

'What are you doing here by the way?'

'We will make sure your father never becomes ruler.'

Mambu raised a hand to silence them and said, 'Come with me, Halay. I want to show you something.'

He led me to the largest hut in the compound, where he slept and received his wives. It smelt of musk. A mat made of colourful cloth covered the floor, and several rifles were leaning against the wall. Mambu reached for something concealed behind a sheet of cloth.

It was a mask, with a slit for lips and tiny flat nose but with eyes so large they seemed to burst out of their sockets.

'I am not making false claims to power,' he said. 'This mask is a symbol of our power. I inherited it from a line of rulers going back to our founder. Your father is a brave man, but that does not make him a ruler. If I don't fight him now and hold on to what is mine, when the time comes he will choose you to succeed him.'

It became evident to me that whatever I said would not alter the course of events, but I had to say it anyway.

'I don't want to become a ruler, Uncle Mambu.'

He seemed surprised by my words.

'You are a child now,' he said. 'As adult you might change your mind. Or others might change your mind.'

'I will never become a ruler.'

'I wish you were your father.'

Mambu led me out of the compound, through a throng of his men who glared in disapproval, and before leaving said, 'I have to see this through, Halay. Tell your mother that I will come and see her. She doesn't need to fear a thing. I will not hurt her.'

The roads teemed with Mambu's men, but seeing me in his company they refrained from bothering me. The moment I was out of his sight and on the main road, a group of his men blocked my way.

They were all armed with cutlasses and rifles.

'Look, Kollie's son,' one of them said.

'How dare he come here?'

One of them raised his cutlass and swung it, as if he was going to cut me in half. As I felt the cutlass sweep very close to me, instead of breaking down with fear or bursting into tears, I gazed into his eyes. He caught my gaze and hesitated, letting the cutlass drop.

'I swear he's like his mother,' he said.

'The child of a woman lusted by evil spirits,' another said.

'One has to be careful with such a child,' a third said.

They let me go, staring at me in awe. I could not explain where my courage had come from, except that a strange calmness had descended on me as the man raised the cutlass.

The smith met me on the road. He had been searching for me.

'Halay, child, we thought our enemy had kidnapped you,' he said. 'Never go to the other side of town. Old Town now belongs to Mambu and his followers. Never walk alone. You might get killed.'

I couldn't tell him that I'd been to see Mambu, for I knew that he would perceive this as betrayal. I followed him home.

'Your father wants me to prepare you for what lies ahead. You must learn to fight and use weapons, including rifles.'

On seeing us, my mother ran over and, without greeting the smith, pulled me away. 'I told you to stay put during this

117

time. What were you doing outside? Why can't you listen to me, Halay? What must I do to make you listen to me! People are talking about killing each other as if death means nothing to them. Why, Halay?'

She led me to the compound and to our hut.

'You are not to leave this place without my permission. You are my only child. I don't want to lose you to crazy people. Just listen to them. They've all lost their minds. Listen to those war cries.'

Indeed, in the distance, the war cries were rising and falling, as each camp displayed its range of power and capability. Sounds of rifle shots and drums took hold of the air, the ground throbbed, and I thought the situation might turn violent before nightfall.

'I went to see Uncle Mambu,' I told my mother.

'You think he cares about you? He could have killed you or held you to ransom. You are not part of this war. I don't know what has come over your father. He keeps listening to that warmongering smith.'

'Uncle Mambu asked why you don't visit your people.'

'You are my people now, Halay,' she said.

My mother was so distressed that she built her world around me, pounding rice within sight of me, all the while making sure that I did not leave the compound.

That same day a group of men with spears, their heads, waists and knees adorned with palm fronds, entered the compound. It was rumoured they carried the secrets of the forest with them, vanishing or turning into trees at will. They filled up the compound and pushed my mother and me to its edge. Under the camouflage of charcoal and chalk, their ferocious eyes glared. Their bodies were painted white. They sang a song and their feet made a trampling sound as they danced. Moving in measured gait, brandishing spears and daggers, the men headed towards my father who sat at the entrance to the compound in full war regalia. They contorted their faces and took up another song. After revealing the extent of their prowess as dancers, the men stood around in front of my father and fell into a silence.

No one stirred for a long while.

'We've come to bring you power beyond that of any rifle or weapon. We've come to bring you the ancestral power. You are our ruler, Kollie, our one and only Masangi – our king,' one of them said.

'You've heard them, Kollie,' the smith said. 'These are our *Zoes* – the intermediaries between our world and the ancestral one – and they have approved of you. Mambu stands no chance against you.'

The men left. That night, the town throbbed with war cries, with songs of masked beings, with threats of blood and a never-ending war.

My mother held me close to her, her whispers an attempt to allay my fears, but nothing could rid me of the thought that at any moment, a cauldron of warriors would burst into our hut and cut us down.

'It is all right now,' my mother said when I woke up the next morning. 'Mambu had a dream and was instructed by his father to give up the power that is your father's. War has been averted. What cannot be defeated in the real world must be confronted in dreams, Halay.'

6

'It's not yet over, Halay,' the smith told me months later, after a period of relative peace in the land. 'Mambu is bound to change his mind.' The smith had met me with the blind Tellewoyan who was teaching me English verbs. 'We have to prepare you for the future. Mambu was heard to have said that if he cannot be ruler, he will fight your father to the end. You have to be wary of that man. Your father asked me to train you to become a warrior. So when you finish here, come and see me.'

This was happening at a time when I was beginning to appreciate what the blind man had been saying to me, particularly his stories of life in Freetown, where blacks who were once shipped as slaves to lands beyond the seas had found a home, much like the stories of the Liberians. Through him, I came to know about your America, Edward, but not enough to form a clear picture of the land. I was anxious to master his few books, so I approached his lessons with diligence.

My mother, who knew that the lessons kept me away from my father and the warmongering smith, had asked me to come home only if the blind man had told me to. 'Help him however you can, Halay,' she had said. And Tellewoyan had many errands for me to run.

Sometimes I would meet him peeling plantain, which I would boil and share with him, or I would fetch firewood, or sweep his hut and its surroundings, and wash his clothes. I had become his student.

'Halay, listen to me,' Tellewoyan said after the smith had gone. 'Your future is here with these books. Not with the smith. The man craves war so much I wonder whether he will not end up inciting one.'

But I could not avoid the smith or my father. Their hold on me had become as hard as metal. The years of childhood drifted by with mornings spent with the blind man and afternoons with the smith.

The smith taught me archery, wrestling, and the use of rifles. He would lead me to the top of a mountain and ask me to charge at him with a spear or cutlass. I would race towards him, but he would stop me. 'You are not agile enough, Halay. You did not howl. A warrior has to evoke fear in the enemy.' And we would begin all over again. After the training, the smith would tell me about war. He would choose a moment when the mountains were awash with the light of sunset.

'War and drought compelled us to move and settle here,' he would say. 'Our founder, a woman of great strength and wisdom, stumbled on this place with our people and decided to stay here. The trees at that time were so tall that days went by without sunlight touching the ground. We lived side by side with the animals. But with time we drove them deeper into the forest and further away from us.'

Sometimes I would dream I was in a battle. I would have no weapons. Enemies would fall and come to life again. The war would drag on until the few still standing fell. But suddenly they

121

would rise up again and the war would begin anew. The dream tormented me, and as I grew older, the dreams intensified. One day I told my father.

'We should consult the Muslim scholar,' he said.

The man suggested sacrificing a white chicken.

'What is the meaning of the dream?' I asked.

'When the time comes, you will know, Halay.'

My father then took over teaching me. He taught me wrestling, and one day he decided to put my wrestling prowess to the test. He invited some of my friends over to dinner and then said, 'My son says he can thrash you all.'

My friends were dumbfounded.

'Yes, he says you are not men.'

'Father!'

'I will let him explain it himself.'

One of my friends said, 'Uncle Kollie, you shouldn't be surprised when your son returns home later with a broken leg or an arm.'

7

I didn't want to fight. I loathed the act of hitting someone and causing him pain. Trained by my father, whose achievement among others was to wage war on his mother's people, a warrior in every sense, I was reluctant to fight. But failing to persuade him, I had no other choice but to follow my friends to the town square. The moon, concealed by clouds and then moments later exposed, dazzled with its effulgence, the distant horizon sprinkled with fading hues. A bevy of girls trailed after us as we walked along, singing our names in teasing voices. In the square, the heart of New Town, the girls formed a circle around us. The boys I was to fight gathered in a single group, facing me. On taking off my tunic, a flurry of cool breeze enveloped me, and I felt the first intimations of cold. I clenched my hands into fists, whirled them around, but felt awkward. To become a fighter, a warrior in the best sense of the word, my father had taught me, one had to be prepared to summon strength at any moment. But I found that I couldn't.

My main opponent, the one who had threatened to thrash me, a tall young man of my age or thereabouts, declared, 'It's time you ran away to your mother. Why are you still here,

Halay?' He turned to the other boys. 'Do you want to see some fun?'

His words were working me into a fighting mood.

'Boys, he is creeping all over with fear.' Turning to the girls, laughing now, he said, 'Form a tight circle around him. He's bound to escape. You are not a fighter, spoiled child, return to your mother.'

This did it for me. For some time now, boys had mocked me behind my back for the fact that even after being initiated into the Poro Secret Society – a process that still awaits you, Edward – I still slept in the same hut as my mother, which was not true.

I threw myself at him then, but found myself lying in the dust and blinded by it. As I tried to stand up, I stumbled into one of the girls, who said, 'Fight, you coward, or I will never sing your name again.'

I couldn't see her because of the dust in my eyes. But her words had cut me to the quick. I attacked the boy again, but he proved a formidable opponent. He moved around the ring made by the girls, fierce, agile on his feet despite his size, trying to pin me down with his bulky figure. But at every attempt, I would cut loose. We tugged at each other for a while, during which I managed to grab him around the waist, lifted him and sent him falling with an ease that astounded me.

I turned in the direction of the girl's voice but did not see her. The girls were singing my name now. The next wrestler did not even have the opportunity to get into the fight. I sent him sprawling in the dust. The girls' song rose. The third wrestler darted out of the group, flashed a blow across my face and cut me on the tip of my nose. I got clear and felt my nose. I was not seriously wounded. Head bowed, hands shielding my face, I moved towards my opponent, raining blows on him. One of the blows caught him in the stomach, and he uttered a yelp like a wounded animal. Another assailant lifted me up and whirled me around, and when we landed on the ground he hit me with steady blows. I shoved him, dug my feet in the ground and jumped up. I was prepared when he came at me again. I dodged him and when he fell, I held his arms behind his back and began to squeeze. 'Halay,' he grunted, but I ignored him. His sobs only served to feed my anger.

The girls began to admonish me.

'Halay, you've taken the fight too far,' one of them said.

'We were trying to have fun here.'

'So, you hate your friends that much, Halay?'

'How can you be so cruel?'

I brushed aside their grumbles and walked home. A figure tore away from the group and called my name. It was the girl who had called me a coward. She was of my height, with slender legs and arms, and hair plaited into little portions tied with black threads.

Whenever she smiled or frowned, her face broke and then coalesced into expressions that made my heart lurch.

She was dressed from chest down to her knees in a single wrapper. She looked me square in the eyes.

'I thought you were clever,' she said.

'You were the one who called me a coward,' I said, determined not to flinch from the embers in her eyes. But the hardness in her gaze did not falter.

'So you think you are a great fighter now.'

How could she have lived in the same town as I did without me ever noticing her until that moment? Yet I knew her. She was Mambu's daughter, Miatta, the daughter of my father's rival, his sworn enemy.

'Is this how you will treat me when I become your wife?'

Sweat broke out on me.

'If ever you lay those hands on me, I swear I will put an end to your life, do you hear me, fighter Halay?'

'I don't like fighting,' I said.

'What a way of showing it.'

'I don't ever want to fight.'

'Then our future will be a difficult one.'

'Miatta, will you agree to marry me?'

'I've been watching you all my life, Halay. I know you.'

'I will tell my mother about you.'

True to my words, I went to see my mother that night. I met her seated before the fire in her hut, staring at it intently. Her lips quavered and her eyes glowed. She was eager to talk with me.

'That's not how you treat a friend,' she said.

'Mother, I did not start the fight.'

'Your friend's mother came over to see me. She said you fought her son like you were fighting an enemy.'

She fretted with the firewood, shoving a piece into the fire and stoking the embers by blowing on them. My mother still bore traces of her youth, of her beauty, which was apparent in her neat set of teeth, in her gentle voice, in her smile and smooth forehead. Was my father attracted to that smooth face that seemed not to have aged? I could not imagine that tiny body, lean and fragile, ever bearing the man I had become, one of the tallest in the town, focused on avoiding fights and trying to know the world beyond the town.

'I was once a centre of attention in my land, Halay,' she said. 'Our home brimmed with hordes of young men who came every day to narrate stories of courage and offered to marry me. My father, your grandfather, was a generous ruler. He had so many children we could fill up a whole village. But for reasons I cannot understand, he doted on me and preferred me to all his children. If I had stayed in my land, if there had been no war, he would have asked me to succeed him. It was not uncommon. We've had women rulers in the past. But your father brought war, put an end to everything, and took me with him.'

'But you can return home, Mother.'

'I belong here now. My father is long dead and his children have scattered across the land. And I care about you.'

As she spoke while blowing on the fire I could detect in her voice something that hinted at a remote origin, at traces of a culture unknown to me. Manifestations of her illness were rare now; she hardly ever stared vacantly or communicated with spirits as she was wont to do during my childhood. My real mother had returned.

'I could go home with you,' I said.

'Don't be a fighter, Halay. By fighting, you nurture enemies.' She snorted and dried her tears with her wrapper.

'I shouldn't be crying in front of you,' she said.

Moved by the grief in her voice, I knelt before her. She took my head and guided it onto her lap and began to ruffle it.

'I met the girl I want to marry, Mother.'

Her eyes glowed, and she smiled.

'Tell me about her. You never talk about girls.'

'She's Mambu's daughter.'

She was silent for a long time.

'Your father will not approve of this.'

'Yes, I know.'

'Well, we will stand up to him, won't we?'

She sang to me in the Kissi language, not a word of which I could understand, but it was a beautiful song, and all the fear I'd had vanished, and I fell into a dreamless sleep on her lap.

8

Why would a girl who had agreed to be my wife the other night prove so impossible during the day? I wondered as I stood in Mambu's compound. I had gone to fetch firewood for Miatta earlier that morning, a bundle of a size meant to impress her, the wood of the best kind, and I had negotiated my way into the compound, avoiding her father, avoiding as many people as I could, to the hut she shared with her mother. I let the firewood fall on the ground with a thud that was meant to draw her attention. No one came out of the hut to receive me. I waited, my exasperation growing with every passing moment, for I was sure that Miatta was in the hut.

I called out several times but received no response. I was about to leave when she came from behind the hut. The embers in her eyes were of such intensity that I avoided her gaze. I found myself scrolling patterns on the ground with my toes.

'Where did you get the wood?' she asked.

The gentleness in her voice surprised me.

'In the forest around our farm.'

'I don't like men fetching wood for me.'

'Why is that?

'They will stop fetching wood later on.'

'Not me. Not when it comes to you.'

'You might change your mind.'

'Never, Miatta. Never.'

'I don't believe you. Forget what I said last night. Take your firewood and leave. Mother is waiting for me.'

She left me standing there and went round the hut to join her mother, leaving me wondering what had happened between the night and this moment to have changed her mind.

'I would not oppose my daughter marrying you, Halay,' Mambu said from behind me. 'But your father has to agree to it. Only then will I give my consent. You two are meant for each other.'

I knew Mambu took to me, but I had not expected such generosity, and knowing him as I did I could not but wonder whether he had an ulterior motive for this gesture. I couldn't wait to tell my father.

But he had left with the smith to lead a punitive campaign against our southern neighbours who were fighting with our farmers over land rights. He had wanted me to accompany him, for in his own words I was a warrior now, better than most.

But my mother refused. 'If you dare take my son with you, Kollie, you will return from that war to an empty home. I will take him with me to my people and you will never see us again, do you hear me?'

He wavered before her threat, which was real, for he could see the determination in my mother's eyes. So he said, 'You will take care of the house in my absence, Halay.' He had more than a hundred warriors under his command. He was in his war gear, a hat and tunic adorned with cowries thought to deflect bullets, and he had a rifle in one hand and a machete in the other, ready to confront the enemy. My father smelt of herbs and the weariness of war, and while he was with me I could see that his mind was elsewhere, perhaps on the battlefield. He drew me aside, as if he was about to impart a terrible secret. 'Open your eyes, Halay, see the world as it is and not as it should be,' he said.

On returning home from seeing Miatta, I could not avoid mother.

'Talk to your mother, Halay.'

'Miatta hates me.'

She laughed. 'I cannot tell you exactly what she feels about you. But she does not hate you. Last night she agreed to marry you.'

'But she refused me today.'

'Wait a few days and talk to her again.'

'I am tired.'

'Never give up pursuing a woman.'

'I have to win her, Mother.'

'You will, son. You will.'

The next morning, I went to see the Muslim cleric. I met him doing his ablutions in preparation for prayer. The man had an attractive forehead and a beard sprinkled with a dash of grey. It was believed that the cleric could perform wonders, transforming misfortune into luck and altering the prospects of barren women with the power of his rosaries. Even though only a handful of people besides his followers espoused his beliefs, some of the masked beings and most of the walls of our homes, our waists, biceps and necks were adorned with amulets he had prepared, using verses from his holy book. Hidden in the ground of almost every home was a pouch he had made to deter malevolent spirits.

'Halay, the chosen one, please approach.'

It astounded me to hear this. What did he mean? How could I ever be a chosen one if all I felt was a terrible apprehension about the world. The wall of his hut was covered with ancient manuscripts up to the ceiling.

'I know why you are here. I can see longing in your face.'

So he could also read minds, I thought to myself.

'It is love, isn't it?' he asked.

I explained. 'She refused me,' I said.

The man went on counting his rosary.

'Are you sure?' he asked.

'She looked at me with contempt.'

'Or was it love?'

'What?'

'Maybe it was love that you saw.'

'It cannot be. I saw hatred in her eyes.'

The man laughed.

'We shall see,' he said.

He spread out a large mat before me with circles, triangles, rectangles and other mathematical figures drawn on it. Strange figures and letters were written in these shapes. Around a large circle were stars and beautiful writings in black, red, gold and blue. The cleric asked me to step onto the mat and sit crossed-legged in the middle. Then he closed his eyes and counted the rosary. Gradually I felt a burning sensation in my stomach. It swelled until it was unbearable, and I stood up to leave.

'You are running away from your destiny, Halay.'

I sat down, and the sensation surged up in me again.

'I can see the sign clearly now. It is in you.'

'What sign?'

He ignored my question.

'Miatta, although part of it all, is very small in the circle of things, Halay. Go to the river. You are destined for great things.'

What did he mean? What destiny? What great things? I left for the river bothered by these questions.

131

The river teemed with people. Not knowing why I had come but obeying the cleric's instruction, I sat under a tree from the top of which young men of my age and older jumped and plunged in the river. I had done this several times before, but it always amazed me to see others do it, plunging from such a height.

Miatta was there with other young women, but she ignored me, which added to my bafflement. Later I was alerted to her scream. I turned to the river to see Miatta being tossed about and dragged towards a whirlpool, which had claimed lives before. Without a moment's hesitation, I plunged in the river, reached Miatta and guided her safely to the bank.

9

Rifle shots and jubilant war cries interrupted us while we were celebrating my rescue of Miatta that night. My father had returned. My mother joined me as I stood with my friends, with Miatta, anxious to see him. 'Your father has brought us victory,' she said, and held my hand. Together with the townspeople, who numbered in the hundreds, we moved towards the western gate to welcome my father and his men. I knew what awaited us. On meeting my father, the people would bear him on their shoulders and would not halt until they had reached the town centre, where he would be gowned in the most precious fabric, a hand-woven cotton tunic perhaps red in colour, to go with baggy trousers. My father would be showered with praises night and day. The land would celebrate him for days, for weeks, for his fame would spread to include other towns and villages, other hamlets and farms.

The crowd reached the western gate but encountered pandemonium. My father, I was told, had been shot. Those who had remained of the defeated enemy had pursued him and his men to our town where one of them had shot him. Confronted with this enemy, the crowd surged backward and fled. The enemy went on a killing spree.

I lost sight of my mother, and I raced about in search of her, in search of Miatta, in search of the blind man, but was hampered by a warrior with a spear. He aimed his weapon at me but missed, and I charged at him. A litany of awesome shrieks and yells took hold of the trembling night. I fought my enemy by employing my rage as a weapon, and in no time I had broken his neck. I did not pause then to take in what it meant to kill a man, only later when the urge to be alone had overwhelmed me. All around me, the dead lay with their faces twisted in eternal repose. I failed to find my mother, Miatta or the blind man. It was impossible to search for them without encountering the enemy, and in the end, routed and in disarray, our warriors took to their heels, and I followed suit.

We met at the Poro Secret Society ground to take stock of our losses and to lay out a strategy as to how to reclaim our town.

It was then that I came to learn that my mother had not survived, nor had the blind man and dozens of others. I couldn't bear the news, and so I left the gathering to amble through the forest. My grief was like a storm that gathered strength with every passing moment and crashed over me, over and over again, until it forced me to my knees. I remained kneeling until day broke with beams of sunlight sprouting through the trees, forming alternately bright and dark patterns on the forest floor. I got to my feet, fighting to remain sane.

I hastened to join the men and reached the Poro ground at noon. No one enquired where I had been. We rehearsed our plan in minute detail. Certain of victory, we left to carry the fight to the enemy. We surrounded the town and then launched our attack.

134

The town was deserted. The invaders, having worked out our strategy, had concealed themselves. War cries resounded as the enemy poured into the town but this time on horses, which I was seeing for the first time. The riders went snatching heads off like a farmer cutting rice stems with a sharp knife. We did not stand a chance against such a force.

Our enemies had solicited help from warriors of a type that we had never confronted before. We ran into the forest, through briers and sharp thorns, which cut us. Every now and then I was assaulted by the sound of horses' hooves, as if the enemy were hard on my heels. Climbing difficult hills, racing into strange bushes with knife-like plants, sometimes falling but never once halting, I ran on until my legs could carry me no longer. When I stopped, the forest seemed to be listening to my heavy breathing. The shrill cry of an animal conquered the silence and was answered with a chorus of other animals. A white form glided past me, and I thought it was one of the wandering beings believed to inhabit the forest at night. Cuddled in a hollow of a tree trunk that I had cleared of leaves, I waited for dawn. Strange birds hovered in the air. An owl hooted. Bats flipped about me, and a leopard, perhaps in search of a place to rest, paused before my hideout, stared at me with its marbled eyes gleaming in the moonlight. I shut my eyes, and when I opened them it had gone. Dawn came when I was about to fall asleep, and I stood up and carried on my flight, following paths no one took any more, heading for an unknown destination. I rambled on for days, for weeks, perhaps for months. I would follow paths I had walked before and finish up where I had begun. A strange thought occurred to me that perhaps I had become a hostage of the invisible dwellers of the forest, of beings who had blinded me and who now dictated my every step.

This fear resulted in a fever of delirium. I began to ramble to myself. At a stream, I gazed at my twin self and rebuked it for an entire afternoon, calling it names and slapping it. Voices spoke to me in a chorus of confused din. But a lone voice would silence the voices and narrate stories I had forgotten. I would repeat the songs of those stories. I ate the wild fruits and drank from the streams. There were moments when everything was clear, and I could gaze into the past and see myself in a different light and into the future and know what lay in store for me. I would speak to the birds, to the animals, some of which were amiable and comprehended my longings and fears. I spoke languages I could not remember ever learning. Gradually, I became one with the forest.

One day, during my wanderings, I happened upon a cluster of shacks with calabashes, pestles and mortars like those on our farm. The palm-mill pit, the grey mortars with their smooth insides and the slender pestles were like ours. On entering one of the shacks, I recognized a smell that belonged to my parents. I had arrived at our farm.

My wanderings had ended. I waited until dawn broke to steal into our town. I was amazed to find that it was populated with my people. The invaders had looted everything and had left.

Miatta had survived the war, so had her father Mambu, my father's sworn enemy, who had been chosen as our new king.

A year after my return, I wed Miatta. On our first night, the women brought Miatta to her new home covered in layers of clothes that I had to remove one after another, as if I was peeling a fruit to reach its core. Alone with her, after the act, lying beside her, smelling her, I thought our future was secured. Many years later, after the birth of our son Salia, the drum sounded and everything changed.

Book Three
The Sacrifice

1

The drumbeat gathered pitch as the town crier drew closer to Halay's home. Halay shifted in bed and his elbow nudged Miatta who awoke from her sleep. Tired of the town crier's message Halay eased out of the mud-bed, groped in the darkness for his tunic, threw it on and came out into the night. The crier was calling for an important gathering. Experienced in affecting hearts, in eliciting tears, the crier drummed the message into the ears of the townspeople, as he had done every night for the past week, his steady, stentorian voice bearing terrible tidings. 'Never before in all our history has our land been faced with danger of this magnitude,' he said. How he emphasized every word, pausing between his sentences, his silence carrying as much portent as his message, got on Halay's nerves. For a while, he shut his ears to the message, but he knew no one could ignore it. He certainly could not.

He returned to the hut to find Miatta awake. She had lit a fire in the hearth. A single wrapper covered her from bosom to knees.

She sat on the bed behind him and caressed his shoulders with her hands, including his nape, and ran her thumbs up and down his spine. Above his waist, below his armpit, she grabbed him and pulled hard, expelling the fatigue of farm work out of him, including the hours spent in the town hall with the elders and King Mambu, deliberating on the crier's message.

Salia, their son, interrupted them.

'I cannot sleep, Father,' the child said.

He was around the same age as Halay when the masked beings visited him for the first time, and Halay feared for the child's future.

'Did you have bad dreams?' Miatta asked.

'No, Mother. It's the town crier's voice.'

A long silence ensued.

'Tell me a story, Father.'

What could he tell the child – stories of the cunning spider, the clever rabbit or the tortoise? He had heard those before. He must tell him about the movement of the people and the founding of the land and of the forces that had threatened to alter its destiny over the ages, including the present. 'The British want us to be part of them, which is what the blacks along the coast in Liberia also want. Edward is one of them,' he said.

'Uncle Edward still has trouble speaking our language,' Salia said.

'He's new here. He's doing his best.'

'He sounds funny every time.'

'But he's a good teacher, isn't he?'

'Yes. He tells us stories of his life in America. He says he was forced to become a slave to people who had no regard for him.'

'It must have been a difficult life.'

Outside the crier's voice swelled. 'War of a kind that not even our ancestors ever witnessed is about to befall us. The oracle has spoken. War is on its way. It has to be averted by all means.'

140

'How can war be averted, Father?' his son asked.

Halay sighed and gazed at his son.

'I don't know. But it has to be averted.'

The crier's voice trailed off, his drum sounding at every interval. Halay stood up and led his son to the hut he shared with other children who had fallen under Halay's care after his father had died.

He waited until silence had settled on the hut and he could hear his son snoring before sauntering into the night. The town had changed. It now boasted a school where many children, including his son, went to lessons. Edward taught them English, arithmetic, and the Bible. Beside the school, he had built a small church, which a handful of his students attended. Once a week, he moved about the town preaching his religion. He talked about things that were already familiar to Halay from his interaction with the Muslim cleric, but some things were still incomprehensible to him. But he admired Edward. Although he was different in many ways, Edward had become a pillar of their society, an adviser to Mambu, the new ruler, the letter-writer to the government of Liberia and to the English in Sierra Leone. Edward gathered with the townspeople to discuss issues pertaining to the land's existence. Within a year of his arrival, he had traded his American clothes for simple tunics. He had become one of them.

The drum sounded again, and the crier's voice rose. 'I swear he takes pleasure in torturing us,' Halay heard someone say.

The crier's voice was now faint, barely audible. Halay thought of the warriors who were yet to come. Would they be the horsemen who had killed his parents, the midwife and the blind man? he wondered. Or would they be Liberians from the coast or whites from Sierra Leone?

On returning home, he sought refuge in Miatta's embrace. He nestled by her side, needing her touch, scared out of his wits by a destiny that was certain to befall his people. She undressed him. The faint rustle of her wrapper triggered the urge in him to have her. Her body scent was of musk and shea butter, and while he relished it, he buried his face in the small of her back. But he refrained from making love, for he was not sure he was fully up to it. Miatta soon fell asleep, her gentle breath rising and falling. Halay went on pondering the fate of the land until the cocks began crowing. Dawn slicked into the hut.

With her usual promptness, Miatta left the hut to warm his bath. The town had awoken. Halay heard an angry and commanding man's voice directed at a woman, followed by the clanking of calabashes. Wisps of water vapour rose from bathrooms stretched out along the edge of the forest. The muezzin of the mosque called the faithful to prayer; his simple, untrained voice rose in the morning air.

Halay listened to his wife admonishing their son.

'You are old enough to bathe yourself.'

Salia mumbled something.

'If girls were to see you being bathed by your mother, none of them would want to come near you again.'

The child grunted.

'As of tomorrow, you will bathe yourself.'

Halay came out and sat in front of the hut in his compound, watching the children having their breakfast. On seeing him staring into space, Miatta's face broke into furrows of weariness. 'Don't ignore us, Halay. This whole house is your responsibility,' she said.

He did not respond. Later she brought a breakfast of eddoes prepared with palm oil and waited for his compliment, which often resulted in an intense session of lovemaking. It did not come.

Halay took the food to his son.

'I brought you this, Salia,' he said.

His son eyed him, astounded, for his father always brought him leftovers and not a whole bowl of food. The child hesitated.

'Eat, your mother prepared it.'

'I am not hungry, Father,' Salia said.

'I say eat.'

His son would not touch the food.

'You will eat this food, now.'

The child responded by drawing the food closer, but the way he ate, slurping, gagging, about to burst into tears, angered Halay.

'Treat the food with respect. Behave.'

Halay bowed over his seated figure, and sucked his teeth; he compelled the child to eat one handful after another until the bowl was empty. The child stood up and darted off.

'Come back here.'

The child returned in tears.

'Wipe those tears and tell me where you are going.'

Salia mopped his eyes. More tears fell.

'If I see a single tear again, you will be in trouble.'

The child wiped his eyes with the end of his tunic.

'Now, tell me where you are off to.'

'I, I am going ...'

'Raise your voice, I can't hear you.'

'Stop hurting him,' Miatta said.

She rushed to her son and took him away.

'You are acting strange. For weeks now, you've not been yourself.'

'I can't bear it any longer.'

143

'Can't bear what?'

'The drum, the voice, the message. They haunt me.'

'They haunt us all and yet we are alive. Your family doesn't have to suffer because of a message. Your son doesn't have to suffer.'

'Life is not just about family. It's more than that.'

'What do you mean, Halay?'

'I cannot tell you.'

'I want to know why my son suffers. Why I suffer. And why my husband hardly ever sleeps. You are not the only one in this town.'

She faced him with fire in her eyes. Her eyes, unwrinkled forehead and dimpled cheeks showed that she was still beautiful. Unaware of it, lost to him for months now, perhaps for years, was a young woman who seemed to have budded in her again.

'It will be all over soon,' he said.

It was all he could do to allay her fears. He left the compound. The morning was the same as the night, shrouded in a tranquillity within which the people brooded, pondered and questioned their destiny. A dog scampered past him, halted, turned in his direction, barked and then made off. On the wall of an abandoned hut, a goat rubbed its back, bleated, rubbed again, and bleated again. Following a tiny path off the main road, Halay saw a woman bathing a screaming child. She was oblivious of Halay. Behind her hut was a line of dyed clothes hung to dry, and a loom set for the day's work.

Halay reached the market centre. The stalls were built of wood and uncovered, like trees bare of leaves after a storm. A few marketeers were setting out their wares of fruit and vegetables. Near a heap of cassava leaves were bunches of potato greens, mangoes and bananas, eggplants, garden eggs and bags of rice. Cutlasses, knives, pots and spoons of various sizes were spread on the planks. Halay ambled through the market and came upon an old man dressed in a kaftan like the town cleric, and with amulets spread out in front of him, hawking them. The man claimed they were charged with powers strong enough to fend off all possible evil.

'Can they fend off war?' Halay asked.

The man gaped at Halay, attempted to say something but was confronted with his customer's relentless gaze. The man lowered his head and mumbled something in his language. Along the path that led to Edward's home, a herd of cattle were being tended to by a man from the savannah.

Edward's home, unlike most homes in the town, was a rectangular-shaped house rather than a round one, and consisted of four rooms in one of which was a sextant, a barometer, a thermometer, a gold measuring device, the books Edward treasured, a small painting of himself, and a pile of books in which Edward often noted down his observations.

Edward was sweeping the front of his house with a large broom.

'Halay, you are here,' he said.

Edward dusted the two chairs he had arranged for himself and for Halay, and before sitting on the chair he glanced at it again.

'The seats are fine, Edward,' Halay said,

'The town crier returned last night again,' Edward said.

Halay nodded.

'There are other ways of averting wars than the one you people are contemplating, Halay. Just pause and think about it. This can't be the way.'

'Tell me about the other ways, Edward.'

'You could do everything to ensure peace.'

'Peace can be ensured only if you know the enemy. But we don't know who our enemy is. How can you avert a war that is predicted to decimate our people, to alter everything forever?'

'What have you decided then?'

'We are yet to decide.'

'You've told me your story several times these past weeks to make me understand fully what you must do to avert this war. Yet, despite your personal story, despite everything, I believe there are other ways.'

'Tell me if you find them,' Halay said.

Edward decided that there was no way he could persuade his friend to act otherwise, and so he said, 'You know I am writing down your stories, for my sake as much as yours.'

'Please be honest in your depiction of our lives.'

'I will be honest.'

'Share some of the stories with me.'

'They are not yet complete.'

'Is anything ever complete?'

Edward prepared slices of pawpaw and shared them with Halay. The two men ate slowly. 'One day, I will return to Liberia or to America. Your stories will be witness that I lived here. I will share them with the world.'

'You are different from all the people who have ever visited us, including the Liberians and the English. Why is that?'

'Maybe I look at things differently.'

Halay glanced at Edward. He had lived among them for years now, and in his presence Halay always felt a sense of pride in his land, in his home, in his family. Edward had left America and had chosen not to live on the coast like most settlers but among them in the forest.

'I don't think you will ever leave, Edward.'

Edward heaved a sigh.

'I don't know,' he said.

'I am going to visit my ancestors' graves.'

'Should I accompany you?'

'No, Edward. Not now. You are not yet fully one of us. The time will come when you will be fully accepted as one of us.'

'I thought I was already one of you.'

'You are still an outsider, Edward.'

'What do I have to do to become one of you?'

'That you should not know beforehand.'

'I cannot wait for that day.'

'I can hardly wait for it myself.'

Halay arrived at the graveyard where his parents, the midwife, the blind man and the founder were buried. Grass had swallowed up most of the graves. Crouching down, Halay searched for mounds that were the graves and found a series of them. He brushed off the grass with his cutlass until he had cleared the graveyard, working for most of the morning. He fetched sands from the river and strewed them on his parents' graves, and then ran his hands on the graves, poured a drop of wetness into the dust and rubbed his face over and over with it.

On leaving the graveyard, the sound of his footsteps startled a squirrel along the path. The animal scampered for cover into a bush. Before leaving home, Halay had not decided on a specific destination. It had all happened without planning: his visit to Edward and now to the graveyard. But the real purpose of leaving home was taking shape in his mind now. It was to visit the Poro Secret Society ground. Situated in a clearing, the home of the initiates and of the masked beings was shrouded by tall trees. Halay entered one of the huts where a huge image rested on a tree trunk, its elongated, crocodile-like beak closed, in repose. Huge rings dangled from its ears, and the back of its head was stuffed full with plumes of feathers – it was the mask from his dreams. But the fear that he once associated with the mask was gone now. What remained was a deep reverence verging on wonderment.

He was aware that the ancestors had led him to the one place that symbolised their unity, the Poro sacred ground. He was at peace with himself. The journey home was swift, his heart unburdened of worries, for he had made up his mind. He would avert the war.

2

But first Halay had to exhaust other means before acting on the decision he had made. He was a prudent man, for life had taught him so. He would deliberate on a subject for a long time, and once he had made a decision, he would not waver. He would not waver now. But other options had to be exhausted. That night he went with the elders, including King Mambu, to consult the cleric. The reclusive old man was almost blind, but his insight into things was as accurate as ever, his rosaries hardly ever failing him, such as when the land was confronted by a severe drought and he had prayed and it had rained buckets. He was in his hut, seated cross-legged, counting his rosary, whispering incantations. The heady scent of the burning incense overwhelmed them. Outside, around a bonfire, his students were gathered, reciting words from their sacred book. There were chinks in the walls of the hut, and the pile of leather-bound manuscripts was shrouded in cobwebs. The cleric seemed to be withering away, Halay thought, perhaps due to the burden of age or to the fear of the imminent war. He coughed, his hands trembled and his voice was fragile.

'The war is inevitable,' he said.

The elders were silent.

'But when will it come?' Mambu asked.

Spreading a sheet of paper with mathematical symbols on it, he closed his eyes, whispering incantations and circling his right hand around his head. Then he brought his index finger down and pointed it at one of the symbols. He seemed not satisfied. He circled his head again and brought his figure down to point at another symbol, his actions seeming not arbitrary but deliberate, compelled by an outside force rather than himself. A weary expression appeared on his face. Halay grew anxious. He repeated the act again, his gaunt face hardening, bewildered.

'I don't know. It could happen today or tomorrow. In the eyes of the knower of the skies, God, time is of less importance.'

'But we have to know the time. We have to prepare,' Mambu said.

'Will it happen a year from now?' another said.

'It could happen a year from now; it could happen ten, fifty or a hundred years or more from now. It could happen today.'

'Can it be averted or avoided?' Halay asked.

'That I cannot say. It's not in my power.'

The elders glanced at each other again and went on throwing questions at the cleric, his stubborn reticence unnerving them. Later, when Halay left with the elders, Mambu asked him to accompany him home.

'How's my daughter faring?'

'You raised a good human being, Father-in-law.'

'How's my grandchild, namesake of my father?'

'Salia is my greatest worry. What will happen to him?'

'Do you know that people whisper that I let you wed my daughter so that you could allow me to take your father's place?'

'People always talk.'

'They say I had a hand in your father's death. You must have heard. Even after your father's death, our people are still divided.'

This was true. There were people who still regarded Halay as the rightful person to succeed his father, and they had told him so.

'Now we are faced with this war,' Mambu said.

'If only there was a way to avert it,' Halay said.

'We could wait it out,' Mambu said. 'Wait until it comes and then confront it. We could prepare for the war.'

'You mean wait until we are no more?'

'Listen, Halay. You are like a son to me. I feel your loss.'

'I don't think you do.'

'We shouldn't be fighting over this.'

'Not if you see it the way I do.'

'The oracle could be wrong. The cleric and other diviners could be wrong. The fear could be unfounded. We could wait and see.'

'What an abomination!' Halay said. 'Sometimes I tend to believe that you are not one of us, that your people did indeed arrive later.'

Halay could not take it any more, and he left his father-in-law standing in the dark and headed home. The elders met him as he was about to retire to bed. 'We heard your exchange with Mambu,' one of them said, after they had gathered around the fire in Halay's compound.

'Clearly he's not one of us,' another said.

'We must put a halt to his foolishness,' a third said.

'He was just expressing his worries,' Halay said.

'We don't understand you, Halay.'

'What do you mean?'

'You gave up so easily. You turn over what was yours, what was ours, to someone who does not deserve it, who questions our way of life. You gave up, and now an incompetent man lords it over us.'

'We will put a stop to this,' someone said.

'Yes, we will. This has to end,' several said.

'What are you talking about?' Halay asked.

'If you don't want to act, we will. That's what we came to tell you tonight. Act soon, put a stop to this man or we will do it.'

With that the elders left. Miatta was preparing for bed when he entered the hut. She noticed his weariness and sat up on the bed.

'What did the elders want?'

'They asked me to depose your father.'

'The world seems to have gone mad. What is happening in this land, Halay? Please, stand with us and be with us through this.'

He didn't respond but sat beside her and held her hands, playing with her fingers, which were slender but rough from hard work.

'What are you doing sitting beside an old woman,' she said.

He smiled and said, 'I like the old woman.'

'You like the old woman?'

He nudged her, and she secured her wrappers firmly around her.

'We are too old for this,' she said.

'You mean too young.'

Halay spread his wife out on the mud bed and brought his hand to rest on the mound of hair below her navel. She let out a moan and held him. He began to swim the narrow river of her world, his every stroke strong, determined to get to the other bank with its brown sand, trees and shades. As he drew closer and could almost touch the bank, he quickened his strokes, and when he reached it he let out a cry and fell on the sand, his body trembling in contentment. Nothing in the whole world, not even the predicament of his people, was worth trading for that moment. He wanted to remain lying on that sand, in the shade of those trees forever.

3

The men surrounded the house. The occupant was asleep. For days, the men had prepared for this moment, had played out this scene, and now they were ready to enact it. As instructed they waited for a sign, which came with a long, wailing call of a masked being. In response, the men stormed the house, headed for the main room, grabbed the sleeping form, blindfolded him with a piece of cloth, tied him up, and carried him out of the house, toward the forest, crossing a river and heading to an agreed destination. Taken aback by the sudden intrusion and the terrible voice of the masked being, Edward called out Halay's name and the names of all the people he knew in the town. No one answered him. The men raced on, winding their way through the forest, the portentous cry of the masked being hard on their heels. Edward could tell by his captors' hard breathing that they were climbing a mountain, and then suddenly they set him down. He attempted to get free from his captors' hold but failed. However much he tried, he could not identify them, for they seemed to be speaking through a medium that transformed their voices into the chirpy notes of birds. His precarious situation as an outsider in a place with strange customs, where for years he thought he belonged, now dawned on him. The thought occurred to him that perhaps he was being held by slave traders with the goal of selling him to a terrible master. A freeman sold back into slavery! It would mean the end of him. He kicked, fought, cursed but to no avail. Unable to fight a force he could not see, let alone comprehend, sure now that his end had come, Edward began to recall snippets of his life in America, where he had pored over books with the intention of sharing that knowledge with these people, learning their ways and becoming one of them. But they had betrayed him.

After what seemed like forever, they set him down.

'It's all right, Edward,' one of them said.

He recognized the voice.

'Halay!'

He got no response.

'It's you, Halay!'

The men were untying him.

'I thought where you came from men were taught to be men and not whimper at the first sign of danger,' Halay said.

'Halay, it's really you!'

'You chose to be one of us, Edward.'

'I thought I was being led into slavery.'

The men laughed. His blindfold was taken off. Edward found himself in a large hut with a burning hearth. On seeing Halay in the light of the fire, he fell into his arms. Halay was amused at Edward's clumsiness.

'This is how we introduce people into our world.'

'But you told me you would teach me your ways.'

'This is our way, Edward.'

'What are you going to do with me?'

'We are going to introduce you to our secrets.'

'Your secrets?'

'We now feel that you've stayed long enough with us to deserve becoming one of us. We will prepare you to become one of us.'

Edward was silent. Tears of joy streamed down his cheeks. He held out his hand to Halay, who shook it. The men shared palm wine with him to soothe his nerves, and Edward gulped down the drink.

The hut's interior was decorated with feathers, with raffia and homespun clothes heaped in a corner. There were bags of rice and dried bushmeat piled near the door. Outside, the men were spinning a yarn.

Other huts on the sacred Poro ground were soon crowded with frightened youths who, like Edward, had been abducted from their homes for initiation. The huts were crowded with activity, but when the masked beings made their presence known, a hush fell on the place.

Emerging from the hut, Halay met the head masked being stretched out before the door, as if the ground was its throne, its task to swallow up each initiate, as it were, and give birth to him again, so that the reborn initiates would be prepared to face the world.

'Child of our king, the chosen one, I see you are here,' it said, addressing Halay, and Halay answered that he was.

'Our children are being reborn into men,' it went on. 'We might not survive the war that is to come, but we need to go on living until it's upon us.'

'We might not survive the war ...' Halay repeated.

'Unless we find a way to avert it,' the masked being said.

'Yes, unless we find a way,' he said.

'Remember who you truly are, Halay.'

The masked being then went on to warn the initiates, including Edward, never to reveal what they saw or did in the

156

forest, for the consequences would be severe. Later it retired to its hut, followed by its large retinue. For most of the night Halay explained the initiation procedure to Edward. And when Edward fell asleep, Halay left for town and reached it at dawn. He crept in to lie beside Miatta and fell asleep.

But his sleep was interrupted by the elders.

'We came to see you, son of our king,' one of them said.

The sun was yet to rise. Halay came out into the first light of morning, bleary-eyed with sleep, irritated for being interrupted.

'Follow us,' one of them said.

They took him beyond the river to a clearing in the forest with a huge tree standing in the middle. Sunlight fell around the tree as though it was an island. Halay thought that he was being brought there to meet the head masked being who perhaps carried a message of the greatest importance for him.

'Look on the other side of the tree,' one of them said.

Halay approached the tree with trepidation. The sight drew a cry from him. King Mambu was tied up like a sack of kola nuts, over and over again, his hands clasped behind his back, his face beaten up, and the soles of his feet lacerated by what must have been harvesting knives. They had tortured him, for he could see that one of his ears was missing, so were his toes and his fingers.

Halay rushed to his father-in-law and began to untie his corpse, while the elders looked on, none interrupting him.

'We told you we would do it for you,' one of them said.

'You are our king now,' another said.

'You killed him.'

'He was never the right ruler. He was a betrayer of everything we held sacred. He had to die for the sake of the land.'

'You killed an innocent man.'

'Innocent? He was attracting strangers to our land; he was in league with the English and the Liberians. He betrayed us.'

'You hated him for speaking his mind.'

'If you think we acted alone, then you are wrong. Consult the masked beings and you will see. We didn't want to involve you because you would have stopped us. It had to be done. You are now our king.'

'I don't want to be a king.'

'You have no choice in this.'

Halay was thinking about Miatta and her reaction to her father's death. The two were close. For her sake as much as his own, he decided not to tell her about this death until he had done what was necessary to rid the land of this perpetual fear of war, a fear that had transformed wise men into mad ones. If it went on like this any longer, the fear of war would plunge the land into chaos. He had to act. He gazed at the once handsome face, upon which a constant smile of mirth played. What remained of the face were a broken nose, bloodshot eyes and bulgy cheeks.

When he turned around to take in his surroundings he realized he was alone. The men were gone.

He returned home after burying his father-in-law. The streets were deserted, which he had expected, for the masked beings' presence always left silence and dread in their wake. On arriving home, he found no one, which was unusual. Miatta, who hardly left the compound but delegated most chores outside of home to her domestics, was also absent. Halay left in search of his household and found them and most townspeople scattered around the thatched building that served as the town hall.

There were visitors from the distant city of Monrovia. Because such visits were infrequent, the people from both Old Town and

New Town had gathered to listen to them. The men were all armed to the teeth. The leader, a young man who tried to conceal his diffidence by looking stern, spoke without an interpreter. This meant he was from those parts, Halay thought. His men flanked him on both sides, their rifles clutched to their chests.

'We've come in peace,' he said.

'But then why the rifles?' Halay asked.

'I belong to this place,' the man said. 'My mother is from here. My parents in Monrovia sent me to school to learn and return to help you.'

He sounded sincere. But Halay remained cautious. The men had rifles and they were, like their commander, trained and educated by the Liberians on the coast who led different lives.

'Your action proves otherwise,' Halay said.

The young commander looked Halay squarely in the eyes.

'What do you mean?' he asked.

'It is he who is asking the questions now,' one of the elders remarked, and the hall burst into laughter. The young militia man dabbed his face with a handkerchief, upset by the crowd's reaction.

'Tell me what you mean.'

'If you don't know what I mean, then return to where you came from. We don't want people with rifles in our town,' Halay said.

Another peal of laughter followed. The young man turned to his armed men, who pointed their rifles at the crowd, and suddenly before anyone could say anything, shots were fired.

The crowd scattered. People were stumbling into each other as they left the hall, which resulted in a stampede. Again, Halay saw what fear could do to men. He sat in the dust, outside the hall, made despondent by the chaos and cries, numbed and paralysed by it all.

The young militia man began to scold his men.

'It was a mistake, believe me. I did not order this,' he said.

No one was listening. The young man turned to Halay. 'This was unintended. I came to help you people and to involve you in the country of Liberia. I am sorry. I am sorry,' he said, and went on pleading.

'But the damage has been done,' Halay said.

The young commander left with his men, promising to mete out justice to those who had opened fire. No one had died, but several had been wounded. It was not a good beginning.

A few days later, the town crier appeared.

'We'd all seen the signs,' he said. 'War is now inevitable.'

Halay, who had been dining outside the hut, in the centre of the compound, lost his appetite. 'Are you going hungry because of that man,' Miatta said. He did not respond but washed his hands.

Every time he looked at Miatta now, she reminded him more and more of her dead father: the shape of her nose, her lips, and her eyes – features that were more honed and sharpened in her than in her father.

The elders had told the people that King Mambu had left at short notice to settle a dispute between distant family members in a neighbouring region, and that he would return soon. 'In a few weeks we will announce that he has been murdered by our enemies on his way back and that you are now our king, Halay,' they had said. Halay had shaken his head.

Sooner or later, he thought now, Miatta was bound to find out what had happened to her father. It was certain to trigger everlasting rancour, and would shatter everything the two of them had worked for.

Miatta covered the food to keep the flies off it.

'You seem to enjoy this, don't you?' she said.

She stood before him, glaring at him.

'Just tell me in all honesty whether you enjoy all this, this strange behaviour of yours, this disregard for your family.'

'Miatta, you are making it impossible for me.'

'You know, there are people who wallow in their suffering. They take on the burden of the world as if it is theirs alone.'

'The burden of the world?'

'They carry it around as if it is their inheritance. Your past does not give you the right to put us through this.'

'You are not being fair.'

'No! I don't want a husband who turns his back on me and my child at the mere sight of a crier. The world will go on despite everything.'

'Not our world, Miatta.'

'Hear him. Not our world?'

She sucked her teeth and left for one of the huts.

'Salia,' she called. 'Your father doesn't care about us any more. You and I are alone in this world. From now on, I am your only parent.'

Halay burst into tears.

4

The initiation period lasted a few months. Halay saw Edward on a daily basis during that time. The town and the land were at peace. The crier had been silent for a while. It had to do with the initiation, Halay thought. He was sure the man would return as soon as it was over. Halay had decided in that period to build a few huts to accommodate the growing number of children who fell under his care; he plastered the walls of the old homes, emptied the granaries and filled them with the new harvest. He had to do something to keep his mind off the inevitable, and because he was a man who took pride in work, who saw the creases in his hands as proof of his labour, he worked on for days. The walls of the huts were already finished, except for the roof, which would consist of palm fronds or grass. Over a brief span of a few months, Halay succeeded in bridging the gap between him and Miatta. He seemed to have discovered her anew, more so because her father's absence had been explained. Miatta received him every night, both of them clinging together as though fearing that the other could vanish at any moment.

One night he slipped out of her grasp and started for the Poro ground. He thought of Edward who had begun to show strain associated with the trials of the initiation. His friend hardly slept, he took to eating fruits of the forest and not the sumptuous dinner presented to the initiates every day. Halay met him in front of the main hut, scraping away at the ground with a stick, pulling at the grass.

Edward spoke in snatches, and to the consternation of other initiates, he spoke in riddles like the masked being.

'Edward, come sit beside me,' Halay said.

'Tell me, Halay. What language do these beings speak?'

Halay shook his head.

'Do they eat like we do?'

'Edward, stop!'

'How come people are so afraid of them?'

'It's enough!'

'Can one of you become a masked being?'

'This is scandalous!'

'How were the masks made?'

'Edward!'

'Do the beings live forever?'

'Lower your voice!'

'Do they bear children?'

'I can't stand this!'

Halay looked about him. The men in the compound and the initiates were hard at work, doing their chores, feigning not to hear him.

'Are they married?'

'Will you stop this, Edward!'

'You have to tell me, Halay.' He looked at Halay, and then said, 'I was told the masked beings change form, how?'

'I cannot answer you.'

'Those beautiful feathers, how did they come upon them?'

All of a sudden Edward went silent. He leaned against Halay and cupped his face in his hands.

'I am not who you think I am, Halay.'

'You are who I think you are, Edward.'

'What if I said it was all for love?'

'The love of a woman?'

'You wouldn't understand, would you?'

'I am not understanding you now.'

'I knew it. My best friend fails to understand me.'

'I am trying to understand you.'

'Well, try a bit more.'

'Edward ...'

'I was such a fool.'

'Tell me.'

'I shouldn't have done what I did. I should have stayed with them, closer to them. I shouldn't have abandoned them.'

'Abandoned who?'

Edward stood up and paced about.

'You will forgive me, won't you, Halay.'

'We are friends, so yes I will forgive you.'

Edward told Halay about Charlotte and their years in America. He told him about their son.

'The longing for them has crippled me. I left a part of me in Monrovia. I am not fully myself here.'

'I understand. You could arrange for them to come. Or you could leave to see them. Monrovia is not that far away from here.'

'Yes, you are right.'

'After the ceremony, I will arrange for you to see your family.'

The two men went on talking for most of the night. In the morning, Halay left for town.

5

The head of masked beings appeared before the initiates for the last time and charged Halay with caring for Edward. Around dusk, on the final day of the initiation, it addressed the initiates. 'You've completed the tasks set before you. You've ensured that our way of life will be passed on to your offspring, that we as a people will live on. This means that we've fulfilled our goal of making you men, just as in a few years, if we are still around, if war doesn't do away with us, our young women will be in the Sande Society.' The masked being turned to Halay and dozens of young men who had formed a circle around it.

'Son of our king, our ruler, we are tasking you with caring for the man who chose to be one of us, who deserves our protection, our love,' it said.

Edward, too unstable to be part of the event, had been kept in a home where he was tended to by two men, and when Halay, who went to fetch him, met him, Edward broke into a plantation song.

'It's over now, Edward,' Halay said, and together they came out to join the initiates. Edward stared vacantly, his steps unsteady; he seemed a broken man, as if he'd undergone a terrible ordeal.

'Don't be afraid, our *wigi* – our westerner,' the masked being said. 'You came to us to meet your destiny, to find yourself.'

'*Kanikokoi* – he brings fortune,' the crowd burst out.

'You've heard them, Halay, he brings fortune just as you do. Take him home and don't leave him till he's well.'

With its task accomplished, the head masked being retired to the largest hut to wait until such a time as the land needed it again.

The next morning, the initiates dressed in new tunics, painted their faces with chalk, and with a solemn song accompanying them they danced towards town. They were met by a procession of mothers singing their praises. The women circled them, danced and sang their names. Groups of singers, drummers, and *salsa* – rattle players – danced about them. The crowd was so huge that there were rumours the ancestors had joined the ceremony. One woman claimed to have encountered a man of impeccable beauty dressed all in white who held his hand out to her, and she was about to take it when he vanished. A child saw a long form whose head was shrouded in the clouds. One man swore that he had met one of his ancestors among the crowd, had spoken to him, but the ancestor had not answered and had then merged with the people. These incidents heightened the excitement of the dancers.

The best drummer in the land could tell stories with his drums. His presence brought the bleary-eyed, the crippled, the blind, the old and the young pouring out of their homes and onto the streets. The sound of his drum rose above the stamping feet and crashed across the hungry mass. The ceremony had begun.

Meanwhile, at Halay's home, Edward's condition seemed to have worsened. Halay sat beside him in the main hut.

'I want you to fetch my notebook,' Edward said.

'What do you want with it?'

'I want to describe what's happening.'

Halay left to fetch the book and on his way met the crowd dancing to the beat of the master drummer. Around him, a group of women had coalesced, fanning him, wiping the pouring sweat off his face, which wore a haughty expression. Halay thought of his father-in-law, whose absence was beginning to be noticed by the people. He left the crowd.

At Edward's house, with its neat rooms, living room and verandah, he located the notebook. It had drawings of the town, the houses, the roads, and a detailed description of daily life – all noted with accuracy. Edward had chronicled their lives as if he would need to recall their life later. When he returned with the notebook and a pen, Edward sat up and asked Halay to give him a few moments.

Night came with Edward still at work. Halay went in to ask him to join him for dinner. He met a man sweating, feverish and yet focused on his writing. Edward looked up with fiery eyes, as if he had awoken from a terrible dream, and Halay asked, 'How are you, my friend?'

Edward did not respond.

'You must eat,' Halay said and put the food in front of him. 'I will not leave your side until you've eaten. No one is going to accuse me of neglecting you. You will eat, Edward, or I will force-feed you.'

The determination in his voice won Edward over.

'You will live to witness it all, Edward.'

The crier's voice interrupted them. Edward stopped eating. The voice was ominous, laden with urgency. The drums, the celebration stopped. Halay came out of the house. The sun was yet to set.

For the first time in months, Halay came face to face with the man whose voice had disrupted every happiness the land had known. The crier was tall, with a slender frame and narrow face; a fretful man with a feline lilt to his gait, his eyes darted everywhere but avoided Halay's.

'Oh! It's you, Halay,' the crier said.

A nervous laughter twisted his lips.

'When will this ever stop?' Halay said.

The crier, almost cowering into himself, answered, 'It will never stop.'

He held his drum as though under a tremendous strain, his limbs were unsteady, but as he did so he lost his grip on the drum and it fell. He cursed as he stooped to pick it up. He was all agitation now, his frail, effeminate features trembling, as if Halay's presence were unbearable.

'You know that such a sacrifice is impossible,' Halay said.

The crier clutched the drum. Sudden tears clouded his eyes.

'You, of all people, should not be saying this,' he said.

'But I mean it. It is impossible.'

The crier's hold on his drum became tighter, his teeth chattered.

'If so, Halay, if so, then we are all lost.'

He broke into a run then, and from a distance Halay heard his voice rise, not with a warning of what was to come, but with a wail, a singular dirge that lamented the end of things as they were.

6

Halay entered the hut and met Miatta not in bed but on her feet, as if she had been waiting for him. Perhaps she had overheard his exchange with the crier, he thought. They did not speak. Later, while in bed with her back to him, she reached for his left hand and folded it within hers, clutching it tight to her breasts, and she remained silent even during those moments when sleep was far from her grasp. She had nothing to say, for the man lying beside her, whose breath she could feel on her nape, was a shell of a man. The real one was gone now, far out of her reach.

In the morning, after his bath, she went to the wooden box where the two kept their belongings and fetched his best outfit, a red and black tunic with baggy trousers bought from a trader across the river. She helped him into them, and while at it she touched the hems of his tunic, touched his shoulders to feel the strength in his arms, the arch in his spine, touched his hands which had become crude as result of farm work, and then she drew close to him, wanting him to hold her, which he did, holding her so tight that she fell into a swoon and didn't want it to stop.

169

She led him out of the hut and through the compound, and stood watching him as he took the road towards the town hall. Miatta had resigned herself to the inevitable, to a life without him, and with the resignation came a deep wisdom regarding the whimsical nature of life. However, as she joined her son, she was yet to fully embrace this wisdom.

The town was quiet, holding its breath, waiting. Halay met the elders arguing in the town hall. He was surprised they were so early.

'We should make offerings of cows,' one of them said.

'Dozens of cows,' another said.

'Will that be enough?'

'It doesn't matter,' another said. 'We have to do something.'

'I will do it,' Halay heard himself say.

The elders looked on.

'I have come to offer myself to save you.'

His own revelation startled them. The elders turned to him, dumbstruck by the tenacity and courage in his voice.

'You are our king now. Soon, we will announce that Mambu has perished during his journey across the river. No one will know.'

'I am not doing it because of his death.'

'Halay, you are an only child and the father of an only child,' the eldest said. He stood up and walked to Halay.

'I've made up my mind. Our people will never suffer the scourge of war again, never. The land will live in peace.'

The eldest fell to his knees before Halay.

'Think this over, son, wait a month or two and if you return with the same answer, then we will do it.'

'I've made up my mind.'

The elders, failing to persuade him otherwise, led him surreptitiously to a hut on the outskirts of the town.

Soon afterwards, the crier beat his drum, announcing in an agitated voice that a saviour had been found. The land will live on.

Halay, alone in the hut, was sure that his son would live to be like him and his land would never know war. His son would wed and bear a child whose name would be his name and he would live on in the child of his child, in the child of that child, the chain unbroken forever.

Soon a crowd gathered in front of his hut. The whole day and night he would spend in isolation. The crowd kept vigil outside. When morning came with a gentle breeze blowing through the thatch of the roof and with a bird singing somewhere, Halay awoke and peered through the cracks in the door. The crowd had not dispersed.

Miatta came in the afternoon with a bowl of food.

'How's Salia doing?'

'I cannot tell him. I will not be the one to tell him,' she said.

'He must know. You must tell him.'

'He will not understand, Halay.'

'How about Edward?'

'He's there. He keeps writing. He says he wants the world to know what happened in our land, what happened to you.'

'You don't approve of my decision.'

'You are saving the land,' she said.

'I am saving you.'

'I cannot understand.'

'But it is simple, Miatta.'

'We could leave this land before the war comes.'

'Where to and what will we live on? On memories, which would fade until we've ceased to remember?'

'What about our son?'

'He will live on, Miatta.'

'But without a father.'

Her objections unnerved him. He accompanied her to the door and stared after her as she took to the road, but as she moved further away, he noticed a tremor in her steps. All of a sudden Miatta stumbled and fell. The crowd rushed to her. She had fallen into a faint.

Halay held her, waiting for her to come to, and as he did so he began to doubt his decision. What will happen to her? What if she did not survive the aftermath? What will happen to their son?

'You are not the only one in the land,' she said after she had regained consciousness. 'You are my husband.'

'Countless people will be saved,' he said.

She didn't respond. The crowd took its place in front of the hut when she had gone and Halay had retired indoors.

Once alone, he gazed at the cracks in the walls of the hut, at a spider weaving a web in the palm fronds and thatch that formed the roof, at a gecko that often emerged and nodded at him; at an amulet buried in a cow horn that hung at the threshold; at a goatskin mat on the floor and at a clay container filled with water. He touched the bowl of food, the mud bed, and the door; he touched everything that could give him a sense of belonging to this world, and all those things felt real. And he doubted.

The days quickly flew by. He began to take particular interest in life around him. The cock crows announcing dawn were distinct, so were the voices of people outside, which came to him as sudden but vivid memories that burst into his mind, lodged there and took on shapes. He could tell by a woman's laughter that she needed her husband to receive her that night, or that she was disappointed or glad. He would analyse the timbre in the voices, the level of anger, frustration, love or tenderness, and attributed stories to them. Images of Miatta and his son would appear in his mind's eye, images of himself alone with his wife, making love to her, the act sending them into a firmament of bliss and to a garden opulent with the freshest vegetables and with plants that had healing powers. Later he would imagine the three of them in the future, imagined himself a grandfather, a great-grandfather, his family at peace, the land at peace, the world at peace. Or he would be beset with doubts regarding the relevance of his action, doubts about his courage, about his strength, about the end. What if it was all for nothing?

On the fifth and sixth day, his anxiety began to wear off. On the morning of the seventh day, Halay was led out of the hut. The entire town was waiting there; thousands had gathered. He paused to glance at the cracks and bumps in the earth he walked on, the shapes of houses and the thatched roofs; the trees, the orange trees, mango trees and avocado trees, the grasses along the road, the ochre colour of the road itself, the overcast sky, the goats and sheep lying idly on the roadside. He strove to imprint on his mind the face of every individual in the crowd: the face of a young man who seemed not to comprehend the meaning of the ceremony; the anxious face of one who questioned his decision; and a face that was overwhelmed with joy, for at last the land would cease to be embroiled in constant war. A face littered with the creases of old age; a serene face that had been troubled by recent events. And a face every angle of which he knew and had touched: Miatta's face? And another face that bore his father's broad nose, his strength, his gait, and that was a replica of his mother's with the broad forehead, the smiles, the laughs, and the gentleness: his son Salia's face. He turned his back to the faces and walked on.

A square-shaped hole came into view when he mounted the hilltop. Palm fronds encircled it. The trees had been felled

173

to clear as much ground around his final resting place. Once again, very briefly, he felt the intimations of doubts, but the longer he gazed at the clearing, at the hole, the doubts began to subside. His future was certain. He was alone now, a solitary figure about to embark on his final battle, his final war, and whose feat would be remembered by his people.

Halay started down the hill towards his final resting place.

Book Four
Exile

1

War met me sitting at the table and reading a book in the light of a bare bulb. My mother had purchased the book during one of her trips to Monrovia, with money I had accumulated by running errands for her and doing chores around the house. The book was about a boy growing up in a town in the savannah, a boy named Kamo who tried to negotiate the challenges life threw his way. There was something about how he conducted himself that appealed to me: he was alone most of the time, conjuring up words in which he was the master, just like I often did when I drew the world around me: the butterflies at the river, my mother's face, the professor's Afro, the chair on which I sat, my table and bed.

Before me on the table were other books, many of which once belonged to my father, books loaded with stories ranging from those about American Indians and the Chinese who lived on the edges of the Gobi Desert. There were other books for school, but my sketchbooks took a prominent place on the table. Nothing mattered to me more than giving shape to the world. Behind me was a poster of a jet plane I had drawn, based on the one I had seen in a film at the local cinema. The drawing

177

had established me as an artist in the eyes of my teacher Mr Wilson, who had taught me to look at the world closely and with deliberation.

I was so buried in the world of the book that when war came I thought it was the sound of fireworks, but soon it was followed by my father's hurried footsteps going towards the room where he kept his belongings, and then I heard the sounds again.

He entered my room with a rifle.

The sight of my father holding the weapon as though it were a toy unnerved me. I stood up to make for the door.

'Halay, those idiots have brought war to our city. I am going out with others to chase them away.'

My mother burst into the room.

'You are scaring the child with that gun, Frederick. Give it to me right now,' my mother said and whisked the weapon away.

'But those brutes are already here,' he said.

He was right. Outside, down the hill on the main street, machine guns were firing.

The three of us made for the door, but my father paused, hesitant to open it as the gunshots came nearer.

'Frederick, we will die here,' my mother said.

Hurried whispers and trampling feet populated the world around us. We darted out of the house. Somewhere in the dark, a cock crowed and a panicky dog barked. Most people seemed to be heading towards the mountains, which was also our destination. My mother had managed to bundle up some of our belongings, including clothes, a tin of palm oil, smoked fish and meat, some vegetables and fruits, a family album and my sketchbooks.

We followed a path once used by people a century or more ago but was abandoned when a bulldozer clearing it had crashed and its driver had claimed to have seen the dead. My mother was silent while my father kept lamenting the sudden transformation in our lives.

'Jowo, your ancestor sacrificed his very life to prevent wars such as this. Yet, more than a century after his death, war comes. This must be the work of not more than a thousand people,' he said. 'Just a handful of people plunging the whole country into a nightmare!'

My mother ignored him. At one point, after we had climbed the mountain and had turned to stare at the city lying below us lit up in flames, my father stopped my mother. 'Jowo, we can't leave. I just remembered that we forgot the professor. He's been like a father to you since the death of your parents. Everything we worked and lived for is right there. We can't leave,' he said.

'You are behaving like a child, Frederick,' my mother said and brushed past him, hauling me with her. My father followed.

Now in the forest proper, we were assailed by the terrifying cries of animals. Thick foliage and sharp entwining plants hindered our passage, but my father would clear them with his cutlass. I marvelled at his dexterity. I had never seen him dig a furrow with a hoe or use a tractor like other farmers did, for his gift lay in bringing those farmers together and harnessing their power in a cooperative society that catered to their needs, selling their crops in Monrovia and supplying them with farming materials. He worked to gain the farmers' trust by being fair and fought corruption to hold on to that trust. Farmers were so taken by him that sometimes we would wake up and see them gathered in front of our house, waiting for him, trusting his verdict regarding their products.

My father was from the south-east of the country, where the ocean joined the land, and where the people perceived water as their god. Part of him belonged to those who sailed across that ocean, but his mother was of the seafaring people, the ones who regarded the sea as an entity that deserved filial treatment and was often given it.

Animals awoke to the sound of our footsteps and ran to safety. Dried leaves chattered as they took to flight. My father led the way, and I followed, and my mother brought up the rear. Near a stream, I realized that my mother was not with us. My father screamed like a wounded animal and darted towards the bush. He tore at branches, broke plants and wrestled with trees. We went up hills, stumbled into caves populated with bats. An animal gave a piercing cry so laden with terror that my knees buckled under me.

'Halay, stand up, stand up I say!' he shouted.

I could not move. He shouldered me and trudged on. We came to a more open place with low trees. My father set me down, cupped his head in his hands and burst into tears. I sat beside him and felt his shuddering body, felt him hold me tight, until the crack of dawn.

The rain that came lasted all morning. We continued our search. The trees and plants wafted a mixture of poignant smells. At an intersection of two obscure paths, we happened upon my mother entwined in foliage of thick brush, tortured and bruised. My father rushed to her, tore the brush off her, and revived her with water from a nearby stream.

'Jowo, you are alive, you are alive …' he kept saying.

We rested for most of the day and resumed our journey at noon. We came upon deserted villages, upon clothes, utensils, farming implements and cans scattered everywhere. In a village over which a cloud of smoke hung, the homes burning, we encountered a pack of stray dogs. They barked at us but did not attack us. A goat tethered to a house that was in flames wore an expression I had seen on my father's face when he entered my room the previous night. My father untied it and the animal escaped toward the bush.

Outside the village, we encountered a heap of masks. Most had been burned and the rest broken into pieces. The one with the face of a woman had been hacked into two and soiled with faeces. A mask with a mirror face had its once proud countenance dipped in mud, and another had its nose chopped off. We paused for a while, gazing at the carnage. My father sucked his teeth and shook his head.

'Who would do such a thing?' he asked.

The sun was bright and the air filled with a cloying, sweet fragrance. Insects chirped and birdsong rent the air. We sat down to rest in a clearing in the forest where a drowsy wind wafted over us.

My mother offered me some pounded peanut, and I nibbled at it, savouring it, knowing it was my last real meal.

Then we heard someone crying, the voice so pregnant with sorrow that we hurried towards it and met a woman standing in front of a house in flames, her hands on her head. We stood rooted to the spot as she grieved the loss of her home. Suddenly, she raced towards the house and, before my father could stop her, had flung herself into the burning pile.

None of us moved, too stunned to cry or moan. My father shook his head and led us on. In subsequent days, we slept in abandoned homes and ate fruit that resulted in dysentery, all the while avoiding people and sleeping while one of us kept watch.

Bedraggled, worn out, having suffered the cold, the noise and silence of the nights, and hunger, we crossed the river that bordered the two countries and reached our destination desperate for food.

2

It was a densely populated place. We moved through the streets, gazing at the people with some apprehension, at students in uniform on their way to school, and at cars piping out dark smoke. We gazed at the world around us as if we were seeing these things for the first time. They seemed separate from our reality and no matter how much we tried we could never be part of them. We came to a crowded market. As we edged our way through the throng of people, I bumped into a girl bearing a basket of mangoes on her head. The load seemed twice her weight. A scarf covered her face and a skirt and blouse shrouded her tiny figure. She wore cheap slippers, patched here and there, but from her clean clothes I thought she must come from a home that took good care of her. Her back was straight under the weight, and now and then she would call out offering to sell her mangoes in a high-pitched voice.

My mother's face had reclined into a smile, perhaps because we had survived the war. My father wore a puzzled look, as if the world had become a riddle he was fighting to decipher. We roamed the city in search of a place to stay until we came to a house on its outskirts, with a piece of cloth as a door and the walls shrouded in bougainvillea. There was a chicken coop on the side of the house, and on the right, giving onto an open field, was a thatched shack that perhaps served as a bathroom.

We called out and an old lady appeared at the door. She wore a white dress that had faded to grey and from whose sleeves emerged tiny hands wrinkled with veins. Her dark, sparkling eyes searched ours.

My father explained our plight.

'We are refugees,' he said in French.

To our relief the old woman responded in our language. She asked our names and nodded as my father answered.

The old woman, whose name was Ma-Wata, lodged us in her immaculate home and fed us a meal of pounded cassava – *toe* – and hot pepper soup. Before leaving that night, she told us that she would be staying at one of her relatives until we had a place of our own or had returned to our land.

After dinner, I moved to a corner of the house and sat on a chair to take stock of our lives. The image of my school surrounded with orange and mango trees came to me, as well as the giant breadfruit tree that stood in front of it, the football field, and the huge bell, which I had been responding to every day for most of my twelve years. I thought of my schoolteacher, Mr Wilson, who had encouraged me to draw and had persuaded my parents to support my talent. My mind drifted to my grandparents, my mother's parents, who had passed on a few years ago. Every morning, my grandmother, an old woman with skin the colour of deep brown earth, would come to fetch me to see her husband. My grandfather would present me with a cup of tea sweetened with condensed milk and served with French bread, which he smeared with margarine and stuffed with sardines. Seated on a mat, facing him with the morning sun beaming through the window, I would bite into the bread.

His great-grandfather Salia was the son of my namesake Halay. Besides stories of this ancestor, Halay, which varied every time, sometimes taking on mythical proportions, my grandfather told me of journeys he had undertaken to lands that went by new names now. He would tell me of a ruler who would force a whole town to bow in prayer night and day and would punish anyone who defied him by pinning his genitals to the ground. The ruler called it the big bowing day. There was another ruler whose reign of terror was such that the mere mention of his name was enough to keep people awake, on edge, afraid he would sack their towns and enslave them. But when the land could no longer condone his deeds, the ruler, while being carried in a hammock, had been ambushed and murdered.

But my grandfather's favourite story was the one involving my grandmother. 'She was not particularly beautiful when I first saw her, Halay,' he would tell me. 'No, there was nothing remarkable about her. And that's why what happened to me later after I had learned to know her better, to eat her food, to spend hours with her baffled me.' He had journeyed to a town in the east of the country to visit one of his friends and had lodged at his place. When dusk fell and it was time to take his bath, a young girl called to him to take his bath. She was the youngest daughter of the house and he had not seen her on his arrival. He was charmed by her smile and by the way she announced the bath. It was when he could not sleep and ate little of the food the next morning and when he walked in a daze and saw everyone returning his smile that he realized he was in love. He saw her once, then twice, but every time he met her, his longing for her heightened. He had asked for her hand in marriage but was told he could only marry after she had completed her secondary schooling. 'I had to wait for a whole year, Halay,' he would say.

At that point in the story, my grandfather would pause. 'Here she comes,' he would say of my grandmother. 'Pretend you are eating.'

'You are telling him one of your fanciful stories again,' she would chide him. 'Did you add that you had to wait five more years for me?'

My grandfather would fidget.

'I don't remember waiting a single day for you,' he said.

'Yes, after high school, I went to university,' she said. 'Don't listen to all those stories, Halay. They are all embellished.'

'But the child has to know.'

'Then tell him the truth.'

'That's what I am doing.'

She would laugh and shake her head. Later, she would spirit me away after my grandfather had fallen asleep during siesta. She would lead me to a room full of jars of coins and stacks of notes not only of our currency but of many other countries, which she had begun to save the day I was born. In various valises, native cotton clothes were stacked. I often spent the night alternating between being enfolded in my mother's arms or lying on a king-size bed in my grandparents' room. When the two died in a car accident years later, I was the sole heir to their wealth.

From looking at the coins and notes, I learned about the flora and fauna of other lands, about their rulers, their artists and statesmen and those who had shaped the destiny of their countries. I would confine myself in the humid, stuffy room for hours on end, rubbing the coins and notes and studying the pictures and strange inscriptions. I would make up a game of trying to decipher the languages and what the images stood for and the stories behind them. Often I would draw them.

Those aspects of my past came to me now in that new home. In an attempt to understand our flight, this house and this exile, I began to jot down my feeling in poems. They were crude lines yet to be honed into something permanent. I turned my attention to my mother with her mysterious smile and my father huddled in a corner, his eyes closed. I watched my mother move to the only bed in the house. She was glowing amid that confusion, and I could not explain it.

'You look happy here, Mother,' I said.

She shook her head.

'But why the smile?'

'We are alive, Halay. We are alive. Have you paused to think about it? We are alive. Thousands will perish in that war.'

So this was the source of her happiness, that we had survived the war. Was that enough? I wondered. What did exile hold in store for us?

Moments later, she fell asleep. Her gentle breath rose and fell peacefully in the mud-scented house. Night had fallen. The flickering flame of the hurricane lamp lit up her face in a golden haze.

The urge to capture that moment led me to fetching my sketchbook and drawing her. I drew her hands tucked under her head as a pillow, and I drew her face, made it look younger, her lashes and fluttering eyelids. Instead of the bed and my father huddled beside her as background, I drew patches of clouds and drew the bed as a garden. And I drew my father, and set upon his head a bundle under which his now spindly legs strained.

On my attempts to draw war, to give shape to our terrors and experience, I found that the results were either detached from my innermost feelings, chaotic or mere fantasies that lacked depth.

The light of the hurricane lamp faded out and left me pondering on the subject of war. I had failed to draw it. I spread one of my mother's wrappers on the cold floor and went to bed. My sleep was capricious. In between sleep, I would hear peals of laughter and snatches of conversation drifting from the houses along the road. Then sleep would overcome me, and I would drift into the realm of dreams. One of my dreams was of a storm that hit the city. The storm headed towards me and was about to sweep me up in its path when I woke up drenched in sweat. By then it was already morning. My mother was absent.

'Where is mother?' I enquired from my father who shrugged, tucked his hands between his legs and went back to sleep.

From a nearby well, I fetched a bucketful of water and had a cold bath. My father was still asleep. The old woman had brought us a breakfast of eddoes cooked with palm oil. She told us that a batch of people had arrived from our land and had set up camp at the other end of the city. I ate a little of the food and came out of the house.

Along the road, down a hillock, a group of men were involved in a heated discussion, and children were playing in the sand. One was rolling a bicycle wheel and chasing after it up and down the road. Seated on a stool outside the house, her beautiful face filled with warmth, the old woman told me that the language that sounded strange to us was in fact a variation on ours. 'Just listen carefully, you will hear the similarities,' she said. And I did. Words I had thought sounded strange were in fact versions of our own. The languages were indeed related.

My mother returned at late noon, drenched in sweat but in a lively mood. She unfolded a bunch of Dutch wax material from a bundle she had put in front of us.

My father who was awake by then asked her, 'How did you get these clothes?'

'I persuaded a businesswoman to give me these wrappers after much talking, telling her who were in our country.'

'She gave them to you just like that?'

'I told her I will return them with profit at the end of the month.'

'Can you do that?'

My mother nodded, and my father did not enquire further but turned his back to us and went back to bed.

After that, my mother frequented the market and returned late at night. My father slept most of the time. When awake, he avoided looking at me and hardly spoke except in snatches. He would sit up in bed whenever the old woman came over after a few days of absence, and he would rub his flabby face and manage a smile. He would grab the food offered us and wolf it down. During one of her visits, the old woman told us of frequent reports of fighting between the refugees and the hosts who had to cope with the huge number of people.

When my mother came home, my father did not mention the fights to her. She told us about her struggles at the market, her rudimentary grasp of the language, and my father nodded and kept silent. She referred to her thriving business before the war, the stores she managed, the houses she let out, and for the first time in weeks, my father referred to the life we had left behind: 'I can't wait to return home, Jowo. I will expand the farmers' cooperative into a national enterprise, where all farmers will be allotted a fair share for their labour. That will be my goal on our return.'

I realized, as he went on, that his dream was ensconced in realities that seemed far-fetched, for there was no guarantee that we would ever go back. I grabbed my sketchbook and I drew the shape of his hands, which had been bruised during our flight. I drew his face, which was robbed of strength and still sagged with fatigue.

Later, by the time I was finished, my parents were fast asleep. I went out into the night and stared at the star-studded skies. How could I draw the one thing I feared most, the one that had sent us fleeing for our lives? I wondered as I stared into the great expanse of sky. The more I thought about it, the more I felt that I did not have it in me to draw war.

During the day, I would often spend hours roaming the forest behind our house, listening to the birdsong, plucking and smelling the flowers, tasting and squeezing them for colour or odour. I would try to put onto paper memories of home, with my parents seated on the verandah of our house at sunset receiving the farmers. My father would note down their complaints and he would surprise them by visiting them on their farms with materials they lacked.

With these memories, came my longings. I wanted to be a great artist, a medical doctor, a saviour of the country, one who would bring peace to it, and I wanted to shake my father out of his stupor. I wanted to be like the bird now perched on a tree close to me, one to which all and sundry would listen and relish its beautiful, enchanting song. When I gazed around me at the lilies of the swamp, heard the croaking of the frogs, the songs of the birds, breathed in the perfume scent of the flowers, the mild wind of the forest, and admired the patterns made by sunlight on the forest ground, I wanted to remain in that forest, far away from everything. I would return home elated, sure now that perhaps I was on my way to understanding what made my mother so resilient, while my father wasted away. Her being alive was not enough of an explanation for me, for in that life her husband played no role.

189

My mother purchased new wrappers, using the profit from the first sales. 'I am right on my way to conquering the market, Frederick,' she told my father one night. The language of this land was yielding to mother. She would repeat sentences and words that she had learned at the market to us.

The old woman came one afternoon, stayed longer and ate some of the food we offered her. She told us about the camps that hosted the fleeing people, which were now spreading along the edges of the city. The refugees were building their own city in the land of exile.

3

For months now, I had confined myself to the house and its environs, leaving only to run errands for my parents in the neighbourhood, or go to the forest to draw trees, plants and flowers or to write awkward poems. One day I decided to brave it to the city. Farms and vegetable gardens lined the road. Some men were tending to their coffee and cocoa farms. Further down the road, women were pinching rice stems into the soggy earth. As I approached the city, the noise of purring car engines and the shouts of marketeers assaulted me. The pervasive odour of gasoline, garbage and sweat hung in the air. Vendors called out their wares and some offered fake jewellery and watches. Girls carrying massive heaps of vegetables, fruit and loaves of bread on their heads moved along the road.

Before a weak corrugated-iron cubicle, I saw a little bald man sitting on a chair. What struck me about him, besides his dwarfish size and baldness, was the confidence he portrayed. He was arguing with a man twice his size. In carefully chosen words, he addressed the giant who at first fended him off with laughter. The spectacle attracted me. The little man hauled himself at the giant and his blow caught him around the crotch. He shouted victory, slapped the ground, and swore to truly show the world the stuff he was made of. His sour epithets and derisions were inventive. The giant turned to the crowd, his laughter revealing a neat set of teeth. He threw a punch meant to knock the little man out, but he missed. The two men went into a clinch. It seemed to last forever. Then I heard a crack. In a second the little man was free. The giant stood for a while and then fell to his knees. The crowd, including myself, thought he would never rise again. His face was contorted with pain, while the little man capered about, sucking his teeth and spitting. It was the roar of the giant, which sounded like a wounded lion, which shifted our attention to him. He was rushing at the little man, but did not reach him, for a group of men blocked his way. They managed to force him to his knees.

The crowd went berserk. From the house I was standing in front of a man darted out, almost colliding into me, and flung himself at the crowd. Utensils flew around and chairs were shattered upon heads. The most inventive of curses rang the air. A child was crying and a man was bleeding, having wounded his leg. One of the men held me by my shoulders, shook me as if I were an empty sack, and then let go of me, butting his way into the crowd. The fighting went on.

It was the police who finally broke it up. I slipped away while a policeman was handcuffing both the little man and the giant, and I moved through an alley of makeshift homes to a bar.

It was crowded. A mother dressed in rags sat at a table with her four children. She was trying unsuccessfully to attend to them all. She would yell at one, pet the other, breastfeed one and called sweetly to another. A man with an empty bottle before him and his head resting on the table was fast asleep. Another was tapping on the table and staring at the ceiling. In a corner, three men were playing draughts. Music was blaring. The singer, who was popular in the late eighties, was singing:

The flowers have withered
The grounds scorched
And the earth longs for rain.
When will it pour?

The barman, an old grey-haired man with uneven teeth, his skin so black that it glinted blue, beckoned to me with a smile. I moved towards him. He leaned on the counter, and spoke to me in his language.

'Do you want something to drink?'

'I don't have money.'

He searched an old refrigerator behind the counter and pulled out a plastic sack of ice water, and I swallowed at the sight of the drink.

He handed the drink to me.

'You saw the fight, didn't you?'

I nodded.

'One of them, the giant, is from your country. The little one was born and bred in this town. He's a troublemaker.'

I was silent.

'Have you been here for long?' he asked.

'We came here a few months ago.'

The music continued playing, and I nibbled at the ice.

'What's your name?'

'Halay,' I told him.

'Did you see the war?'

'We fled on the very first day.'

'So you don't know how it feels going through war?'

'We fled under volleys of gunfire.'

193

'But that's not enough. To be a true victim of war, you must have experienced war itself,' he said.

'Did you ever experience war?'

'Yes, a bigger one.'

'Which one?'

'The Second World War. I fought in it.'

'You were a soldier?'

'Don't mention that word. I am not proud of being a soldier.'

The music rose to a crescendo, and the singer was displaying his mastery of the guitar. The man who had been gazing at the ceiling was now hitting an empty bottle in tune with the music. The sleeping man had awoken and chimed in to the song. He stood up and swung his hip, snapping his fingers as he danced. I took a bite of the ice.

The barman said: 'Yes, we fought that war like men. We fought in trenches, in rain, in forest, in cold, side by side. You should have seen me then, a young man who fought not because he had to but because he believed that justice must prevail. I saved lives in that war. Perhaps that's why I am a poor barman today. Perhaps it takes all the courage in a life to save another. I don't have a life now. Long ago, I gave it up to save others in the trenches of those snow countries.'

He stopped and eyed me, his gaze intent.

'Any word from home?' he asked.

'No,' I answered.

'That's how it always is. Remember this, child: whenever the silence breaks, it is accompanied by the most fearsome noise.'

Some people came into the bar, and he left to attend to them. Looking at him as he cheered up his customers, I could not believe he was the same man who had fought in the Second World War. My father had seen war and it had turned him into a man who spoke in snatches and hisses. Maybe the barman had witnessed something in that war that had made him capable of managing a smile or even a laugh.

I was about to leave when he said, 'Come and see me again.'

I nodded and stepped out into the sun. The streets were deserted, the air shimmered. A flurry of dust swirled and headed towards me but I dodged it. On the roadside, a girl with eyes that had become blood-red from the fire called out to me to buy the plantains she was frying. I smiled at her and moved on. I met my father in front of the house, working on a fishing net. He looked up when I approached.

'I am going to be a fisherman,' he said.

A twinkle of light leapt to his eyes. He continued working on the net until my mother came home. She seemed surprised.

'Your father is becoming a fisherman,' she said.

'I will start small, Jowo, watch me. Then I will expand. I will go on to unite all the fishermen in this place. Watch me.'

We were interrupted by the old woman. She had come to tell us something of the greatest importance: the signs of things to come.

'What things?' my mother asked.

'Can't you see the signs?'

'What signs?'

Perhaps she was referring to the fight I had witnessed in town earlier that day, I told my parents after the old woman had left. The two shook their heads, but did not enquire further. The next morning, my father left to go fishing and asked me to join him.

'I am going with mother to the market.'

'You will miss the silences.'

'What silences?'

'Of the river. Fish hate noise, you know.'

195

My father promised to bring us a catfish. My mother looked beautiful. Her silver earrings dangled from her ears and her bracelets clanked to the movement of her hands. She owned a stall in the market now, where we sat till midday without selling a thing. Vendors, young girls moved with their wares, their strident voices rising above the noise of the market. We waited. I tried to sing, but struck the wrong note and my voice trailed off into silence.

A bulky woman from the stall next to ours informed us that a handsome man was going around the market saying he would only purchase from the most beautiful woman at the market. My mother laughed, and I did too. Soon we saw a man walking up to our stall. Tall and with a shaved head, he wore a skullcap decorated with images of the crescent moon, and he had applied kohl to sharpen the outline of his eyes. He was clad in a white gown with flowery designs upon it. His handsome face sweated a little as his gaze rested on my mother. My mother stood erect, elegant and graceful, and I saw what the stranger saw: pitch-dark skin shrouded in colourful wrappers, a woman so radiant that her beauty held the man in thrall.

With a voice that sounded like a revelation, the man said: 'Truly, you are the most beautiful woman I've ever seen.'

My mother blushed and I noted her smile, but her face quickly regained its normal expression. Even when the man went on to purchase all the goods in our stall and placed an order for the next supply, my mother's expression did not alter. In fact, as his long, slender arms counted out the notes and handed them over to my mother, her face clouded with anger that verged on repulsion. I wondered why. The man bundled up the goods and left the market, never turning or speaking to anyone.

196

My mother chose not to mention the day's incident. But the spectacle had not gone unnoticed. We packed up and returned home earlier amid the envious glances of the market women.

The next day, the women turned against my mother. Her neighbour, the bulky woman who had helped her set up her business, now tried to draw her into a fight. Some days, she would return home, complaining about the market women and their fights against her. 'They are making it impossible for me to do business, Frederick,' she would say. During those moments, my father would be close to her, cracking jokes and reminding her of life before the war. He would stay with her all night.

4

One day my father caught a trout. He moved about the compound displaying his catch, his gentle face aglow with pride. Despite objections from my mother, he decided to prepare the fish himself. The result was an over-seasoned sauce not fit for consumption. While we were trying to eat the food, focusing on the rice and not the sauce, my mother remarked, 'It's too spicy, Frederick,' and this sent him into a rage.

'In your eyes, I never seem to do anything right here,' he said, and stood up, fuming. 'Yes, look at me and say it, Jowo,' he said.

And my mother, her eyes fixed on the food, replied, 'Say what. I am not saying anything.'

My father sucked his teeth. 'You will say it, Jowo. Say what you think of me. I can see it in your eyes and in your behaviour whenever you return from that market of yours. Say it and then Halay here will know what you think of me!'

My mother stood up but as she tried to lay her hands on her husband's shoulders, to calm him, he stormed out of the house and returned late, wearing a sombre look accentuated by the flame of the hurricane lamp. It was not because of the food, he said. Our house, he told us, a proud mansion with six rooms, one of the best homes in our city, had been demolished, our furniture stolen. Our city was now a deserted place where not even a dog barked. All the domestic animals, dogs, chickens, sheep, goats have been consumed by hordes of fleeing people. 'It's that fact that's slowly killing me here, Jowo,' he said.

She nodded, and as she went on to console him I turned away and thought of the war. Would life be the same even if one day we had the chance to return home?

The next morning, my father took to singing old and new songs, songs sung by men and songs sung by women, nursery songs and songs forbidden to my ears. Later, he began humming a single tune which went on the whole day. He gave up fishing for a while and confined himself to the house. He would try to lull my mother into a fight but would fail every time. He would throw strange glances at me, bare his teeth and grunt. He would ask me questions I had no answer to. Why did people choose to slaughter each other? Why did they demolish homes that did not belong to them? Who was behind those destructive forces? Tell me, Halay, you are the artist, explain this war to me? I would slip out to escape his temper.

For weeks I had not been to see the old barman.

'You are here, Halay,' he said when he saw me.

I nodded and took a seat on one of the bamboo benches.

'Why have you been away for so long?'

'I draw most of the time.'

'What do you draw?'

'People mostly and nature.'

He was silent, and after a while he said, 'The artist's life is a difficult one here. Too much passion could end up killing him. I remember meeting an artist during the Second World War who drew only women. I could not understand why a man would choose to draw women and nothing else until I met my wife.'

The barman broke off and shuffled to the other end of the bar to change cassettes in his tape player. A Congolese song began to play, the most recent to hit the stores, and many were taken by it. The old man swung to it as he moved towards me.

'Halay, have you ever wondered what it feels like to find yourself at the centre of things?' He smiled and tapped his head. 'No, not the centre of things. I mean the centre of war.'

I shook my head.

'It could be exhilarating, especially for an artist, what with all the explosions, the cries and screams, the confusion. Nowhere is human courage more evident than in war.' He shared such vivid and minute details of his life as a sniper that a chill ran down my spine.

I was about to leave, but he served me a drink and told me about his wife whom he met in France. He married her just after the war. In the years that followed, they had three children. He was penniless during that time, sleeping and waking up to a hungry wife and children. Matters turned for the worse when his wife delivered their third child. He came home one night and met his children famished and his wife throwing him looks that reduced him to nothingness. Wretched and no longer capable of bearing her gaze, he waited till they slept, then packed a suitcase with clothes, taking along the photo albums, and stole out of the house and into the night. The next day, he boarded a ship bound for the land of his fathers. He never returned.

But he loved that woman, he told me. He loved her blue eyes and short brunette hair, her faint dimples, and the smell of mashed potatoes that seemed to always linger about her. He loved how her gentle gaze would sweep across the table as they shared their meal. Most of all, he loved the feeling of being in love and being loved. He understood then why the artist who painted only women never lacked inspiration.

Years later, after their first child, he would learn that she came from a prosperous family, a descendant of a long line of musical instrument makers. Her family had all perished in the war. She had survived a bombardment because she happened to be in the garden and not her father who played piano at that hour of the day, nor her mother who was sitting before the window doing some embroidery, and nor her brother who was in his atelier painting horses and cows.

The barman was about to say more when a handsomely dressed young man strutted into the bar. Before serving him, he asked me to accompany him to his home after he closed up.

It was a tidy house with a living room simply decorated with gilt-framed pictures. It had a verandah that looked out onto the ochre street. He showed me to a seat, went to his bedroom and emerged with a pile of picture albums. Pictures had always fascinated him. He would cut them out from books and newspapers and date them, including the hour and how he had come upon them. He would note down the country, the continent and the world's reaction to such an occasion. Now he had pictures of every major event since the Second World War.

The pictures were many, each with a story. In one of the pictures, he was standing and smiling, wearing the uniform of a soldier. In another he was in a suit and stood beside a seated woman whose hands were in her lap. There were his children, the eldest with a severe expression, the second with closed eyes and the third a cheerful baby.

He told the story of the family portrait with such tenderness that I wondered why, surrounded with such love and beauty, he had chosen to abandon them. I thought of the longings of the heart. Had his love for his wife driven them apart instead of bringing them closer together? I wanted to draw him as the man he once was, and draw his children and his wife before her gaze had become unbearable.

5

My father was sitting in the shade of the mango tree in front of the house. 'You are here, Halay,' he said, and shifted his attention to the fruit on the mango tree, which were still unripe. My mother had taken to returning home earlier from the market because of the constant friction between her and the market women. They would not let her be. After sharing a few words with her, I ate my meal of pounded cassava and peanut sauce, a combination that had grown on me. I decided to draw the barman and his family. I pictured them seated around a table in a room with a sofa that served as a bed, a burning candle and a small painting of flowers. I drew his wife and children with their anticipating stares, drew them lanky from hunger, drew them walking hand in hand on the main thoroughfare of their city, drew them with healthy limbs and faces, evoking a time when they seemed at ease with the world until poverty began to gnaw away at the foundation of their lives. I drew nothing else but the barman and his family for days on end and in different shades and moods.

Then I went to show him the drawings. He was busy clearing the bar for a performance. An acrobat in baggy trousers, a Fulani perhaps, was dancing in the cleared space, accompanied by his flute player. Soon the bar was crowded. Whenever the acrobat jumped, cheers and applause rose, and the crowd tossed money at him. The man left the bar and climbed to the rooftop from where he somersaulted and landed on the ground. He repeated this many times, as though his body was of steel.

I happened to shift my attention and my gaze rested on a girl whose hair was tied into little knots with tiny black ropes. Her eyes were wide with excitement, and beads of sweat were coalesced on her nose. The acrobat ceased to amuse me. A boy about her age approached her and whispered something in her ear. She laughed, and her face lit up like sunlight on a river. There was something peculiar about her. She was part of the crowd but stood apart, and whenever someone touched her, her face would flame up with irritation. Her plainness, the fact she was not a great beauty, fascinated me. She would stand on her toes, straining her neck to watch the performance, but afraid of being touched. The urge to draw was stronger than the desire to watch her, and so I left.

My mother noticed my sunny disposition. 'You look different, Halay?' she asked, but I chose not confide in her. I wanted to relish the moment alone.

I did not share in my father's victory when he returned from fishing with a basketful of his catch. 'If this goes on like this, I will start selling fish here, Halay,' he said, but my mind was elsewhere.

I drew the girl, concentrating on her slender figure, her hair, her full lips and sharp chin, and on her nose and on the drops of sweat gathered on it. Dusk met me still drawing her, and I slept soundly that night.

The next morning after my mother had left to wage her war against the market women and my father to fish, I went to the bar, hoping to see the girl. The place was empty, except for the barman.

'You are early, Halay,' he said.

I nodded.

'The acrobat will not be performing today.'

'I am not here for the acrobat.'

'Why are you here then?'

I was silent.

'If you are not here for me, then you must be here for someone else.'

I could not tell him.

'It happened to me before, Halay.'

'In France,' I said.

'Where else,' he said.

'What should I do?' I asked.

'Fight until you win her. It's winners who count.'

He broke into a love song, and I left him in search of the girl. I had not gone far when I saw her with a huge basket of peeled oranges on her head. Surprised, confused, I turned my back to her.

'Do you want some oranges?' she asked.

I was tongue-tied. My poetry, every sentence I'd ever forged, now failed me. I cursed every poet who had ever lived. What did their lines mean if they could not guide me through this moment?

'I saw you yesterday,' I managed to say.

'You couldn't take your eyes off me,' she said.

'Who was that boy with you?'

'So you are jealous?'

'I just want to know.'

'He is my brother, okay?'

I didn't know what to say.

'I know I cannot love you,' she said.

'Why not?'

'My father says that refugees carry filthy ways with them.'

'Do you think so?'

'You have to wait until I finish school.'

'Why finish school?'

'Because we are poor,' she said. 'I don't want to always be reminded of something I want to forget.'

'Do you want to forget poverty?'

'No, I don't want to be reminded of it.'

'You talk like an adult.'

'I am an adult.'

'You are not older than I am.'

'You think so? I am an adult because I see the world as it is,' she answered. 'I cannot love you for example.'

'You can't stop love,' I said.

'Who says so?'

'It's always been so.'

'That's not true.'

'Do you love me then? Can you love me?'

'I do. You are the first boy who ever looked at me that way. It's as if I was the first woman you've ever laid your eyes on.'

'Did you like it?'

'I couldn't sleep last night.'

'What do we do now?'

'Do you want some oranges?'

'Yes. I will buy one.'

'They are not for sale.'

'What will you tell your mother when she finds out that a few oranges are missing?'

'The truth.'

'What truth?'

'That I gave you some oranges.'

'It has to be a secret.'

'But I keep no secrets from my mother. I tell her everything.'

'What's your name?' I asked.

'Nafisat, and you?'

I gave her my name. Then I went on to tell her about life before the war and about our flight. I told her that I wanted to be equal in talent to an artist whose work I had encountered in one of my books. I told her that my single goal was to draw war, to capture on paper what had brought an end to our lives in our country, to explain war to myself. I became so excited that I stumbled on my words and stopped.

'I will tell my mother about you,' she said.

Later we parted, agreeing to meet the next day.

6

Unsure of my father's reaction to Nafisat if he met her, I took her instead to the refugee camp that was stretched along the city's outskirts. It was a boisterous and chaotic world, as if when my people fled they had taken their disordered world with them. Everything was for sale: zinc sheets, doors, timber, furniture, cars, nails, screwdrivers, mats, brooms, portraits, pans, cupboards, valises, second-hand clothes, shoes, rice, dried meat, yams, eddoes, palm oil, gold, silver, everything. In and around the makeshift camps, with homes built of plastic and mud, zinc and wood and thatch, people haggled over goods. Women, desperate to feed their children and themselves, sold their wrappers, their footwear, their bodies and everything else for ridiculous prices. Men let go of their precious possessions with heavy hearts. A man was lauding the long and loyal service of his jeep as he sold it. I saw a woman with a child seated before her, her feet swollen with jiggers, while flies flew around her and her child. She was a beggar. Her scrawny eyes shot me a look that made me want to break into a run.

'I don't like this place. Let's leave,' Nafisat said.

'No, I want to see this,' I said.

'But it is such a wretched place.'

'That's why I want to see it.'

On a hillock a thatched mosque stood a few feet away from a mud-built church. A crowd had gathered around a reverend and an imam who were discussing Jesus. A stone's throw away from the two places of worship was a bar that also served as a shop. We entered it. A woman with a vacant stare sat at a table. Flies hummed about and settled on the drinks, the glasses, the bottles, the openers, the lollipops, the sweets and toffees, and on the woman. A cassette player hiccupped and broke into a harsh tone. A child as thin as a teacher's cane raced into the bar, darted a look around the counter and seeing no one behind it snatched a sweet and rushed out. After a while, a group of young men entered chatting in a language that was both familiar and strange to me. It was my language. But the pitch in their voices, the break in their sentences, the laughter, the nuances, the rhythm seemed new. I felt close to them but at the same time lost in my own exile, unable to attain the level of mirth and confidence being displayed in their strange, chaotic world. Was I forgetting my language or had I been speaking in a different tongue with my parents? I wondered.

We went out. Along the muddy and cramped road, we met a group of boys playing a game of marbles. One of them broke away from the group and hungrily eyed the basket of oranges on Nafisat's head.

'How much for the oranges?' he asked.

Nafisat told him.

'They are too expensive. Do you want a marble for an orange?'

Nafisat shook her head. The boy joined his friends.

Under a huge tree sat a group of elderly men arguing about the war and what had led to it. Their voices rose with passion.

The war could only be explained by going to back to the beginning of the country, one of them said.

Another argued that the beginning had nothing to do with the war. 'It had to do with greed,' he said, but a third disagreed.

'The war had to do with tribalism,' he said, but another shook his head.

'It had to do with nepotism.'

One of them stood up. 'Wait, wait, listen,' he said. 'The war had nothing to do with any of these, but with outsiders who were pitting groups of our people against each another.' The rest did not agree.

We strolled past them. On one side of the road, close to the forest, rice paddies stretched out. Men and women were hard at work with hoes. An obnoxious smell that summed up the depth of deprivation of the camp hung like clouds over the place. Shacks that housed dozens of families rose up before us.

We came to an area of the camp that could boast a certain degree of decency. Between the mud-built homes was a shop stuffed full of provisions, and there was also a small market. A group of men had gathered around a girl selling fried fish and *callas* – fried doughnuts.

In front of a big house, in two lines that stretched to almost a kilometre each, desolate and beaten people stood, holding out bowls for their daily rations. At every turn, a refugee would push forward a bowl, the gaze almost always fixed on the azure blue skies. Was it anger I saw on the faces or the stark expression of people resigned to their fate?

'Where are you from?' an old man asked me. Before I could get around to answering him, he said, 'Child, you are looking at us as if you don't belong to us or as if you don't want to belong to us.'

Nafisat pulled my arm to go, but I couldn't move.

'People, look at this child who pretends he is different from us,' the old man said. The people in the queue laughed.

It took a while before I could take hold of myself. I promised that upon my return to the house, I would persuade my parents to move to the camp and become part of this world, our world.

On the roadside, we saw a man in a gown too large for him. One of those men who grew no beard despite age, he seemed to be the leader of the camp and was overseeing the building of a school. Men and children were labouring around him, digging holes, building mud bricks, fetching wood from the nearby forest to be used as poles to hold the building together. He was an agile man, he moved about shouting out orders, pausing with a frown to listen to one person and berating another.

By then we had covered the length of the camp and were now at a place where the clearing ended and the forest began. Under a giant cotton tree, a group of men stood trading in currencies, exchanging ours for those of the land of exile. On seeing us, the men fixed their gazes at the skies, hurriedly puffing at their cigarettes, pretending not to have seen us. Here and there, new shacks were being put up by fresh groups of refugees.

Nafisat was overwhelmed by it all. I offered to help her with the basket of oranges. The camp was far behind us now and the noises and smell were replaced by a pleasant freshness when we arrived at the river, which was said to run as far as our land and beyond it, winding its way like a giant python through several countries providing fish, bearing people and goods on its waters and inexhaustibly falling into the ocean.

I set the basket of oranges down and we sat on the sand, in the haunting silence of the languid river. After a while, a fisherman rowed along the river in a slender canoe, humming a tune as slow as the current until he disappeared beyond the mangroves.

Nafisat enquired about my drawings. I told her what I had done and planned to do. I did not hide the fact that occasionally after making a drawing I would shed tears. Or, out of dissatisfaction, I would tear my drawings into pieces and would not draw for a while. I told her about my mother and how difficult exile was for my father who spent his days fishing.

A movement in the river interrupted us. A tortoise was swimming across the river to the other side. We watched it crawl up the bank and get lost under the canopy of dried leaves.

'Why do you want to draw war?' Nafisat asked.

'Because war haunts me,' I said.

'What do you mean?'

'I see war in everything.'

'In everything?'

'Yes,' I said.

'Even in me?'

'Yes, even in you.'

'Do you often dream about it? I mean the war?'

'I do,' I said.

I had laid bare my soul to her, but instead of feeling exhilarated, free of the burden I had borne since the war, I felt I had betrayed what had held me together by sharing it with someone who had not lived it or could not understand. Would Nafisat understand that my obsession with war went deeper than the loss of property or a home? That it had to do with my past and with my family and its history?

Nafisat embraced me as if she understood. She held on to me for a long time, and when she let go she said: 'Let's swim.'

We swam in silence, crossing the river to the other bank and then swimming back again, until we were worn out, and

212

then we lay on the sand under the full glare of the sun. Our bodies were dust-white from lying too long on the sand. Before leaving, we washed the dust off.

'You are special, Halay,' she said when we parted.

7

'Where have you been all day?' my mother asked that evening. We were alone in the house. My father had not returned from fishing. I told her about Nafisat and about the remarks of the old man we had met in the refugee camp. 'Please, Mother, let's move to the camp and be with our people,' I said, and she smiled.

'Come and sit beside me,' she said.

I stood and moved towards her but stopped short of sitting next to her.

'No, here on the bed,' she said, patting the mattress.

When I eased down beside her, she held my hands. There was light in her eyes, as if she were about to impart a very important message to me. She rubbed my hands to reassure me, her gaze seeming deep in the world she was about to evoke.

'Once upon a time, not so long ago,' my mother began, 'our land was confronted with the probability of war. It was believed that this war would be the sum of all wars. Past experience had taught the people about the true nature of war. Indeed, their migration was not only to seek greener pastures but to escape wars that had resulted in famine and death. The war had to be averted at all costs. Only one man stood up to confront the threat head-on and to avert that war and all other wars, to bring about peace in the land. He was your ancestor, Halay, yes, your namesake.'

My mother stopped ruffling my head.

'Why then this war, this flight?' I asked.

'I've asked myself the same question. Have we done something terrible? Are the ancestors playing havoc with us? Why this war?'

We heard a shuffle at the door and the old woman who owned the house greeted us and entered. My mother offered her food but she refused. She was worried about the rising tension in the city. There were rumours that armed men were preparing to launch an attack from across the border. The old woman suggested that we return to our land. When my father came back from fishing and heard what the old lady had said, he nodded.

'Jowo, let's keep our eyes open,' he said. 'From now on, we will not leave the neighbourhood. You've earned enough to keep us alive for a year. Let's begin to prepare for our departure.'

I left to visit the camp the next morning, telling my parents that I was going to the forest to sit and draw. The shacks and the shops were being evacuated. The rice swamps were empty but alive with the chattering of insects. The roads were dead silent. 'War is coming,' people were saying as they rushed to gather their belongings and leave. The desolation in the camps was such that I turned around and headed back to the city in search of Nafisat. I found her with her mother. The woman looked a spitting image of her daughter except that her gaze was severe.

I was about to take to my heels but for her laughter, which meant she knew who I was. We stood facing each other, like two wrestlers, one of whom was sure of crushing the other. 'Are you not man enough to face the mother of the one you love? I thought you would know how to deal with the inevitable. Or did you think you would never meet me?'

Nafisat tugged at her mother's wrapper to silence her.

'Suppose I decided that you will never see my daughter again?'

'Mother,' Nafisat called.

'Suppose I were to forbid you now to see my daughter?'

'Mother, please,' Nafisat pleaded.

'Madam ...' I tried to say.

'Don't worry. My daughter told me everything. We have a relative residing in your city; he's my uncle, my mother's brother. You hail from a special family, Halay. The story of your ancestor is well known here. Be careful, and treat my daughter with respect.'

She left without Nafisat. Our relationship had been approved and sanctioned by her mother. We headed for a meadow. A place once used as football field but now abandoned. We walked on the grass, feeling the softness giving way under us. We lay on the cushion of grass and held each other, and as we did so I thought of life without her and of the tension that held the city in thrall. Soon I would be forced by war to abandon her and to return to a war-torn country. What would that mean for me, returning to a place that was still at war with itself?

The next day I went to bid farewell to the barman. He was alone, and there was no music. 'I will be joining the army to defend the city from intruders. Once a soldier always a soldier, Halay,' he said. And he leaned across the counter, and in a soft voice said, 'Once it's over, I will travel to France to see my wife and children.' He shook my hand, and I left the bar for good. The city seemed to hold its breath in anticipation of war. People

216

were stockpiling food and vehicles with loads of belongings were moving out. Clearly we were late fleeing the city. I rushed home where I met Nafisat with my parents. She had come to see me.

'We are leaving for Conakry today,' she said. 'We will be safe in the capital.'

'We will leave soon,' I said.

She held out her hand to me, and we strolled to the river where my father fished, and we sat on a fallen tree trunk. We stared at the undulating river, and at a flying fish, jumping and diving. We relished the mild rise of the wind. Nafisat's eyes clouded over.

'Will you remember me?' she asked.

'My drawings will be dedicated to you,' I said.

She smiled and let go of my hand. We sat in the soothing silence for a long time, and when we returned to the house at late noon, she hugged me. I held on to her, never wanting to let go.

'I saw you on the first day of your arrival,' she said.

'What are you talking about?'

'I stumbled into you,' she said.

'You were the girl at the market!'

She laughed and broke away from me, and I watched her moving along the dusty road. Before rounding a corner, she turned and waved and was gone. A gentle breeze rose in her wake, and I felt alone.

Book Five
The Drawing

1

Armed men converged on the city at the same time as rumours reached us that there was a lull in the war in our country. 'It's time to return home, Halay,' my father said. He was the most elated of us all, for exile had broken him and he wanted to escape it. But I was reluctant to leave. I had begun to appreciate this new land, the nature and the people I had loved and drawn on the pages of my sketchbooks. But exile was a metamorphic realm where we would perhaps never be at ease, despite everything. Home was certain to offer us a sense of stability and continuity. I couldn't help but question that stability, for I was leaving Nafisat behind, the one who fed my passion and made me want to be better and to perfect my art. Would leaving her not mean the end of that passion? And what would home offer us after such a long absence?

My mother distributed what was left of her things among the market women who had fought her, and my father gave his fishing gear to a neighbour. The old lady returned to her house.

'I am not leaving,' she said. 'I've seen enough of this world. I will be right here when they come. If they decide to kill me, so be it.'

Moments before our departure, we paused in front of the house that had been our sanctuary for a long time, and my mother heaved a sigh and without looking at me said, 'Never forget what your ancestor did to prevent this war, Halay. We bear more responsibility than others. We feel more pain and suffering than others. Remember that.'

She seemed to be preparing me for the future and for what was at stake when we returned home. But the future was so clouded with uncertainties that I did not know how I would fare within it.

On crossing the river that bordered the two countries, we encountered thousands of people heading home. Every vehicle was moving – old trucks, motorbikes, bicycles. Children were strapped to the backs of mothers who bore huge loads on their heads, while men transported the old and the sick in wheelbarrows. The mass of people trudged on in slow steps, weary of the fate that awaited them. Our number thinned out at every junction, at every fork in the road, as groups split up and took roads to their various towns and villages.

Our city, when we reached it after days on the road, exuded the odour of death and desolation. Weeds had grown along the roads, mould had begun to cling to bullet-ridden homes, and the painted walls, the green, blue and yellow, had been scorched by fire until they had turned smoky black.

We walked through Old Town without encountering a soul, as though it was yet to be populated or would never be. In New Town, the streets looked narrower, the sewers broken, the lighting poles like scarecrows on burnt farms. The large store in town, the one my father had managed as part of the farming cooperative and which sold farming tools and building materials, was empty, the roof gone and the walls burned.

People we encountered wore haunted expressions that pursued us as we climbed the hill to the place where our house had once stood. Nothing was left of the place, not even the walls. My father took a handful of the ashes and let it run through his fingers and then he turned to us. 'Well, we are left with the task of rebuilding it.'

I happened to glance down the hill at the city sprawled below and I saw George Richards, alias the professor, moving towards us. A descendant of Edward Richards, he was born in Monrovia, but for as long as I could remember, he had been a friend of our family, especially with my mother, and he treated me as if I were his grandchild.

The professor often wore simple clothes, his Afro uncombed, and with the habit of drifting through the city with a cane in one hand and an old manuscript in the other, telling stories and predicting the future. During his university days, he would correct his professors and arrive at mathematical solutions to complicated equations with a speed that astounded them. He taught for a while at the university, where his fame grew. He acquired so much knowledge that it was believed his brain could no longer contain it and he had gone out of his mind.

The professor hugged mother.

'Daughter, how did you survive this war? You know, I did not leave. And when the fighters caught me, they thought I could be some help to them and kept me alive. But in the end I was of no use to them.'

As if a thought had occurred to him, he said, addressing my father, 'They turned your store into a warehouse where they kept their arms and ammunition, Frederick. Yes, and when they left they burned it down. Some of them are still in town. You will hear them tonight.'

'I am going to meet some of our farmers today and we will rebuild the warehouse and start all over again,' my father said.

Soon afterwards he left with the professor. My mother and I retired to the shade of the tree where we had often had dinner. My gaze shifted from the ruins of the house to the city below us with its rusty roofs.

'The city looks like it has been worked over by a bulldozer. There's nothing left, Halay. We've lost everything,' my mother said.

She was referring to her two petrol stations, to her store across from my father's store; she also meant her position in the city, as a prominent member and one of its most privileged.

'We will make it our home, Mother.'

'Tell me how? How do you make a home out of a place where everything is gone? There's nothing left for us here.'

She sat under the tree, gazing about her, at a loss as what to do. Later my father returned with more than a dozen farmers, and the men set to work, clearing the place of weeds, burned wood, and dirt. While some fetched water from the river to pour on mud mixed with dirt, others fetched trees to be used as poles to support the foundations.

'This house will be finished in no time, Jowo,' he said.

This must have incited my mother to wake up from her reverie, for she left to purchase some rice and greens, which she prepared for us, and we ate in the shade of the tree, as the men shared their war experiences with us. It surprised me how much they remembered.

'Chief,' one of them called my father. 'War met me on my farm, right beyond the mountain. It was harvest time, but I found myself running away, leaving everything behind me. When I returned, everything was gone, my wife, my children, my home, my farm.'

224

'They killed so many people that the river turned red. I swear it,' another said. 'Yes, our river turned to blood.'

'You are exaggerating,' a third said.

'If you don't shut up, I will turn your face to blood. I mean it. I was here when those deaths occurred. The river was all blood, chief.'

No one dared contradict him again, and as each narrated his personal story, gradually our own experiences, our flight and exile, began to pale in comparison to the stories told and we had nothing to say.

The men worked until nightfall, and we slept in the corners of the newly built house, refusing the professor's offer of a place in his house.

I often joined the men to work on the house and then on the warehouse, and when not needed I went to swim in the river. I forgot about drawing, for the new reality, worse than I had imagined, was too stifling to nurture creativity. Instead I stored up everything – the images of the burnt churches and mosques, the stories of the men, and the cries at night which were often interrupted by gunfire, by men bent on warring with each other even after the war had formally ended. The gunshots would continue till morning. No one dared go out at night.

We were told that the fighters were so used to war for so long that it had become their second nature. No one and nothing could make them stop. They would come to the city and fill it with gunfire and as dawn approached they would disappear, as if they were ghosts.

One day, I met our city mayor at the river. He was a diminutive man with a booming voice and slow steps. He seemed indifferent to what was happening to his city. But he was not always like that. Just after the war, we were told, he had bustled with enthusiasm. He would often tell the people that the city would recover and become better. 'This is our opportunity,' he would say. 'We have to start anew. This time, our foundation will be stronger than ever before. This time we will not fail.' He tried to rally the people around him to rebuild the roads, the homes, the wells that had been poisoned, and the schools. He sent out people to deliver his messages, but few listened. In the end he gave up.

'What are you doing alone at the river, child?' he said.

The warning in his voice compelled me to leave the river and change into my dry clothes. I walked up to him.

'How is your mother?' he asked, and before I could answer him he added, 'I am ashamed to face her after this war. I cannot face her.'

The mayor often wore a safari helmet, and I could not remember seeing him in any other clothes but grey suits and the boots of a logger.

'We should have avoided this war after what your ancestor did for us, Halay. But we forgot all about him, neglected him. We have to learn not to forget. We have to learn to remember.'

The river was wide at this point, where drivers brought their cars to wash them. It had not occurred to me that being alone in the aftermath of the war could be hazardous, for the people who had killed in the war were still roaming the city at night and could kill during the day.

'Give your mother my regards. The school will soon be ready to receive students again. Don't waste your life away,' he said and moved on.

I returned home to meet my mother who was as fretful as ever.

'I want to open up my shops again,' she said, but there was no conviction in her voice, and she seemed to seek assurance from me.

'I will help you with the shop after school.'

She was silent, her gaze intent on me.

'You can feel our suffering,' she said.

'Mother, please, don't.'

'You carry our burden.'

'Stop now, please, don't go on reminding me.'

She shook her head.

'I was told that school will reopen tomorrow,' she said.

My father was away, visiting villages, organizing the farmers. He was hardly at home, as if he wanted to make up for lost time.

A sudden but crippling lethargy appeared to have taken hold of my mother, and many a time I would meet her seated where I had left her.

'I will make you proud, Mother.'

I went to bed thinking of my ancestor and of his sacrifice, and wondering what I had to do to become worthy of him.

2

I awoke shivering from the cold of the early rainy season, but it was soon alleviated by a warm bath my mother had prepared. Later I rubbed my body, face, hands and hair down with Vaseline, and I threw on my uniform, a yellow, short-sleeved shirt and brown trousers. For lunch, my mother gave me French bread and a small can of condensed milk as a spread, which was one of my favourites. On turning round after covering a few paces, I saw her standing in front of our newly built house, simply dressed in a deep-blue wrapper, her hair loosened and not plaited. The sun beamed on her face, accentuating her beauty, and I saw myself waving to her. Perhaps bowled over by the gesture, she smiled and waved back to me.

Several schoolmates joined me down the hill and we talked about the war and the nightly gunfire. We met the professor on his way from his house, which was located outside the city, and he called out to me.

'Are you drawing again, child? So much has happened.'

I had tried to draw umpteen times, but the torrents of images prevented me from capturing and committing anything to paper with the passion that I felt was necessary. I had lost my craft.

'It's abandoned me, prof,' I said.

'It will return. Be ready when it does.'

'Why do you carry that old book with you all the time?' I asked.

'It's my most treasured possession. My ancestor Edward Richards wrote it.'

'What's in it?'

'Our history.'

He clasped the manuscript to his chest.

'Study hard and help us all.'

I ran to join my friends. The school boasted a library, a football field, and a plot of land where before the war we had cultivated pineapples, eddoes, cassava, melons and beans. Under a tree was the huge bell whose peal launched the beginning or end of the school day.

Our principal, who had lost an arm during the war, stood before us after the bell had rung and waved his left hand as he spoke. We had seen things not even grown-ups should see, he said, things that had marked us forever. Now we must have the courage to go on. He announced a new set of rules, a new curriculum that would enable us to become better students. 'If this war has taught us anything, then it has to be that it is terrible. Out of our loss we have to forge a new beginning. For the sake of those we lost, for the sake of the man who did everything to avert this war.'

One of us hoisted the flag and we saluted it. The reverence we held for that symbol at that moment was so profound that none of us stirred or coughed as the flag rose, fluttering in the cold morning air.

The history teacher, my mentor Mr Wilson, entered the classroom. We stood up to greet him but he ignored us and went to the window. He gazed at the birds, nodding as if he had unravelled the mystery of their language.

Before the war he had been severe, punishing latecomers or ill-dressed students by caning them or compelling them to work on the school farm or to fetch firewood for him or the other teachers. We all knew his story. His wife had died in the war and he was left with his two daughters. Unable to bear the responsibility of raising them, he had abandoned them and taken to the mountains. After two days of absence, the city mayor had launched a search for him. They found him sitting under a giant tree believed to be inhabited by spirits, babbling in a strange language. The men who found him did not approach him for fear of being haunted by evil spirits. They called in the help of a Muslim cleric, who concluded that Mr Wilson was talking about things to come and advised that a sacrifice be made to help restore him to normality.

Mr Wilson then took up the habit of gathering millipedes. Before dawn, he would set out for the forest and then return with basketfuls of the coiling insects. He would divide them according to colour and size, giving each a name and claiming they were incarnations of his ancestors.

Now he diverted his gaze from the birds to the millipedes in a jar on the table in front of him, then to the birds and back to the jar.

A student threw a paper aeroplane at him. Others followed. Mr Wilson did not stir. I tried to stop the students, but they ignored me. Our teacher wore such an intense gaze that looking at him I felt a chill run down my spine, and I feared what he would do next.

Then he moved to the blackboard and with a chalk drew our city, drew its major buildings, the city hall, the hospital, the church and mosque, my father's farming cooperative store.

He drew our mayor and reduced his figure to that of a crawling child; he filled our school with disfigured children. He drew a map of our country, drew every county and every district, every city and town, every river and mountain. He drew with a red chalk, then yellow, then white and then blue. He drew our flag, the red against the black board, like the red teeth against the black beak of our dreaded masked being. He drew a woman who looked like his late wife and drew his two daughters with strength in their limbs and arms.

No one spoke, we were all held in thrall.

'The genies taught him,' one of us said.

Mr Wilson went on drawing until the school bell rang, and we left him still drawing and went out to roam the forest.

It was an old habit. Streams and the shade of tall trees had appealed to us before the war. We came upon an opossum burrow and decided to light a fire to smoke it out. We waited patiently, our hearts pounding with excitement whenever we heard a squeak or a scuffle from the burrow. That was our prey, perhaps two of them, we told ourselves. We dreamed of building a fire like we had seen our parents do and roasting and relishing the meat. We sang songs about masked beings and of spirits of the night without fear, for the war had taken away the tradition associated with them. The Poro Society had become ceremonial. War and time had made it so. It had ceased to function as a symbol of unity. Alone in that forest, we had become masters of our own destinies and could do whatever we desired, and we did.

One of us suggested we dig a hole to reach the opossum and trap it. 'My father does it all the time,' he said, but it would involve a lot of work. We did not want to work. We went on smoking the hole, by turn throwing branches at the opening. Our eyes became blood red from the smarting smoke, and because we had yet to catch our prey, the oldest of us decided we stuff the hole with wood, so that the animal would have no escape. We were about to give up when the nervous animal jumped out and scurried away to safety before we could catch it.

Our failure only fired our determination to go on hunting. We set our sight on the birds. We used ropes to set up a net and picked fruit to spread below the net. But it was all to no avail. We cleared the surroundings of small bushes, hid the ropes attached to the net, and lurked in the brush. After a few hours we gave up.

Our adventure led us to an abandoned farm with its huts still intact. I moved away from the group and touched the front door of one of the huts to open it. The door fell apart. The birds that had made it their home banged away into flight. Outside there was a pit for milling palm oil. Around the huts there were pawpaw and banana plants, which were not ripe for consumption. We left the farm to return home.

On our way, not far from the farm, we came upon a yellowish skeleton. The eldest in our group decided to assemble it. We watched him, stricken with awe but fascinated, as he joined the skull to the neck, the arm bones with the shoulders, the ribs with the spine, the hips with the legs.

'Let's fasten a rope to it,' he said.

'No, that's enough, let's leave,' I said.

'You, what's wrong with you?' he said.

He was of my height and my build, and before the war he had depended on me to help him with homework. Out in the world, he seemed stronger, invincible, as he toyed with the skeleton.

'They say your ancestor died to avert the war. Well, did he? Tell me? Did he really offer himself to avert this war?'

232

'You are desecrating the dead,' I said.

He threw the skeleton at me, and before I could react he was on me. I did not know where the blows came from, but they were frequent, sustained, directed at my head, over and over again.

'If he died to avert this war, then explain why my mother died in this war. Explain why my sisters perished. You will explain it to me.'

No one intervened, and the thought that he would kill me or wound me terribly became so overwhelming that I managed to throw him off and took to my heels. He chased after me.

'Don't let him go, catch him,' he told the other boys. But I was too fast for them, and I escaped and headed home. By then my eyes had swollen and I was bruised all over. I washed my face at the river, and at home I tried to avoid my mother, but failed.

'What happened, Halay?' she said.

My father was not home. I went to my room without answering her, and she did not bother me. I didn't want to tell her that the fight had awoken in me a keen sense of belonging to my ancestor and what it meant to bear his name. Did my very presence in this world, my every action depend on the past that involved him? Was my very being locked up and my future determined by the consequences of his deed?

I was alone in my room when the professor visited. I was thinking of the skeleton. Was it that of a man or a woman? I tried to give it a form and a face. I tried to picture the person as a living human being, with different shades of moods, happy, sad, irritated and angry, a person with a home, a family, a trade and a past. But my pencil failed me.

The professor knocked at my door. He bore with him the smell of dust and sweat, but his eyes were stern, which made me apprehensive. I could not remember being nervous in his presence. I realized that my fear had nothing to do with him but with my mother who was standing just behind the professor, her rage bottled up.

'Child, how was your first day at school?'

'It went well, prof,' I said.

'I mean outside school.'

I did not answer.

'Halay, will you tell us what happened outside school? Will you look at Professor Richards and tell him what happened when you left school. Will you tell him the truth? Yes, the truth,' she said.

'Jowo, the boy is exhausted,' my father said from the living room.

'Frederick, stay out of this. If you go on encouraging him, it will be the end of us, you hear me? Now, Halay, we are waiting.'

I couldn't speak, her anger had paralysed me.

'Some children were caught playing with a skeleton today,' the professor said.

'Playing with a skeleton, Halay. Do you hear that, Frederick. Children playing with a skeleton and you want to defend them.'

My father burst into the room.

'Were you among them?' he asked.

I maintained my silence.

'Halay, you more than anybody else should be the one to tell the truth. Why are you silent?' the professor said.

'Frederick, talk to your son,' my mother said.

'Halay, tell your mother what happened,' my father said.

The professor shook his head.

'Never play around with a skeleton, child,' he said.

With that, the professor left. My mother sucked her teeth.

'Frederick, what's happening to us? Why would our child, who should know better, play with a dead body? How would that reflect on us, on our name, on our past? Do you realize what he's done?'

I could not remember my father ever whipping me before. He told me once that whipping marks a child forever, but now he fetched a cane and used it with a force that left me dumbstruck. I sought refuge between his legs, and when he got confused, overwhelmed, dazzled by his own fury and weakened by it, he gave up.

It dawned on me, lying in bed that night, that I had withheld the truth from my parents. I hardly slept that night as the shame mounted with every passing minute and with it the guilt of my action.

In the morning I rushed out of bed with the intention of throwing myself at my mother's feet to beg for forgiveness. No one was in the house. I came out only to be grabbed by two men sent by the city mayor.

The skeleton belonged to one of the farmers who had worked with my father. He had taken his family to safety across the border and was returning to help others when he was shot. He had died on his farm.

3

There were six of us. We stood on the verandah of the mayor's house while a huge crowd waited in the square below us. The house, one of the largest in the city, was built of concrete with steps leading to a spacious verandah that had bamboo benches as furniture and a black swivelling chair that the mayor sat on, flanked by a group of elders, including a retired judge. The mayor was munching a kola nut. A huge black and white portrait of him in a richly patterned gown stared down from the wall behind him, the eyes weak and sad. He was old, he could remember the first missionaries who came to our city and helped maintain the school Edward Richards had built and his career rested on a singular achievement: he had made it possible for a road to reach our part of the world, starting a flurry of activity that led to a boom in business across the borders and with other cities in Liberia.

My eyes swept the crowd for my parents but could not find them. They had abandoned me. I could hear people spitting on the ground to avert the evil we had awoken in their midst, our crime being that we had played with a dead body, with a skeleton, an abomination.

The mayor was silent, munching his kola nut. Mr Wilson broke the tense silence when he walked through the crowd with a jar of his millipedes, and the mayor shook his head. Mr Wilson climbed the steps and stood before us, gazing into my face as if I alone was at fault.

Over and over again the mayor shook his head as Mr Wilson left. And when he spoke, his voice was low, fragile. 'Child,' he said.

He was referring to me, and I felt my feet about to quake under me. 'Child,' he repeated, and I moved away from the group and flung myself on the floor before him. 'You of all people,' he said.

'Let us render the severest punishment,' the retired judge, famed for settling disputes outside the courts said.

'I will come to that; I will come to that,' the mayor said. 'But do you know who this child is? Do you know?'

The elders nodded.

'How could he then commit this … this …'

He stopped and held his face in his hands.

'We should banish them from the city,' the judge said.

'But we cannot do that,' the other said.

'Why not?' the judge said.

'One of them is a relative of our saviour,' the other answered.

'Which saviour?'

'Don't you know our past?'

'Which past?' the judge asked.

The elder sucked his teeth.

'I mean the past that concerns Halay, our saviour,' he said.

'He was not my saviour,' the judge said.

'What do you mean?'

'I lost my household in this war.'

'You must all stop this,' the mayor said.

But the judge pressed on.

'After years of waiting and when we had forgotten all about it war came and I lost my children. Don't talk to me about a saviour,' he said.

'Silence,' the mayor said.

'The children have to be punished,' the judge went on.

'I said silence,' the mayor said.

He stood up to address the crowd, but just then we heard the sound of a car, honking as it came to a halt in front of the crowd. Cars had become such a rarity after the war that the mere sight of one was enough to interrupt the proceedings intended to alter our lives forever.

An elegant woman stepped out of the car. She wore a chequered dress of precious material and white shoes. Her hair was braided in two rows, and there was a mole on one side of her upper lip that accentuated her nose and pronounced lips. She carried a leather bag with a brass lock. Her driver, a sullen-looking man with a trimmed moustache, followed her, as if he were her bodyguard.

The mayor hurried down the steps towards her, and we followed him. When he greeted her, his voice seemed to belong to someone else, someone much younger, confident, playful and august at the same time. The mayor seemed to have recovered from the horror of the incident with the dead body. We waited, anxious for her response.

'I came in search of my ancestor,' she said, and the crowd stirred. I edged my way closer to her. 'His name is Edward Richards. He died here, in this town. I was told one of his descendants lives here.'

'Fetch the professor, child,' the mayor turned to me.

I bolted into a run and raced toward the professor's house. I met him asleep, for he had no clock and took no notice of time. His house was strewn with books, on shelves and tables – books on every subject, ranging from mathematics, literature to astronomy, which was his favourite subject.

'You honour me with this visit, Halay,' he said.

The house smelt of dust, of old books and of the forest, where the professor sometimes wandered for hours. He was smiling. He had on a simple long-sleeved shirt and trousers, his Afro as impressive as ever.

'You bring good tidings, I suppose.'

'Yes, I do, prof. Someone is here to see you.'

'I have no friends, no family but you.'

'This woman says she's family.'

'A woman? Now I am curious. Let's go and meet her, Halay.'

The crowd seemed not to have moved since my absence, as though everyone was waiting for what was to unfold.

The woman turned to us, her eyes fixed on the professor as we approached, and, suddenly, she was trembling. She rushed and flung herself at the professor, who held her reluctantly.

'Tell me who you are,' he said.

'Father,' she said. 'Father, you are alive. I was told you were dead, that's why I did not go in search of you. You are alive.'

We were astounded as much as the professor, for as he held her, he wore a weary look on his face, as if he were in the dark concerning this woman. The professor had a daughter? The man many of us perceived as mad had a daughter as elegant as that woman?

'This calls for celebration,' the mayor said. Turning to me he added, 'Child, we will deal with you later, but for now we welcome the professor's daughter. Let's fetch her something cold to drink.'

The mayor tried to dismiss the crowd, but no one left, for everyone was anxious to know the woman's story. But she did not seem to be interested in our curiosity but in the professor, who led her up the steps to the verandah to calm her down. The professor was sweating; he was yet to recover from the shock of the revelation; he was lost for words.

Her name was Elizabeth. She told us her story when the professor brought her to meet my parents who had been too ashamed to witness our trial. Her mother had met the professor at the university, where the two had had a brief relationship. Her mother had not told her about the professor because she thought he was not one to raise a family. Elizabeth was brought up in America, and it was only years later and after much insistence on her part that her mother told her about her father and her ancestor Edward Richards who had built the famous high school.

'I left America in search of you,' Elizabeth said.

'You have a sister now, Jowo,' the professor said. 'You are not alone any more. When I am gone, you two will live on,' he said.

And I saw a light flash in my mother's eyes.

'So all is not lost after all,' she said.

4

'Wake up, Halay,' my mother said. 'Why must I do this every morning? You are not a child any more. You will be late for school.' There was no hint of anger in her voice, in fact she sounded mirthful. Her life had changed. In one of the rooms of our house slept a woman with whom she had not stopped talking since the professor introduced her to us weeks ago. Aunt Elizabeth's presence had altered her mood, but she was not alone. For the first time since our return from exile, I could sense a vague but persistent urge growing in me to draw again. I had been suspended from school for the past month, and I spent the time nurturing that urge but failing at every attempt. But the urge remained, unmistakable.

By the time I had woken up and had taken a shower in the bathroom behind our house, the two women were sitting on the verandah, whispering like two friends who had known each other all their lives.

'We have plans to rebuild my stores and gas stations. Your aunt will run one store and I will focus on the other,' my mother said when I came out to head to school. She had found her strength.

The two went on talking as I went down the hill to join other students. At school we waited in our classroom for Mr Wilson.

He entered dressed in clean clothes. His two daughters were with him. The two girls, seated on a bench in a corner of the room, had on white dresses, their hair plaited in two rows. Mr Wilson taught them himself, for he believed they had nothing to learn at school. His table was empty of millipedes, and while the birds twittered and flew across the window, he paid them no attention. He was staring at us and not through the window, the change in him so visible that it affected us.

Before he began with the history lesson, he walked up to me and said, 'I want to see you after school, Halay.'

We were unusually courteous during the lesson. We listened as he spoke of the past and recent history. His voice was captivating.

Before the war, during lessons that did not appeal to me, I would draw as the teacher lectured. One day I was caught scribbling a portrait on an exercise book that captured the preoccupied look of our biology teacher. When he saw it he was so worked up that instead of caning me or forcing me to do twenty-five push-ups as was the rule, he asked me to walk to the blackboard and write a hundred times: 'I will never draw again.' But I went on to draw, with much more vigour and passion. In the end he gave up on me.

Now, as Mr Wilson unfolded our history, touching on aspects that were unknown to me, as if intent on resurrecting the past, I listened attentively. I had no urge to draw during the lesson.

I confined myself to the school compound during recess. Here and there students were engaged in various sports. Two students, a brother and sister, were selling sweets and toffees and tiny cans of sweet condensed milk, attracting hordes of students about them. Before the war, the brother and sister had sold all kinds of sweets at school, and from the proceeds they paid their own school fees, bought school uniforms and exercise books. Girls were clapping hands and counting from one to a hundred in time to the forward movement of their legs. I strolled around, moved to the rear of the school and encountered our principal seated under a breadfruit tree, chewing kola nut, spitting it out and squinting at the sun. His trousers had many creases, and his black shoes were so old they had turned grey.

'Halay,' he called out to me and I drew closer. 'How do you feel hearing all the gunshots of those mad people?'

'They frighten me, sir,' I answered.

'Have you seen them?'

'I haven't,' I said and sat beside him.

'I can't stand the gunshots. I can't stand this city. Don't you see?' he said. 'No one seems to see.'

His fetid sweat was overwhelming.

'They are all blind,' he said.

He whirled his stump around in agitation.

'You draw, so perhaps you can see.'

He told me how he had survived the war. The first gunshot had woken him up and he realized that fear had paralysed him. He remained in bed as the gunfire sounded over the city and until a crack sounded at the door. Men dressed in the garb of war grabbed him and led him away to a small house and locked him in with other people. For days, he went without food. The room reeked of urine, faeces and fetid sweat. He longed for fresh air, for a tiny beam of sunlight. One night, some men with the eyes of war entered the cell, blindfolded him and took him to the outskirts of the city. He heard volleys of gunshots and then a sudden, deafening silence, and he fell to the ground and did not move until fiery brightness appeared on his face and he knew it was daylight. On opening his eyes, he saw nothing around him but dead bodies. He broke into a run, avoiding the main road until he came to a deserted village and made it his home. He would slip into the village at night in search of food and then return to the forest during the day. It was an exhilarating feeling of being a master, a lord over a domain as huge as a village. He would move about it at night, searching for its secrets. He found buried trinkets, iron-money, a staff with an animal bone buried deep in it, a beautifully crafted dagger with strange inscriptions written on the blade, an abandoned pot of stale stew with an army of flies feasting about it, a carved sculpture of a heavily bearded man, a bale of leaves like one used to support bundles of firewood on the head but that was now used as a block for carrying out fiendish acts. He slept in a room with a round bed that had the flag of the country printed on the bedsheets. He would play with a bunch of coins left under a bed in one of the biggest houses in the village, counting and recounting them. There were instances, during the night, when he felt no fear and would sing until the dawn of the morning. One day, he came to the village and found it suddenly populated by people and he left in search of another village. He could not tell me what he saw during his flight because it was simply too terrible.

He spat out the kola nut and waved me on to class. I left him with my head filled with the sensation that he might have felt in the village.

After school, on our way to Mr Wilson's home, we met the professor. He was going to see Aunt Elizabeth. He had his manuscript with him, and when he saw me he waved to me.

'Come over here. I've been struggling to understand what my ancestor wrote about your namesake. It's all here in this manuscript.'

I had often wondered about the book, and his reference to its content drew my attention.

'I understand it now, and I understand you. You are here to remind us of him. Time will tell how valuable you are.'

'What are you talking about, prof?' I asked.

The professor drew mathematical figures on the ground with his cane, and filled them with strange but beautiful letters. He kept chanting to himself as he drew. He studied the figures from different points.

'I am almost there,' he said. He circled the figures again. 'Just a while longer,' he implored. 'Yes, it is clear now, Halay.' He paused and turned to me, his gaze so filled with sadness that I cringed.

'It says here that you will remain a stranger forever,' he said.

I stood as if nailed to the ground, and then I broke into a run towards home and met my parents sitting outside with Aunt Elizabeth.

They were lunching on bowls of pineapples, mangoes, oranges, and a host of other fruits. It was Aunt Elizabeth who caught the despair in my eyes. What did it mean being a stranger in one's home?

'You look as if you've seen a ghost,' she said.

I ignored them and went to the rear of the house, which overlooked the valley. I sat on a tree trunk. Aunt Elizabeth came to me.

'What happened?' she asked.

She sat beside me, folding her skirt carefully. Being so close to her, I realized that she was not much older than my mother.

'Your father says that I will remain a stranger all my life.'

'That scared you, right?'

I nodded.

'I've been a stranger all my life,' she said. 'But now I've found home. The yearning to feel at home kept me alive in America. I think when you've done what is necessary in life, you might find home.'

'But I am yet to find out what's necessary.'

'One day you will. In America, I always felt something missing in my life long before I confronted my mother about my father. I questioned every aspect of my mother's story about his death, and her failure to fill in the gaps in her story about how the two of them had met and how he had met his end bothered me. She was not being honest with me. Now I know.'

She caressed my shoulders, calming me.

'I want to draw what's happening around me. I want to capture war on paper. But every time I try, it ends in failure. My talent's left me,' I said.

'So you draw?' she asked.

'It's the only thing I know.'

She was silent for a while.

'I had a son in America,' she said. 'He was an artist like you. But his love of art and the urge to represent images on paper and canvas drove him in the end to self-destruction. He would often gaze at things in peculiar ways, his eyes could be disturbing. While bringing him to school, during his childhood, he would be lost in thought, sometimes gaping at passers-by, his whole attention riveted to their faces, just their faces. The people he stared at would feel so embarrassed that they would smile to conceal their unease. 'Stop looking at people like that,' I would tell him, but he seemed not to hear me. He talked about faces, about the shapes of mouths, lips, noses, lashes, brows and foreheads. How could a child notice all those features and with such intensity the way he did, I often wondered. His first real drawing was of me. People praised and recoiled from it, for it was grotesque and terrifying in its beauty. He was a young man then when he did the drawing, and I knew that I'd lost him. Art ruled his life. Many a time, he would fall into depression, a deep and bottomless hole out of which it took months and sometimes a year to creep out of, only because he had failed to put on paper or canvas an image that had haunted his imagination. To me, Halay, art is a discipline, but it becomes much more than that when an artist spends a whole night and day on his feet, standing before a canvas and making paintings that horrify and fascinate people to the point of screaming or shedding tears. Then art becomes an obsession, an addiction; you must remember that, Halay. It becomes a religion with a different dimension. This was what my son desired. Don't let your art own you, child. When my son was gone, I could not live in America surrounded by his ever-haunting presence and I decided to leave to start a new beginning. This is the new beginning.'

When she was finished, in the lingering silence, I felt so close to her that I lay my head on her lap and she put her hand on my head.

5

Mr Wilson's home, located in Old Town, was a three-room house that had survived the war and now stood amid ruins of concrete and mud-built houses, some burned to the ground. There was a house in that part of the city that still functioned as the occasional home of the masked beings whenever they appeared in the city, which was very rare. Nowadays masked beings of all statures, including the dreaded ones, were considered less important. The tradition had waned long before the war, and after the war it had become irrelevant or merely ceremonial.

Once, before the war, I was out with my father to see the masked beings who were in town to receive the president of the country. It was a boisterous event. My father and I moved through the crowd, seeing one masked being after another until we came to the one with the crocodile beak. It was dressed in an impressive raffia skirt, and on top of its elongated beak, close to the forehead, was stuck a black triangular nose. The masked being was spinning around to the songs of its retinue.

When it paused, I approached it and stood in front of it, which in the time of my ancestor was forbidden – for I was not an initiate – and I began to gaze at it with relentless curiosity. Its red teeth, the beautiful, chiselled nose, and the dark and red of its features fascinated me. The masked being ignored me at first, but because I kept staring at it and had begun to draw it in my mind, to imagine the fear it once evoked, the deep mystery it was once shrouded in, the masked being suddenly broke into a song about a boy who had dared to gaze at it.

I did not realize it was singing about me until I saw the crowd around me begin to disperse and I was left alone, face to face with the masked being. There was no sign of my father. I took to my heels.

The masked being and its retinue gave chase. Every time I turned around, I saw them hard on my heels, as if my action amounted to the greatest abomination ever. In my fright, the world turned garishly bright before me and my fear was as white as sunlight. The bell announcing the presence of the masked being rang on relentlessly. I decided to head home. Meanwhile, the masked being was raising dust and havoc in its wake. It seemed bent on punishing me and would not let me be.

I dashed into our house and hid behind the door but forgot in my panic to bolt it. Before I realised my mistake the masked being was on our verandah. Through a chink in the door, I could see it standing still as if it were a statue, while the ceiling and the floor trembled to the power of its hard breath. Then, when I thought it was about to turn around and go down the hill, leaving me in peace, it glided towards the door until its long beak came to rest on the door behind which I stood. I gazed into its eyes which were like a mirror in which I could see myself floating towards a man climbing a hill. On the hilltop, the man suddenly paused, and when he turned around I saw

249

myself in him and the destiny that awaited him. I screamed out of fear of that destiny.

This was followed by the voice of the masked being, which rose with a song, the voice ancient and august, bearing with it the terror and enchantment of old, the song sweet and in languages some of which I could understand and some not. Then it fell silent.

'You are a descendant of our saviour,' it said. 'I can see him in you. You bear his burden, child. Bear it with courage, for none of us can.'

The masked being then glided away, followed by its retinue. I remembered my parents' reaction when they found me home. My father was beside himself with rage. 'What will people say about me if you go on behaving like this?' he said. 'They will say I'm bringing you up to behave like this because I'm not from here. Don't shame me, Halay.'

My mother was so furious that she refused to talk to me all day. At night, she came into my room and saw me lying in bed awake.

'Halay, you cannot afford to behave like this,' she said. 'Our family cannot be seen to be doing disgraceful things. Every eye is on us.'

She sounded so grave that when she left me I couldn't sleep a wink. I kept thinking about the words of the masked being, of the burden I had to bear. What burden? I felt no burden on my shoulders or on my head except the terrible urge to draw, to give shape to the world.

I was thinking about the masked being's words on my way to see Mr Wilson. What did they mean? What role was cut out for me in this world? I met the daughters sitting in front of the house. I greeted them, and walked to the study where I found Mr Wilson, busy drawing.

He looked up when he saw me.

'What do you think of the professor's daughter?' he said.

'Aunt Elizabeth is doing her best to settle down.'

'Have you tried drawing her?'

'No, but I've had the urge.'

'I've attempted several times but failed,' Mr Wilson said.

He pushed the drawings towards me. They bore no resemblance to Aunt Elizabeth at all, perhaps because Mr Wilson had not studied her enough. 'I want you to draw her for me,' he said.

'I am not yet ready,' I said.

'If you wait to be ready it will never happen.'

'But you draw better.'

'I have tried but failed.'

I didn't want to disappoint him, so I agreed to draw my aunt. Night found me staring at the empty papers. How could I give Aunt Elizabeth a face that was hers in every sense? As I bent over the paper, making lines that had no passion in them, a volley of gunfire crashed across the city. The fighters had returned. I thought of my parents and how they would be worried about me. I stood up to leave.

Mr Wilson stopped me. 'Go on with the drawing, Halay, and when you are tired, sleep here,' he said.

'Mother and father don't know my whereabouts.'

'Going out in the night can be fatal. Stay the night here.'

Occasionally, soft giggles rose from his daughters' room. Perhaps they were talking about me, I thought. Mr Wilson left and returned with a mattress. He read for a while in the light of a hurricane lamp, then he bade me goodnight and went to his bedroom.

I could not keep father and mother in the dark regarding my whereabouts. So I tiptoed to the door, opened it and sneaked out.

I groped my way through the pitch-dark night, and along the way bumped into a bucket, the clanking noise crashing through the silence around me. Whispers floated in the air like the whistling of the winds. Not a single light burned. Following my instinct, careful with every step in a city without current – for the hydro-generator had been bombed during the war – I came to a house I recognized as the mayor's. I climbed the steps and banged at the door, hoping to see the old man's face. No one answered. It was the same with other homes in his compound. The houses were quiet and still. Soon it began to rain. I heard a voice screaming as though someone was being beaten, and I hastened towards the sound but crashed into a wall. In a flash of lightning, I saw a figure dart across the street and disappear in the darkness. There was no sign of the fighters.

The rain had begun to gather force, pouring in buckets like sliding muds intent on burying me. My path was lit by the occasional flash of lightning. I went about searching for a way home until I stumbled on a road that I recognized. The lightning flashed on our house on the hilltop, and just as I was about to break into a run, a pair of hands grabbed me. The fighters, I thought. My end had come. I tore at the hands, fought as if I was fighting death. It was not fear that incited me as I struggled to break free, as I thrashed about in the rain, but the will to survive, to see my parents and to continue to draw and to fulfil my destiny in the world.

But the hands were trying to calm me, to enfold me, to dispel my fear. And when I yielded to them, I heard a strange voice, and I thought that my end had truly come. 'You are the child,' the voice said, and I realized it belonged to one of the fighters. I tried again to get myself free.

'If I wanted to finish you off, I would have done so a while ago. What are you doing out alone in the rain?' the man said.

The next lightning flashed across a face that perhaps was as old as my father's. The fighter was tall, had a wide gap in his teeth, and two Kalashnikovs strung across his shoulders. His grasp on me, I realized, was becoming tighter and with it my ever-growing panic.

'We came to bring peace. We hate war,' he said.

I was not listening. My mind was working out scenarios about the end, about how it would feel being shot by a Kalashnikov.

'You understand. This injustice must end.'

I could make out our house on the hill, and the fact it was so close and yet impossibly far brought sudden tears to my eyes.

'Come, I will take you home,' he said.

Indeed, he led me up the hill and waited until I had knocked at the door and my parents had let me in to merge once again with the night.

No one berated me. For the first time, I was confronted with fear of another kind, the fear that is triggered by the unbearable thought of losing someone dear to one. I saw it in Aunt Elizabeth, in the professor who was spending the night at our place, in my mother and father who received me in silence, their voices affected by this fear.

My mother dried me with one of her large towels, and after I had changed into fresh clothes, she led me into my room. Aunt Elizabeth went on to prepare some soup for me. My mother felt my forehead.

'It is hot like coal,' she said.

She took my head and rested it on her lap.

'You will get better soon. The soup will be ready.'

Meanwhile, my father and the professor were standing in the room, gazing at me, their anxious smiles replacing their words.

'I must have scared him to death. It was my fault,' the professor said, referring to his prediction. 'A child doesn't

253

have to be burdened with what is yet to transpire. I should have known that, Frederick.'

'No, prof,' my father said. 'It has nothing to do with what you said.'

The professor approached the bed.

'Halay, you will forgive me, won't you?'

I nodded.

'It's not your fault,' my mother said.

'Daughter, you are too generous.'

Aunt Elizabeth entered the room with a bowl of soup, peppered so much that when I tasted it I felt my face swelling, about to explode.

But it was my favourite soup, to which three fat pieces of catfish had been added and spiced so well that the fish melted in my mouth. I disregarded the hot pepper and soon felt thirsty.

The soup did me good. The professor and his daughter, along with my parents, were awake for most of the night, talking in low voices.

6

Mr Wilson's voice woke me the next morning, Saturday, and when I came out of my room the late morning sun was already fierce and implacable. My family was gathered on the verandah, while Mr Wilson went on with his apologies. He wore his blue tailor-made suit that accentuated the sooty darkness of his skin, the same suit he would wear on special occasions before the war, on the last day of the school year or on Independence Day. He looked small in the suit, bony, underfed, but not as gloomy as on that first day at school.

'I held him up last night. It was not his fault,' he said.

'Teacher, he's all right now,' my father said.

'I should have sent him home earlier.'

'We understand,' my mother said.

'I will never hold him up again.'

'Teacher, tell us about the school,' my mother said.

'Well, we've just started.'

'How is our son faring?'

'If only he can take up drawing again.'

'Let him concentrate on his education first,' my father said.

'But he's better at drawing.'

'Don't fight over the child,' my mother said.

'Halay told me about his drawings,' Aunt Elizabeth said.

Mr Wilson turned to her, saying, 'He was trying to draw your portrait last night. I had tried but failed. He's better.'

'No, you are better, Mr Wilson,' my mother said. 'You are the one who taught Halay how to draw. You are better.'

'But the boy is much more gifted,' he said.

I happened to turn around and saw the city mayor climbing up the hill with an umbrella in hand, and when he mounted the hill, he drew himself upright, and sauntered up to Aunt Elizabeth.

'I had to pay a formal visit to a young lady who's honoured us by leaving America to see us, just like her ancestor did,' he said by way of greeting. He was out of breath but was doing his best to regulate it.

The mayor boasted of his accomplishments. He told Aunt Elizabeth that he had been the one who had introduced hydroelectricity into the city, which was destroyed during the war.

'I worked day and night for forty years building this city, and all my work was destroyed in a matter of a few days.'

He paused to let us digest what he'd said.

'My father knew your ancestor,' he said. 'Edward Richards came to us as a friend. He's an example to all of us.' He looked around. 'Where is your father?' he asked Aunt Elizabeth.

'He's asleep. Halay, go fetch him,' Aunt Elizabeth said.

I met the professor lying in bed and staring at the ceiling, his eyes so fixed on a point on the ceiling that I thought he was in a trance or in the thrall of an invisible being. My presence seemed to have startled him.

'I was dreaming, Halay. I saw you drawing. You must draw.'

'Prof, I don't know what's happened to me.'

256

'Don't doubt. Doubt smothers ability.'

'But I just can't.'

'Don't worry, it will come.'

'The mayor wants to see you.'

'That old man lusts after my daughter. Since her arrival, he's been hounding her, never letting her be.'

He sucked his teeth and said: 'Here's what we will do, child. I kept some money from my teaching days at the university. I will buy you the best drawing materials. What do you think? Come on now, don't disappoint me.'

But what if, with the new materials, I still failed to draw? Because I didn't want to let him down, I said, 'I will give it a try.'

'Now, let's see what that old lecher wants from me,' he said.

The mayor was telling Elizabeth about the school Edward Richards had founded, and about his student years.

'We paid our school fees with bags of rice, with sacks of coffee or cocoa, palm oil or chicken. Most of us were from poor families.'

'Professor,' he said when he saw us. 'You can be of some help to us. Yes, you are the one with the knowledge.'

'If only you would leave my daughter alone.'

'Professor, I regard her as my daughter. No, what am I saying? I regard her as my granddaughter. I am impressed by her courage. Look at what she's done in the short time she's been here. She's changed you, she's changed us all. I barely recognize you, Professor Richards.'

The professor seemed disarmed.

'Now tell us what happened to Edward Richards. You say he wrote that manuscript you carry around with you.'

The professor's voice broke as he attempted to speak. Except for our family, no one had cared for him or for his manuscript.

Often, he would show up on our verandah, his clothes in tatters, needing care, which my mother would offer. Sometimes, after a meal or a hot bath, he would hug my mother tight, saying, 'Daughter, daughter, daughter!'

'Edward Richards did see Charlotte again,' he said. 'In fact, after Halay passed on, he left for Monrovia and stayed there for a while. Once again he became a father to his son, my great-grandfather, and a partner to Charlotte, my great-great-grandmother. He was one of those who participated in outlining the boundaries as we know them today. He made sure that this part of the country did not fall under British or French influence.'

'I remember my father telling me about the boundaries,' the mayor said. 'We were cheated out of many towns and villages.'

'Edward Richards did return to this place. He lived and passed on here. This is why we are as much a part of this place as we are a part of the rest of the country. My roots are here. The Richardses belong here.'

'We've never considered you otherwise, professor,' the mayor said. 'Look, your daughter's returned home.'

The mayor stood up, about to leave.

'Teacher Wilson,' he said. 'Do your best for our children. We need to prepare them for the future even though it's still uncertain, what with all the shootings every night.'

'But you are the authority,' my father said. 'You could put a halt to the gunfire. You could talk sense into those fighters.'

'They are beyond our control. No one controls them. For some the war is not yet over, will never be over. We have to live with the presence of such people in our midst,' the mayor said.

'So the fighting continues,' my mother said.

'Yes, until such a time when those young men realize that there's nothing to be afraid of. It's fear that's driving them.'

258

The mayor turned to Aunt Elizabeth.

'Daughter,' he said. 'We should meet soon to discuss the future of the city. I hear you are helping Ma-Jowo with her stores.'

Aunt Elizabeth nodded. As soon as the mayor left with Mr Wilson, the professor took his daughter to his home. My father decided to mend the front door whose hinges had been weakened by the storm of the other night. He covered the leaks in the zinc roof with stones, the occasional sound of his hammer disturbing the silence around the house. My mother swept and cleaned the house, but no matter how hard she worked, dust managed to settle on everything at the end of the day, which hadn't always been the case. Before the war ours was an impeccable home.

Alone in my room, trying to recover from the fright, I pondered the words of the fighter. Why fight if you hated war? It made no sense. What injustice was he talking about? The thought of being close to him sent a shiver through me. I had stared war in the face and it had spared me. In my mind I tried to give shape to the face with the gap in its teeth, but the face eluded me.

My mother urged me to come out to take some fresh air, and when I did I found it carried the pungent odour of the bushes and of dust, which was swept up by an occasional wind. I sat in the shade of the orange tree, and gazed down at the city, which seemed in thrall to the heat, so much so that I could hardly see a soul on the street. By evening, I was famished for food.

We had a sumptuous dinner. My mother applied her culinary skills in preparing the potato greens enriched with meat, shrimps and fish. It was served with red rice, which the farmers belonging to my father's cooperative society had grown. Aunt Elizabeth, who had returned from visiting her father, joined

259

us around a large tray. We had hardly begun when we heard the professor at the door, clearing his throat to announce his presence. He entered, washed his hands and joined us.

We ate in silence. From the beginning, all eyes were fixed on the chunks of smoked and oil-soaked meat that topped the heap of steaming rice. Because meat was considered the best part of the meal, surpassing in importance the shrimps and fish, we chose to avoid it. We brushed against it as though it was meant not to be eaten. Often, the meat would be preserved until after the rice and stew had been eaten, then divided among the adults. But Aunt Elizabeth made an exception to that rule. She threw most of the meat in front of me. And her father said, 'I don't know how you do it over there, but a child does not need so much meat here.'

My parents laughed.

'He needs good food to recover, Dad,' Aunt Elizabeth said.

'But not so much meat,' he said.

When we were finished, the professor leaned against the sofa and began to pick his teeth with a tiny wooden splinter.

'You are the only family I have left in the world,' he said. 'I came to tell you something about the manuscript. I've kept it all my life. On returning home today, I realized someone else needed it much more than I did. It's time to pass it on to someone who deserves it.'

The professor turned to me.

'Halay, child, you need this manuscript to help you to draw again. It might inspire you. I hope it does.'

'He's still a child,' my father protested.

'No, he's not. He thinks great thoughts. I see our future in the child. He needs these writings.'

'Let him have it,' Aunt Elizabeth said.

My father protested but he seemed alone. Later, the professor returned home, and I retired to bed. In bed and with the manuscript in hand, I browsed through the handwriting of Edward Richards. He was a meticulous man: he had described our rituals and customs, some of which had survived, but it was the story of my ancestor that had the most impact on me. Edward Richards wrote that Halay was an inconspicuous man whose courage was only revealed at the most crucial time. 'I knew him for years,' he wrote, 'but even at the last moment I doubted he had it in him to become the man he was in the end, even after he had told me his story. I had survived slavery, one of the most gruesome crimes committed against mankind, I had encountered difficulties, but mine paled before Halay's. Indeed, he seemed to encapsulate all those experiences, to bear it in life as much as he's doing in eternity. The past lived in him and the future even more so. I understand his choice now.'

As I went on reading, I was interrupted by gunfire but of a kind that was not sporadic. It evolved in intensity, and this time with loud explosions accompanying it as the night wore on. We had been plunged into another war and all desire to flee had abandoned us.

7

The warriors of the night were still fighting each other well into the next day and night and for days on end. Through chinks in the door and windows, during subsequent days, we tried to figure out what was happening but to no avail. No one dared to venture out of their homes. Our world consisted of the four walls of the house within which we discussed and arrived at incredible conclusions. 'It must be a new group of fighters who had launched an attack on the city,' my father said, but my mother was of the opinion that it was the same men who were fighting each other.

'Soon, they will depose our mayor and take over the city,' she said.

The days were long, monotonous and shot through with anxiety, and they dragged on slowly like a reluctant sheep being led to slaughter. 'Don't worry, it will soon be over,' my father said on the fourth day.

But the explosions down the hill, the constant quaking of the earth, the edgy sound of bazookas, the whistling of bullets through the air, the ever-present sense of peril, went on unabated. I could hardly sleep. Our roof would often shiver to an explosion close by, sometimes behind our house, and fetid and suffocating smoke would find its way into the house.

'What do they want?' Aunt Elizabeth whispered and my mother sucked her teeth and said, 'They want to finish us off first and then each other.'

Aunt Elizabeth worried about her father, the professor. 'He will not leave his home,' my mother said.

Then we would escape to our rooms to avoid each other, for boredom had set in. With the boredom came hunger. Our supply of food had run out.

'I will go to search for food,' my father said.

'Frederick, you are not leaving this house,' my mother said. She stood before the door.

'Move, Jowo,' he said.

'I am not budging, Frederick. I lost my ancestor because of this war. We've given our all to prevent this war. You are not going to die in it. You hear me? We've given our all to prevent this year. You are not going to die in it.'

'I can't bear to see you like this.'

'You will have to bear it. We have to bear it.'

'Don't make me hurt you, Jowo.'

'Halay, your father is talking about hurting me. Did you hear him, Elizabeth? Come on now, hurt me. Frederick, go on.'

I rushed and stood between them, and I turned to my father, whose gaze was fixed on the bolted door.

'Father, let's wait for a few days. Then you and I will go out in search of food. Mother, he's not leaving. We will wait.'

In the absence of food, we existed on water, which we collected through a hole in the roof, so that every rainfall became a windfall.

By then, more than two weeks into the fighting, weakened by hunger, I began to feel as if we were living in a dream, for my power of perception had become hazy. So that now I cannot tell whether what transpired was in the real world or in a dream.

One morning I woke up and began to draw, not the face of Aunt Elizabeth, which had become gaunt and which stared into the distance as if somewhere along the path we had not chosen lay a solution to our problem. I did not draw my mother whose face had taken on a solemn expression, and not my father whose face was clouded with rage as a result of inaction. No, I was drawing my ancestor Halay. Now in the grip of a feeling that I was not in this world but in a deep trance-like dream, I left the drawing undone, unlocked the main door without being interrupted by anyone, and went down the hill to the main street and walked on amid the ruins of the new fighting until I reached a point where I could see the fighters, including the one who had taken me home. He was shrouded in smoke and wore dark glasses that covered half his face. He had a bazooka in his hands, aiming it at houses he was about to destroy. He noticed me as I approached and turned the weapon on me. His brow was furrowed into a grimace, and as I drew nearer, his men surrounded me. They followed me as I went up to the muzzle of the bazooka and felt it touch my chest, felt the heat from it.

'It's you again,' the commander of the fighters said.

He took the bazooka away from my chest.

'He's not afraid,' one of them said.

'Why is he here?'

'To stop us,' the commander said.

'A child stopping a war?'

'Let's finish him,' another said.

As I gazed into the commander's face, I began to draw war through the expressions in my eyes – war as I perceived it. I drew without pausing until the drawing was complete in

264

my mind, until I had drawn war as I had always dreamed of capturing on paper. When I looked around me, I found I was alone. The men had disappeared.

In their place I saw my father holding a drawing in his hand, shaking it before my face. So I had not left the room after all. I had been dreaming. The drawing was not a drawing of war. Instead of war, I had drawn the most dreaded of all our masked beings, the one with the crocodile beak, the one with the terror of the night and the power of the ancestors. The drawing was so grotesque that I could not believe it had come from my pencil. Someone else must have done it.

'Halay, you cannot draw this masked being,' he said.

I dropped my gaze.

'A child should not draw these things.'

I was silent. I kept drawing with my fingers a spiral form on the surface of the table I was sitting at, sweating now, dipping my toes in the floor as though by doing so my father would vanish from the room.

'This is an abomination. Look at this, there's no masked being alive that looks like this. This is a desecration, Halay.'

He was shaking the drawing, his lips twitching with anger, afraid of my mother overhearing him. He tried to contain his anger but it seemed not to work. Soon he was shouting at me.

My mother heard him and came into the room. Instead of joining my father to reprimand me, she held me by the hand.

'Let my son be,' she said. 'We've seen worse things.'

My mother pulled me away from my father. Surprised by her remark, he gazed at my mother and then began to crush the drawing and I thought he was about to throw it away.

'Why are you saying this?' he said.

'Because it is the truth,' my mother said.

'But he is also your son,' my father said.

'Don't you think I know that?'

There was a menacing edge to her voice that did not escape him, and that was why he turned to Aunt Elizabeth who, as feeble as a feather, had come into the room.

'Elizabeth, talk to your sister. Come here, Halay, forget what your mother said. What you did is unforgivable.'

'He's an artist, Frederick,' Aunt Elizabeth said.

'Now you two are ganging up on me.'

There was a slight tremor in his voice, for he seemed aware of the vulnerability of the situation; his family was now on the other side of the river, the other side of the valley, and a harsh remark from him was bound to make everyone turn against him. In another time or place, he would have wrenched me from my mother's grasp and whipped me.

But times had changed. We were now prisoners of an ongoing war, confined to a place we could not escape. It was a time governed by forces beyond our comprehension. Never have I seen such an expression on my mother's face, which I found I was beginning to draw in my mind, her defiance, her stone-hard look, her ability to do anything.

'My son has done nothing wrong,' she said.

'You are making a mistake,' he said.

'Halay will draw whatever he wants,' she said.

My father stood there for what seemed like forever, wrestling with what he could say to right the situation, while my mother gazed into the distance, her sweaty hand clasped around mine.

She started for the door, but my father reached out to stop her and she did not move, but turned to him with tears in her eyes.

'If we remain here any longer, there will be nothing left of our family. This war has to stop, Frederick,' she said.

How could I pretend not to be affected by the things that challenged me to give them shape; things that bore hidden beauties and enigmas that dared me to recreate them on paper; things that were not meaningful until I captured them and put them into another perspective, like the flowers on the bushes we walk past on our way to and from school? It was like rendering nature a face and an importance that hitherto was not obvious. What was my responsibility and to whom? To society with those like my father who had forbidden me to draw the essence of such a society? Was I not responsible to no one but the subjects of my drawings? What was wrong with drawing our masked beings? Was it because of tradition or because I was still a boy without the full knowledge of my role in such a society? What if it was Mr Wilson who had drawn the masked being? How would my father and society have reacted to him? These were questions that I had no answer to.

For the first time in weeks, the sounds of war petered out. The silence that fell on the city was so deep that it took on a shape of its own, much more portentous and ominous than the gunfire. The silence crept into our houses and under our skins and kept us awake and on edge, for experience had taught us that when such silence broke it resulted in unimaginable acts. But the silence persisted into the next day as sunlight poured through chinks in the roof and windows of our home. By noon, the silence took root in our consciousness and stayed.

Later voices outside lulled us out of our house, and when I caught sight of the full sunlight and the trees in our compound I felt alive like never before. A deep fountain of creativity welled up in me and burst across my vision, and when it cleared I knew exactly how to draw war.

8

I went to my room and sat at my table. I tore a page out of my sketchbook and sharpened my pencil. I willed it to draw the perfect lines and curves, and in my hand it felt at home. I knew now that I could not draw war in the form of falling men, scorched homes, famine, dead rats, cats or dogs. Not even in the form of plagues and diseases often associated with war. Not in the form of children with guns or women humiliated or killed. And not in the form of skies that rained blood. I was certain that I could draw war only by contrasting it with love. So I drew my ancestor Halay, the man who offered his life to avert war. Human aversion to war could arise only out of love for other human beings. And Halay's will to stop war could have arisen only out of his love for other people. So I drew him.

With confidence hitherto unknown to me, I drew Halay with a body in the shape of our land, with all its challenges and differences and with its terrible past and present. For a face, I gave him that of the dreaded masked being, paying close attention to the sharp lines of the nose, the curves of the beak, the pyramidal features of the whole face, and in the eyes I drew the terror and the longing of the commander of the fighters.

Seven arrows of pain were pointed at Halay, sharp arrows that dug deep into his sides. From his eyes dropped tears that stood for the sorrow of the land. As I drew, concentrating on the stream of tears, over and over, erasing and redrawing, striving toward perfection, I imagined him coming down the hill, bearing the faces of his people with him, hoping they would remember his act, and seeing what they could be and could still become despite everything. I imagined him in the hole that was in fact a grave, alone for seven days and nights, fighting his doubts even at that moment, his heavy sighs being borne by the winds to the ears of his people.

When I felt I could add nothing to the drawing, not a stroke of the pencil, I stood up, moved a distance away from it and stared at it.

I had given life to death, a voice to the past and present and a face to the unknown.

I had resurrected Halay.

9

This is our fate. This is the life of a people with a history and a present that keep shaping the future. In my eyes burns a flame that sees how our lives have changed, a flame that sees how beauty can change even the most wretched of lives. Now, whenever I stroll through the forest, I sit by the silent river and draw Aunt Elizabeth, the professor and my parents, the mayor and the fighters who had left the city, as if they had never been, but their presence is found in bullet marks on houses, in the dead we had buried, and in the cries of a man afflicted by a nightmare. Our lives go on as they were meant to. And I draw that life as it is and sometimes as I want it to be, and always with doubt at the edge of my confidence, egging me, holding me in check, and plunging me into a feverish burst of creativity.

Acknowledgements

In writing part one of this novel, I relied on many sources, the most helpful being *From Slavery to Freedom* by John Hope Franklin and Alfred A. Moss, Jr. I am grateful to my brother Omaru Fomba Kamara for believing in me, after we had fled Kuwait and Syria and during the war in Liberia, which resulted in a trying period on a refugee camp in the Netherlands where the first pages of this novel were written. My gratitude to all my friends and family scattered across the globe. To my muse, the jasmine of the north and the fountain of inspiration. You make my dreams valid.